WESTIN'S CHASE

A TITAN NOVEL

CRISTIN
HARBER

DEDICATION

For TeamCT

CHAPTER ONE

He saw no point in being the leader if he couldn't guide his men home at the end of every job. His team. His operation. And right now, his disaster. Fire exploded around Jared Westin as he rolled for cover. Gravel dug into his cheek, and branches scratched at his eyes. Acrid smoke billowed, leaving the bitter taste of accelerant on his tongue.

Radio silence was a bitch. He was fine. He would survive, despite the bite of the bullet in his calf and the shrapnel in his shoulder. His men and the rescued hostage were his concern.

Stuck on the side of a mountain in Afghanistan, he saw that his only way out was through a hostile mess of turbans and firepower. Not the best strategic position. Jared's only comfort was knowing the released American would soon be on their helo and out of enemy fire. Rocco and Brock had hustled the guy down the side of a cliff toward the pickup zone before the firefight got bad.

Thump, thump.

The enemy's aim was blind, but close enough to cause harm. Dirt and rocks flew at him each time the bullets found groundcover instead of flesh.

Popping up his head, Jared eyeballed the area. He had a third man in this melee. Roman remained somewhere nearby, drawing enemy fire. A flash of a grenade hit ten yards to Jared's right, followed by Roman's return fire. *He must've had the same damn thought. If I'm going to die on a cliff in Afghanistan, let me do so in a pile of empty brass shells.* There was no way either of them was dying without a fight.

Jared checked his super-mag clip—full, with lots of potential. Plus he had a Sig Sauer strapped to his thigh. It had a solid reputation of accuracy, and he needed those bullets to hit their mark.

Fire burned through the brush nearby, and he caught sight of his man. Roman's shadow danced in the fiery glow cast against the rocky mountain. He was hunched against a boulder, reloading.

Jared reached into the gear pack strapped to his back. He needed something explosive. A bloody distraction. In the background, the *chop, chop, chop* split the night as the helicopter neared the landing zone. It was right on time, and he needed to get a move on. If not, they would be on their own.

Moving too quickly, his head spun. *Blood loss must be worse than I thought. Spectacular.* Jared rifled through the bag. More ammo. Two knives. And… thank the gun lords above, a handheld grenade launcher and two big-ass rounds.

Palming the launcher, he recalled the sexy woman he had to thank for this beauty. She went by Sugar. He had no idea of her last name or her real name, but, damn, he loved working with her. She handed out grenade-launching hand cannons as gifts. *Now if that wasn't a turn on…*

And if this thing saved his life, he would have to come up with a decent way to say thanks for the cover.

He snapped the metal handle into place, loaded up the first 40 mm grenade, eyed Roman, and shot out a blast. The explosion ripped open a possible escape route. Jared slammed the second cartridge into place. *Locked and loaded.* After a nod to Roman, saying this was their chance, he let it rip.

Jared covered his face and ran toward the hellfire with his super mag firing. Brass casings spurted from his weapon, leaving a trail behind him. He pushed through the burn in his body and the pain in his leg and shoulder, ignoring the heat that seared his clothes. When his magazine clicked empty, he tossed the piece into the flames.

Behind him, pops of firepower said Roman was behind him. Jared took a harsh breath. The smoke burned his throat. Gun pulled from the holster on his thigh, he pivoted and picked off enemy tangoes. They hit with bull's-eye precision. Sig Sauer deserved a thank you when this shit mission was done.

Their chopper hovered two hundred yards away in the pitch black night, hanging motionless off the side of the mountain.

Roman was fast on Jared's heels, and the two of them beat feet as quick as they could toward the bird.

As Jared closed in, Rocco and Brock became visible, hanging from the opening, providing cover. Bright explosions ripped through the night as bullets rained down behind them. Two rappelling ropes blew in the violent mountain wind. *Hell yes!*

With no time to overthink his moves, he launched over the edge of the cliff and into the inky-black abyss. He crawled through air, reaching for a lifeline. The seconds took too long. Without the ropes, he knew death was certain. A free fall down into the rocky mountain spikes meant lights-out for good.

Gravity took over, and momentum lost. Jared's weight began a rapid descent. His skin prickled as he splayed his fingers, reaching—hoping— for success.

One hand fisted the rope, his wounded arm taking the brunt of his body and gear poundage. With a grunt and heave, Jared growled up to a second handhold. He had two hands tight on the rope, and Jared looked over at Roman. Swaying in the obsidian night, Roman screamed, "Hoorah!"

Crazy bastard.

His heart screamed, punching his bruised ribs. The jump was the best damn adrenaline rush he'd had in a long time. Jared took a painfully deep breath as the helo pulled up hard and swam off into the sky.

The devastating sound of the chopper leaving brought tears to her eyes. Gunfire and battle cries in a language she didn't understand screamed into the chilly night. Her saviors had come for one of them, but not both. It didn't make sense. They hadn't tried to find her. She heard them show up, create hell, and leave after finding her counterpart—the only other American in this camp.

They have no idea I'm here.

That was worst case scenario because that meant they weren't coming back. Big time bad news. Maybe she should have listened, stayed stateside, and handled her *work* headache differently. But, no, she needed an adrenaline rush. Needed to get her mind off everything at home that she wanted to avoid.

And when a Middle East gun-tracking assignment popped up through black-op back channels, she'd hopped on a plane without even telling her friends.

Not that they would let her pull a stunt like this. Because… well, she would've been captured.

Hanging out with the elite gun-slinger types was problematic. Even if she was decent on the trigger, she wasn't elite or even as good an operative as she thought. Her background was intelligence gathering. She was only a *former* ATF agent with a desire for something bigger and too much time on her hands. *Pathetic.* All she had was an ego that rivaled the size of this goddamn mountain, and—

Sugar. Shut. The. Hell. Up.

She shook her head, then rubbed her eyes. "You *will* survive. You *are* that good. Who the hell needs a military rescue?"

It'd been more than forty-eight hours since her dumbass partner had stumbled into enemy hands and she'd tried to rescue him. That hadn't worked out according to plan, and she was tossed into a makeshift cell and given nothing more than dirty water and rock-hard bread. As a foreign woman, they could've done much worse to her—and that threat still loomed. *But I can handle this.* She could kill each one of her captors and walk off that mountain before she had any more woe-is-me thoughts.

Jeers came her way from her captors who'd survived the rescue operation, and her cage allowed no escape. She stepped away, feeling the earthen walls at her back and the lump at the back of her throat. She laid her palms flat against the cold dirt and dug her fingernails in. Two men approached, shooting into the night like it was Mardi Gras. *Celebrating? Oh, yeah, because they still have me.*

CHAPTER TWO

Jared wasn't in the mood for any shit. Never was. But today, his alpha flare was on fire, as if he'd guzzled a six-pack of testosterone and chased it down with a pound of jerky. He would be at the firing range later, working off this... energy until his buzz died down.

Something was wrong. His gut said it. His instincts screamed it. But as he wrapped up the debrief meeting with his team, nothing amiss had surfaced.

He needed to go for a run. Damn the gunshot wound in his calf that was healing at a glacier's pace. He wasn't one to listen to the docs, but the bullet had nicked the tibia and scrambled some nerves. Messing with his health meant messing with his livelihood, so he planned to sit on his ass for two more weeks. Begrudgingly.

The war room was rowdy after the ending of what had to be the closest thing to an office meeting that his team would ever have.

Nicola, Jared's lone female operative, cursed loud enough to quiet the room and tossed her cell phone to Cash. He looked at the screen, then chucked it to Winters, who did the same, sending it to Roman, like a game of cell phone hot potato.

Annoyed and knowing this was the detail his gut said he'd been missing, Jared scowled. He wanted an explanation. Right away. "What?"

Nicola sat down at the table, her brow pinched and lips pursed. Cash and Winters traded glances.

"Cut the shit," Jared growled. "Two seconds until I knock faces for answers."

Roman threw him the phone. The screen was open to an e-mail from Parker, Titan's tech genius.

FROM: Parker Harrington
TO: Titan - all users
SUBJ: Whiskey Tango Foxtrot
What the fuck? Jared scrolled down to the message.

Afghanistan captive count was TWO. Confirmed the second hostage is Lilly Chase. Will be on the news in ten minutes.

Jared looked up, and everyone stared at him. He shrugged. "Not the first time Washington bureaucrats got it wrong."

They could go back in and grab hostage number two, assuming they got the contract for the job. If not, he was fine with that. His gunshot wounds needed more time to heal. Sometimes, nabbing a contract wasn't worth the headache.

"You don't know?" Cash asked, dropping into a chair, his face tight. He looked ready for the next world war.

Parker burst through the doors like his ass was on fire. *What the fuck? Whiskey Tango Foxtrot was right.* Every member of his team stared at Jared, waiting for a reaction.

No one said a word. Brock nodded to Parker, who clicked on a flat screen in the middle of the room. He flipped the channel from ESPN to CNN. Commercial. He flipped the channel again to Fox News, and—

"What the...?" Not believing the screen, Jared pushed out of his chair, balled fists supporting his weight on the table.

"That's Sugar," Parker said.

"I know"—his jaw ached as he ground out the words— "who the fuck that is."

Everyone looked at the screen, then at him. Anger bubbled inside his chest. His mouth went dry as a thousand insane questions mocked him.

"Sugar's an ATF agent. *ATF.* Alcohol, tobacco, and firearms, not some military operation. Not some..." His pulse pounded. Tunnel vision was in full force, and he couldn't put the words together. It didn't make sense. Jared swallowed his reactions and refocused. "You mean to tell me Sugar's on the side of a goddamn mountain in Afghanistan, and we fucking left her there?"

Parker nodded.

Jared threw Nicola's phone across the room, and it shattered. No one moved.

His chest tightened. "Unmute it."

Parker flicked the remote, and a news anchor's voice filled the room. "...but what we do know is a state department spokesperson reports that diplomatic efforts are being made, but since this woman made an unsanctioned trip to—"

"Turn it off."

The screen went black.

"Diplomatic effort? They just sent us there and didn't tell us there were two fucking people." He took a growling breath. "Unsanctioned, my ass."

They all nodded, knowing it had been an official op gone bad. The government pulled this shit, and then had Titan fix their mistakes. Often.

"What's a fuckin' ATF agent doing in Afghanistan?"

No one answered. Probably, no one knew, but he didn't care. Jared slammed his hands onto the table. "Parker, find out. Now."

Roman and Brock slipped into chairs at the table, and everyone sat there, with the exception of Parker, who'd likely started hacking into every classified federal database that existed.

Jared dropped into his chair and scrubbed a hand across his face. "Her name is Lilly, and she's a Taliban playtoy right now."

"You didn't know her name?" Cash asked, raising his eyebrows. Jared knocked a glare at Cash, who threw his hands into the air. "Sorry, man. Thought you two were vibing."

"'Vibing?' Shut it, Cash," he growled.

"You two aren't... weren't?" Winters asked.

"Oh, for fuck's sake. No. She's our arms dealer. She's part of the Titan network. I don't have to fuck everything that's hot. Case in point—Nicola."

Cash smirked. "Easy, man. Leave my wife out of that comparison."

"And don't say that shit about my sister." Roman sneered.

Nicola rolled her eyes. "I think we all thought that you and Sugar... saw eye to eye on some things."

"Everyone, shut the hell up." He needed to think. *Goddamn, my gut aches.* Not his leg or his shoulder, where fresh wounds were healing, but his gut. "Gear up. We're going back in."

No one moved. This wasn't his typical "calm, cool, collected, plan everything to the nth degree, then execute" reaction.

"Now!" He slammed his hands on the table.

Brock stood up, looking ready to pull the second-in-command card. "We don't have a contract."

"She's our girl, and I owe her more than one favor."

"We don't have State Department approval."

"I don't need it." Jared smirked. "I'd call over to Sixteen Hundred Penn Ave and buzz the president if I gave a damn about protocol, which I don't."

Brock crossed his arms. "We don't have a plan."

"Do what we did before, but finish the job this time." *Why am I explaining myself?*

Brock countered, "You're recovering and aren't thinking clearly."

No shit. "If you want to keep your paychecks coming, you'll be ready to move out."

Jared stormed out of the room, not caring about the opinions behind him. The *clack, clack, clack* of Thelma, his bulldog, followed him from the war room to his office. Now *there* was some loyalty. That dog could eat the carpet, the drywall, and the silverware off his kitchen table, but she always knew when to fall in line and come along.

The secure door closed behind them, making him wish Sugar was standing there, too. Intense eyes that distracted him. Lips that gave him wet dreams. And one killer body. From tits to ass, that woman had it going on. Besides that fun-land of a figure, she nipped at his pissed-off personality, tossing grenade-style sass and a smile that knocked him senseless. He hated it. Sugar was IED-dangerous. One misstep, and *kaboom.*

They both knew it. Both avoided the other. Apparently, to the detriment of learning, she'd hightailed it to hell's playground.

Jared's phone buzzed. He swiped the handset to his ear, didn't listen, and then grumbled. "The only thing I want to hear is, 'Wheels up in thirty.'"

Chewing on cinnamon sticks was a nasty habit. But Kip Pearson embraced the god-awful taste. Since his childhood, the scent had always soothed his agitation, though the damn bark turned his mouth the color of Indian clay and chased away the ladies.

Twenty minutes were left until he had major explaining to do, and that shit was for the grunts.

Working for GSI's Internal Affairs Division meant he didn't have to deal with the headache of following the rules. He only enforced them as he saw fit. That was why he loved carrying on with the IA routine, and that title meant he didn't need to sit in his truck, contemplating where to tell his boss to shove it.

Kip glanced in the mirror, wiping orange spittle from the corners of his mouth, and then opened the truck door. He flicked the spit-covered spice stick like a cigarette butt and ignored the guard on the way in to GSI's main headquarters.

Growling at people in the halls, he swung open the pompous doors, emblazoned with "Buck Baer."

Buck's secretary didn't bat an eye when Kip announced himself. *She must be used to the ballbusters who work for Buck. Very well-paid ballbusters.* And considering that the rocks hanging from her ears weren't knock offs, Buck's secretary was making serious dough, too. *Everyone's on the take. Impressive.*

"Mr. Baer will see you now," she said from the desk, not taking her eyes of the monitor.

Yeah, I bet he will. Good thing Kip hasn't wasted time resting his ass in some cushy chair. Buck's place was too nice, had too much glitz. Kip would rather have hard-nosed furniture that'd been beat up and torn down. *That* would fit his demeanor. But not Buck. He liked the show. But if that's what the prick wanted to do with his moolah, it wasn't worth a second thought to Kip.

He elbowed through another set of solid-wood doors that were meant to impart how well GSI was doing in the private security industry. Other firms tried for high security and impenetrable walls. Buck wanted in-your-face success.

The jerk stood from behind his desk. He always looked angry, at least when Kip walked into the room.

"You stink like cinnamon." Buck clapped his hands onto hips. "Thought I told you to cut that shit out."

"Back off, Buck." What he wouldn't do to face off with him and see who could really take who. It would stop their supervisor-subordinate dance. One good ass whipping, and his boss would wise up.

"I sent you to evaluate the outpost for a simple reason— cover our tails. Now I have the goddamn Secretary of State and the goddamn Defense Intelligence Agency wanting answers."

Kip shrugged and pulled out another cinnamon stick. "Sounds like a personal problem."

"We made a deal, Pearson. You earned your money, and I earned mine."

"Don't worry so much. All ends are almost tied nice and pretty for ya." This conversation was an annoyance. He didn't see his boss as his superior. They were on par. *Strength, check. Tenacity, check. Intelligence, nah.* Kip would have to take that one. But all in all, Kip wasn't subservient, even if the man signed his paychecks.

"That woman is alive!" Buck slammed his hands down on the desk, stout fingers stretched on the expensive-looking wood that was so damn showy.

"Not for long. You have any idea where I left her? In the hands of some very… eager beavers. She's probably wishing she'd died in a car bomb."

Buck pointed at the television. Its muted screen showed his former partner's face. That made things slightly more complicated. "So they know she's alive. Big deal."

"Damn government contracts. I'll never accept a stipulation for an outside observer. Hell, I'll never let you find a fall girl again." Buck rubbed his temples. "They want us to go get her."

Kip used air quotes. "So 'go get her.'"

"You're a piece of work." Buck leaned back into his executive desk chair and cursed. "If this was clean, her death wouldn't have raised an eyebrow. I told you, find a throwaway observer to bring with you. Suspended ATF agent? Few family or friends? She sounded easy, perfect. But now it's messy."

"Price of greed, my friend. I can't help how shit went down. I certainly didn't foresee The Titan Group thrown in the mix. Imagine my surprise when they arrived to save my ass. I'd sooner expect you."

"I don't go into the field anymore." Buck crossed his arms.

Kip laughed. *No shit.* Buck was a face guy these days. He'd packaged up all his brutality so that he could shake hands in DC and secure jobs. *Glad-handing son of a bitch.* "I know. That was a joke, man. Seriously, though. What do you want from me?"

"No complications. That's what I ordered. That's what I expect."

"No complications? Christ, you and your boys caused enough problems that IA had to get involved. No one would've noticed a few missing millions."

"Pearson—"

"Greed always trumps good ol' common sense. You had to go for multi-million. And selling the guns? Not the smartest move, ol' Buckaroo." Kip twirled the cinnamon stick in his finger. Its burnt-orange stain was already set deep on his knuckles.

"You took the money, too." Ignoring the name-calling, his boss levied the charge like it should scare him. "If I go down, you go down."

"Shaking in my Levi's." Kip couldn't help but urge the bastard on. He'd walked in wanting a fight. But no matter what he wanted, Buck wouldn't step up to a ring-side showdown.

"I will pummel your face. Don't care if I am wearing a tailored suit."

Yeah, right. "Unless you're down for blows, Buck, let's finish this up. I was a dirty cop before you hired me. No shame here." And there wasn't. He'd been on the take for years, and he had a nice life to show for it. Big house. Kickin' truck. Cell phone full of pros who would roll out of his bed with a smile. "You offered me this job with a solid explanation of my future duties and compensation. I've been covering up your good-time ways and cashing my paychecks. It's all good."

Buck smoothed the front of his suit, and his irritation was as clear as the cost of the Rolex on his wrist. "How do you propose we fix this?"

"Well, shit, man. I'm not one of your special operations leaders—"

"Stop pushing me, Pearson. I know what the fuck my ground team will do. Your report. Your fuckin' paperwork." He sucked in a long breath that didn't help with his red face. "I want your official report ready in an hour. I want a clean bill of health for my outpost job. I want a report so pretty that the fucking president of this damn country will call me and extend his regrets that *anyone* dared to think GSI's on the take."

"But we are." Kip was having too much fun at the risk of giving his boss a coronary.

"Goddamn it, Pearson!" Buck raised his fist and snarled, but then paused for a breath, steadying himself.

Too damn bad. "Look, Buck, you can't fire me. I'm in a great position. And the sooner you realize that, the better it is for both of us. I'll write a report you can send to your government friends. Hell, I'll testify before Congress. But it'll have some dirt smudges and a red flag or two. Nothing that'll lead to anything. You can't turn in a report that's pristine and shiny. Shit, man, you'd think this was your first time at the rodeo."

Buck's head bobbed. "Watch yourself, Pearson."

He laughed. "Yeah, I'll do that. And if I were you, I'd watch Titan. Rumor has it, our fall girl, she's part of the tight clutches Jared Westin calls his family." Kip probably should've dug a little deeper into Lilly Chase. But when a fine piece of ass like Sugar made herself available, he offered her the gig, only feeling the slightest bit bad that he would have to kill her.

Buck's forehead veins protruded. *The old bastard was probably a respectable bad ass back in the day. Back when he started GSI.* Anyway, he was just an inch away from giving out blow jobs to bureaucrats to keep his money flowing.

The desk phone rang. After staring at it, he finally answered, without dismissing Kip. "Buck Baer."

Buck's face returned to its normal color as he breathed through his nose, his nostrils flaring. "Blow the side off that mountain. I want a crater where an outpost used to be. And I want Lilly Chase dead."

CHAPTER THREE

Dawn cracked over the mountain. It was beautiful, despite the crosshatched cage impeding her view. The frozen air had chilled Sugar all night long as she'd huddled against the dirt floor. Her aches and pains were accentuated by lack of sleep and her concern for her safety.

She sat up, rubbing her hands over her arms for warmth. Movement caught her eye. The small hands that had thrown her pieces of stale bread the day before reappeared, as if waiting for her to wake. They waved hello.

"Hello?" Sugar whispered.

An inch at a time, a navy scarf pushed into Sugar's cell. Caked with mud, the thing was crusty and rough as Sugar pulled it through and wrapped it around her shoulders. An added layer of warmth soothed her shivers.

Then she saw the hands again—really saw them. In daylight and without explosions, those hands were more than small. They were… the size of a child's.

Please… no.

She crawled to the cage barrier and pushed her face against it, hoping to see a man or a teen, and not a poor kid caught in hell. But she saw nothing other than the rocky landscape and wind-billowed tents. No kid. No adults.

Sugar rocked back on her knees and wrapped her scarfed-covered arms around her shins, balling up to preserve body heat. A tiny head poked in front of her cell and then drew back.

It *was* a child. A little girl. Sugar's heart broke. Tears would've flooded her eyes had she not been dehydrated. *No, no. Why does hell have to house babies?*

Crawling back to the edge of her enclosure, she put her fingers through the holes and whispered again. "Hi, out there."

The curious head popped forward, staying near the edge of Sugar's makeshift cell. The girl had big brown eyes—the most inquisitive Sugar had ever seen—knotted hair, and dirt-streaked cheeks. The image wrenched her heart.

Sugar wiggled her fingers through the barricade again. The little girl did the same, putting a finger onto the crosshatch and imitating her.

"Hi," Sugar whispered again, smiling. She pointed to the lock. "Can you open that?"

The little girl shook her head, but curled her finger again.

What language would she speak? Dari? Pashtu? Sugar knew a few basic words, but nothing that would translate well to an... eight-, nine-, ten-year-old. How old was she?

The finger disappeared. Maybe Sugar shouldn't have asked about the lock. Any minute, she would have to deal with the fuckers keeping her caged. Any minute—

The little girl was back, bearing a gift. A piece of bread squeezed through a hole. Sugar pushed her finger through the hole in acknowledgement. "Thank you."

The bread wasn't much, but did the job. Leaning against her enclosure, her fingers still snaked toward freedom, Sugar finished the scrap in two bites and ignored the taste of dirt. A soft touch met her finger, and she looked out of her cage. The little girl sat on the other side and had locked a finger around hers.

Sugar whispered hello again, scared that they would both get into trouble.

"English," the little girl whispered back, nodding.

"English," Sugar repeated, unsure if it was a question or an affirmation. "You know English?"

She nodded, and a little smile spread across her face. Their locked fingers stayed in place, while the girl played in the dirt with her other hand.

"My name is Sugar."

"Sugar," the little girl repeated, not looking away from a tiny dirt pile on the ground. "You are bad?"

Bad? Had the little girl ever seen a woman like Sugar behind makeshift bars? If she was out here, she'd seen too much, like the shootout during the night. Sugar tightened her finger around the girl's, trying to sound trustworthy. "No. Not bad. Good."

"Good." Big brown eyes reached into her heart and squeezed.

"Yes, good." She nodded, reassuringly. "What is your name?"

"Asal."

"That's pretty."

The little girl smiled, showing all her teeth. Sugar heard something move in the background, and Asal scampered away. She was all alone again. For a few minutes, Sugar hadn't been stranded in a rudimentary cell, freezing her ass off on the side of a mountain. She was making a young friend, who she had a feeling hated this damn place, too.

No better way to fix a fuck up than with a little cash and coercion. Wasn't that the American way of doing business? Sure was in Buck's book. And his book was nothing but corrupt commandments and legendary loopholes.

This plan was worth the eye roll from his secretary when he'd sent her running off for the impossible—a simple phone number that would dry up his worries.

Buck leaned back in his chair, cradling his phone against his ear. He had a small window of time to pull this off. Jared Westin was as predictable as he was loyal. If Lilly Chase had a connection to the Titan Group, that devoted jerkoff would run all the way back to Afghanistan to find her. Some people couldn't help being the good guy.

"Yeah, hello?" a clipped voice answered.

His secretary had been successful, worth every Benjamin he threw at her and all that jewelry he gifted on the regular. "This is Buck Baer, and I have a proposition for you."

"Excuse me?"

That reaction was to be expected. *Let's try again.* "This is Buck Baer."

"Are you looking for—"

"No. I'm not. I want to talk to you." *Time for business.* He cracked his neck. "Let's table your surprise for when I really toss something buzzworthy your way."

"What do you want, Baer?"

"An open mind, for starters." He waited and was rewarded with silence. *Bingo.* "Don't breathe a word of this, don't fiddle with recording gadgets, or link up to whatever toys you boys have at Titan until you know the stakes."

"And the stakes are?"

"The stakes are simple. Your worst nightmare. The daughters you think no one knows about and the sweet wife you've hidden from your mercenary life are with me. You might keep a secret life from Titan, trying to keep your pretties safe and sound, but nothing gets by GSI."

"Bullshit."

"I have your wife's phone, and I see you're calling her right now. Cute."

The voice growled, "You will die if you hurt them."

Buck shrugged. "I don't want to hurt them. Really. But here's what I do want. Lilly Chase."

"You kidnapped my family because of *Sugar*?"

"I'm not even asking you to hand her over. I only want intelligence. I suspect Titan will be on the ground before GSI plans to mobilize. If you want to see your family again, all I need is the where and when after you have hands on Lilly Chase. Then—presto—you'll get your family back. Unharmed. And I'll even throw in a couple hundred grand for your worries."

Ensuring Buck's victory before nearing the finish line, the voice again growled, "I'm going to find you, slit your—"

"You might, but your family will die. So it's a lose-lose for everyone. Don't bother bringing Titan in on this one. I know how great your cocksucker boss thinks he is, but do you believe he's better than me? Would you stake your family's life on it?"

"Why do you want Sugar?"

"I took you for a smarter man." Did the world not see she was the one thing that could crumple his empire? Women talked more than they should. She would certainly come back to the States and tell the world what he was actually doing in Afghanistan. Buck shook his head. He was betting that she wouldn't mention what a great entrepreneur he was. No, her focus would probably lie in the terrorists he was aiding in exchange for cash. "It's better not to ask questions."

"Jared will come after you. Me. Both—"

"Titan's days are numbered." Buck gestured nonchalantly. "Jared and I have a not-so-friendly game of Annihilation running. Stems back from our Ranger days. This is more personal than you realize."

"Probably not." The man's voice was harsh and knowing.

The man's comeback was unexpected, but men under duress rarely behaved as they should. "So, do we have an agreement?"

"You take my family, return them at your leisure, then I let you live another night?"

Feisty son of a bitch. Too bad this guy works for Titan. Buck sighed, uninterested in explaining himself, but needing to shore this up. Time was ticking. "No one will take me out. Not you. Not Jared Westin. Not a rogue ATF agent who should've minded her own business and died in the Middle East. You'll always know in the back of your mind that I took them once, and I could do it again."

Silence. Silence was golden. It meant: "Yes, sir. I'll do it, sir. You've got me by the balls, sir."

Just the way Buck liked his friends and enemies. "We'll be in contact. And until then, know everyone is safe. Temporarily."

Jared didn't care about inciting fallout in the Middle East or pissing off people in power. It wasn't his concern. Loyalty ran like blood through his veins. Sugar was a part of his network, which roughly translated to being part of his team. The Titan net had been cast over her, and he would do just about whatever it took to get her and shake some sense into her. *Afghanistan? Shit...*

The knock on his door made him wish for good news. But he wasn't counting on it.

"Get in here," he yelled.

The door opened, and Parker walked in with a folder in one hand and a tablet in the other. The look on his face wasn't promising.

"Speak."

Parker slid the tablet onto Jared's desk. "Details on the hostage we pulled out."

Jared grabbed the electronic device. He tapped on the screen, and it lit up. *Kip Pearson.* The file gave Pearson's generic stats like height, weight, and profession. "He works for GSI?"

Global Security International was Titan's rival. *Wish we'd known that shit when we flew Kip home. Wish the asshole had shouted, "Hey, buddy, you've left my partner on the side of a Taliban-infested mountain." What the fuck was that all about?*

"Yup. As their version of internal affairs."

"Damn it." He bunched his forehead. "IA left a partner behind? That's a stretch. What was their objective?"

"I hacked into Sugar's e-mail and—"

"Great." She would have both their butts for hacking her e-mails.

Parker shrugged. "Most everything from GSI were invoices—"

"She works with them?" *Of course she works with them.* He wasn't her sole client. Actually, he was a newer client. Jared scrubbed a hand over his chin. How much Titan business would it take for her to drop GSI? He had other branches of Titan that she didn't know existed, and they all needed weapons. *Why does it matter?*

"She works with everyone worth a damn." Parker opened the folder. "Here are the details on the job. GSI had a contract with Uncle Sam to arm and train Afghanistan outpost police. But there were red flags that made it to Washington—missing guns and moolah."

"Get to the part I care about, Parker."

"Reports were inconsistent. Military Blackhawk UH-60 did a flyby and reported what looked like Taliban fighters and

Afghani OP police training together. Washington folks complained. GSI jumped to investigate. Cue their internal affairs. Sugar's on suspension with ATF for—"

"Yeah, I know what for," Jared growled. He didn't need reminding. She had ousted herself as an undercover agent to protect his ass and watch out for his team member. Sugar saved Nicola and Cash a lot of worry, and him from a giant headache. He couldn't forget that kind of honor and allegiance.

Parker shifted on his feet. "Kip sought Sugar out after hearing she was on indefinite desk duty. The guy thinks he's smooth, but looks like she was itching for something to do. The rest is in here." Flicking the folder, he paused, then laid it on the desk.

Jared snatched it, then paged through. It held nothing interesting. "Tell Brock I expect an approval of our return within an hour."

"GSI already has the job. They went back and asked for it. Something about trying to save face since we had to go in and save their man."

Jared slammed his hands on his desktop. "Excuse me?"

"They already—"

"Find me Kip Pearson's location. Now." He would hunt the bastard down and find out what wasn't on paper. All the training in the world wouldn't keep Jared Westin calm and collected, but it would help him interrogate the piece of shit who'd left his partner behind.

"One more thing."

He didn't have the patience to read the entire file. "What?"

"Turn the page. There's a fifty-page report from Washington explaining why we only knew to pick up one hostage."

Jared thumbed through the thick wad of paper. "Short version."

"Before Kip was captured, he transmitted a status report that said Sugar pursued a lead solo and was killed by a car bomb. No one would have thought twice about a fatality like that, but I guess some bureaucrat double-checked. No one wants to see a US contractor die in a bomb. But, more importantly, no politician wants to hear about a female civilian dying like that.

Analysts checked several sources and came up empty. There was no car bomb."

"What? Washington read the transmission wrong? Or..." Too many possibilities came to mind. "Or GSI had no intention of Sugar leaving Afghanistan alive."

Parker nodded. "They've always been sketchy."

"You're telling me." He rubbed his temples, deciphering fact from bullshit. He'd known GSI far too long to trust them. "Let's assume the red flags were correct. GSI had the contract to train Afghani police, but were also training Taliban. Uncle Sam requested their internal affairs to follow up with an independent observer like Sugar..." Jared cracked his knuckles, thinking of the ways he wanted to take down GSI. "Fuckin' traitors."

Parker nodded. "Here's the kicker. No one's picked up on it. They had no reason to look for it, but Kip's transmitted message was on a timed delay. He sent it before Sugar landed in Afghanistan."

Anger pounded in his chest. Blood thumped in his neck. A roar started deep within in his lungs. "She was set up."

"Looks like."

"GSI's gonna kill her." He took a deep breath. He excelled in these situations. Shut off emotions. Factor in problems. Execute solutions. Save Sugar, and rain hell along the way. "Time to suit up." Jared bounced a look to Parker, expecting to hear the hold-up list again.

"Everyone's on it." Parker paused as if he had to explain. "You said to suit up twenty minutes ago."

"Fine. Out." *Well, shit.* He'd been so wrapped up in *vibing* talk and Brock's crap about a contract that he'd assumed his team wasn't on board. He shouldn't have assumed. He was distracted to the point of forgetting how loyal his team was to him. To Sugar. To the detriment of any order or contract.

Parker walked out the door, leaving Jared with the report and his thoughts. His team seemed to know how high the stakes were for him. Hell, they knew even before he did. An ache in his chest punctuated that realization.

Jared skimmed the report Parker had left on his desk— Sugar's e-mails. She would kill him for reading her private messages. Then again, she would have to be alive to do that. A live Sugar was better for all involved.

He skipped past pages and stopped. His name appeared in an e-mail to someone he didn't know. By the looks of it, the message was to a girlfriend she worked with.

Thanks for helping with GUNS while I'm gone. I couldn't do this without you, and right now, I need the distraction. This job couldn't come at a better time... Damn, I don't know what it is about him.

The last time he'd seen Sugar, the situation had been tense. *But to run across the world?* He scowled at the paper and kept reading.

When he's not being a dick, I want to kick him to get a reaction. When he is... it gets my blood going. Seriously, how grade school is that? So my decision is made. I won't be tempted. I won't be interested. It's my new motto. Hell, my battle cry. Stay away from Jared Westin.

Jared tore the page out of the folder. Parker hadn't pointed it out, but he had to have seen it. Why else would it have been included? Parker wouldn't see it again, but Jared needed to. He smoothed it out and stared at it.

This was unacceptable. Walking into a mountainside firing line to avoid him was completely, categorically unacceptable. And a battle cry of avoidance? His chest felt tight. His fists clenched. *Sugar.* What he wouldn't do to get his hands on her and say—

And say what? Jared looked at his dog, who looked back, head cocked and wrinkles furrowed. She offered no answers.

He folded the paper, then shoved it into his back pocket. He would make her explain herself after he figured out why he cared.

CHAPTER FOUR

Words Sugar didn't understand floated closer as the night drew darker. Another day in this hole was another day she wouldn't lose hope. She hadn't found a way out yet. But a plan was formulating. If only she had more energy to corral her scattered thoughts.

Her captors were coming for her. She knew it. She felt it. And when they did, she would summon what was left of her waning strength and fight to survive.

A campfire roared in the distance. Dinner and drinks sounded well on their way to being done. Asal had come by with food she'd obviously snuck away with, and the calories might've been what kept Sugar from delirium.

Again, the little girl showed up, knocking on Sugar's enclosure. Her little face was streaked with tears. Sugar's heart pounded harder. She had a soft spot for neglected kids, and Asal took the cake on that title. She'd never met a less fortunate child who survived in circumstances Sugar couldn't fathom. Sugar's childhood had been so-so. But that was due to her self-absorbed parents and had nothing to do with surviving the elements and avoiding grenade launchers.

Even with all that weighing down on the kid, Asal still smiled. Until that night. That night, she was crying, and heaven help whoever had made Asal cry. If Sugar could hurt them, too, it would make this cold day a little better.

She pointed to Asal's eyes and cheeks. "Why were you crying?"

Asal said something Sugar didn't understand, then pressed her hands to her chest. "Husband."

Her throat cracked as a prickle cascaded down her spine. "Your husband?"

The girl nodded, rubbed her face, and stopped, seeming to search for words Sugar might understand. "I go to him soon."

"You haven't met him?"

Asal didn't look as though she understood.

Sugar tried again. "Your husband. Is he here?"

"No." Her tiny face shook.

"How old are you?"

Asal held up fingers, making an effort to count, then shrugged. She finally held up eight fingers, but shook her head.

"How old is your husband?"

She looked around and pointed at men older than Sugar was. The air crushed out of her lungs as if this godforsaken mountain had caved in. The baby in front of her, with the sweet and innocent face, pained her.

"Do you have a mom and dad? Family?"

She nodded. "Uncles."

"Are you scared?" Sugar asked.

Asal nodded.

God, I'll kill them all. "Go hide. I will help you."

The girl didn't move, but the drunken voices had come closer. The men who held her captive drank and gestured. This was about to get ugly.

"Asal. Go. Now."

The little girl looked at the men, then at Sugar. "Hurt you."

The English was halting, but the sentiment was dead on. The men were coming for some fun, and Sugar didn't want Asal around for the show. "Go." She tried to push her away from the cell door. "Now, Asal. Run away."

Asal stared at the men and tilted her head. "Uncle."

Shit, that's her uncle? Well, Uncle was about to have a fight on his hands. Sugar had no plans to be the evening's entertainment.

"Go."

Asal stuck her finger in the cell, wiggled it, then pushed something to her. It fell, and the little girl ran away. Sugar looked down—a rusted, bent blade. US military issued. Broken handle. It was more than enough of a weapon.

She looked up, and Asal was gone. Thank God, because that bent blade was in for some see-saw action if Sugar could help it.

Two men staggered to the door of her cage. They stank of desert booze and highland sweat, of dirt and mountain living. Her stomach retched. The gleam in their eyes issued their threats. But their drunken squabbling gave her time to get ready.

She couldn't stand in the makeshift cell, but she could fight. Tucking the knife into the waist of her pants, she rose to a kneeling position, ready to be pinned down or dragged out. The lock scraped, and the door opened wide.

Each man took an arm. Dragged out it was. She could scream, but she didn't see any reason to waste the energy. *Get me to a place I can stand.*

Once in the clear, she powered up, moving her weight from one man into the other. Their drunken asses stumbled, but that wasn't enough for her to get away. Sugar lunged into one of them; the other fell on top of her.

Fight. Kill. Survive.

Labored breaths heaved through her nostrils. Her stomach threatened to spill the remnants of the stale bread. The men laughed, and a slap rang clear through her brain.

The stars spanned seconds, too long to regain her focus, and her face was slammed into the rocky ground. Pain sprayed through her nerve endings. Stars spun again. One arm tore from the socket and was pushed above her head.

Sugar focused on her training, on how to endure. She wrapped the pain in a box and punted it out of the game. She reached into her waistband and found the blade. It scraped into her palm as she grasped it, but she ignored the bite of pain. She slashed the blade sideways, connecting through the thick burlap clothes until she heard a man's yell. A small victory.

He released her hand. The second man dove onto her, but she rolled. Her elbow cracked him in the temple, stunning him and allowing her enough time to find her feet. Her breaths came fast in the frozen air. Adrenaline was her partner, treating her far better than that GSI jerk had.

She jumped up. The world spun round like a toy top. The dark mountain and inky sky blurred. The fire in the distance became her focal point, and she blinked hard.

Both her attackers came at her, their hands up and their faces angry. They hurled threats she couldn't understand. But she comprehended.

An explosion ripped through the air behind them. Rapid blips of gunfire lit the distance. Gas bombs catapulted, flipping and zigzagging into the tents.

The timing couldn't have been better. Someone needed to tear this place down, and she needed the distraction. The men forgot about their conquest-in-waiting and ran back toward camp.

Asal.

Sugar rotated a glance over her horizon for the little girl, but she came up empty. A fire bomb boomed, and she needed cover. Running toward a rocky ledge, Sugar snagged an automatic rifle propped against a boulder. She swiped as much ammo on the fly as she could carry, then climbed into the thick mountain brush. Thorns scraped her skin but didn't slow her down.

Behind her back, artillery detonated. Her captors hadn't been ready for an offensive strike. Sugar turned from her perch on a sturdy inlet. Was this a rival tribe attack? Was this military? She couldn't tell through the smoke.

Men scattered, fleeing the main camp, and one by one, the tents were ransacked and brought down. Cries of pain accompanied screams of defiance. The offense was on a search-and-destroy mission. Like a tiny town swallowing itself, the area was consumed.

Then all was quiet.

Objective met?

What was that? she wondered. As long as they didn't bother her, Sugar didn't care. And where was Asal? Sugar would find that blade-gifting girl and get her the hell out of this mountainous crapshoot. *That kiddo isn't marrying some sick fuck. No way.*

Through the billowing clouds in the fire-lit night, Sugar couldn't see much. Somewhere, a goat bleated, and someone shuffled through tents. *Must've been a rival tribe attack.* There was looting. As long as Asal was safe, they could hunt and gather all night long.

A branch cracked. The hair on her arms stood up, as if on lookout. Her breath stilled, her mind listening, hoping to hear nothing.

Nothing. Not a peep. Too quiet. But wasn't that what she wanted?

Someone was near. A shiver of awareness said so. Or was that paranoia? Dehydration could do that. Men threatening to rape her could do that.

Trust your instinct.

She closed her eyes and forced her senses to attention. Smoke burned in her nostrils and coated her tongue. The harsh wind bit her cheeks and... carried footsteps. Closer. Close enough that she had to move.

Sugar crouched, then crawled down the narrowing rock path, which became a brush-covered ledge. Loose stones slipped away, cascading off the side of her foothold. *Not good.* Shadows danced far below the sharp drop-off. She positioned forward, aiming the AR-15 for whatever came her way. As long as it wasn't a little girl, it was dying.

Another crack. Branches scraped beside her. Above her?

She couldn't get a bearing on the source. The camp activity echoed against the mountain. It was too distracting, and she was too panicked. Her pulse pounded in her ears, and blood pounded in her throat.

Another gust of wind carried the sound of shifting fabric. Her skin prickled. A solid force dropped on top of her, knocking her rifle from her reach, holding her to the ground. A hand wrapped over her mouth, twisting her body against her attacker's.

Her stolen breath was knocked away. Instinct took over the fight. Her knee went up, and her fists punched, then clawed.

Eyes. Groin. If she could hit either, her chances increased. All she sensed was strength and power. That wasn't going to take her down. She would fight until she died.

No! Not die. Survive. She centered, assessed, and jerked back her head, connecting with a jawbone.

A grunt of pain followed. A minute win. She turned and—

"Sugar."

The harsh whisper stopped her, stunning her, and she began trembling the instant she registered the deep timbre.

"Stop."

She pinched her eyes closed. This was a delusion or a nightmare. But her body stilled as pinpricks of awareness popped, and her mind galloped after logic.

Strong hands turned her and forced her eyes open. Tactical gear. Night vision goggles. Blood dripping off his chin.

She didn't need to see his face. The confirmation was innate. Instinctive. Jared Westin had found her. Saved her. Another round of shivers spiked down her spine.

"We gotta go." He stood, pulling her up and wrapping her to his chest, then backed down the incline.

Her shock wore away. Heated embarrassment took its place. She had run away from him, only to have him come across the globe, guns ablaze. *Only goddamn Jared Westin could pull a stunt like this, the prick.*

Ignoring the all-consuming need to cling to his chest and sob her thanks, she pushed back from his hold, but her head spun. "I can walk." *Maybe.*

Adrenaline made her strong. Emotions and dehydration made her irrationally determined. He didn't let go, just kept moving them down the side of the mountain, toward the decimated tent village.

Where is Asal? "Jared, stop."

He ignored her. She became dead weight. That didn't stop him, though. He lifted her with one arm and kept on.

"Wait." She struggled against his body-armored chest. "Wait. There's someone else."

That put on the brakes. He pulled them against the rocks and took off his goggles. "There were three of you?"

He looked pissed. *Welcome to the club, buddy.*

"No—"

"GSI? POW? What?"

"Her name is—"

"Her?" His eyes darted over her shoulder, watchful and protective. "Not here to sort out the local bullshit."

Of course the *her* would be a local, because women didn't come here. Fury built in her chest. He grabbed her to move on, but Sugar rocked against his grip, struggling to free herself. "A girl. A child. Put me down, goddamn you."

He stilled but didn't let go.

"She's a kid. And if you didn't kill her, she's alone on the side of this mountain 'cause you killed everyone else."

"My mission's to bring you home, Sugar. We'll deal with the GSI crap later. So shut up and—"

"Then leave me. She's a goddamn kid. Scared out of her mind. Find her or leave me. I didn't ask you to come get me, and I sure don't need this bullshit." She knocked him in the chest, hurting her cold, numb knuckles. "Give me a gun and go away."

He tightened his grip on her. "I don't know who the hell you think you are. Look the hell around. You'll die or be captured again. Raped. Sold. Killed. That's your future—"

"Same with that kid. Except she's eight." Sugar tried to swallow. "Just a baby."

Fires exploded around them. The temperature was falling quickly. Clouds of their breaths burned between them. He locked eyes with her, making her stomach catapult. Her mind pleaded that he was more than a machine. His stare broke away, skittering over the barren rockscape. Nothing could live out there in the elements, certainly not a kid. He had to see that.

His dark eyes, bright and furious, stole back to her. She would have held her breath if the anticipation hadn't already put her lungs on strike. "The girl snuck me a knife. It was my only chance, and it worked. Now we're hers. I owe her."

Jared reached for his mic and barked. "Hands on the package. One more to pick up. Repeat, one more to grab. Give me eyes on the outskirts." He paused, studying Sugar. "We're looking for a small girl, boys. Easy with the takedown."

Warmth bled down her neck and into her chest. The bastard may have had a sliver of a heart after all.

CHAPTER FIVE

Jared pinched the bridge of his nose. The side of a cliff with Sugar, who was pulling the unwilling-evacuee act, wasn't the best place for a negotiation. She knew it. He knew it. But she was holding the aces when she dropped intel about abandoned kids on war-torn mountainsides. It was enough to make him revisit his extraction plan.

His team, clad in heat-seeking goggles, was on an efficient but gentle manhunt for a child. *Great.*

Around Sugar, plans never worked out, including his current one to stay huddled in a cave until the kid was found. He hoped she was alive when they found her, but he wasn't holding his breath. Sugar was attached to the child. This had the potential to be a shit storm.

He checked in with the men, who had nothing to report. In another thirty minutes, he would have to call off this rooster run. Sugar wouldn't take that well. He wiped a hand over his face, then eyed her in the dark. She obviously wasn't happy to have a helping hand, and she shivered in silence.

After pulling off his top layer, he pushed it toward her. "Take this." Her eyes flashed angrily. What the hell was her problem? "Take it, goddamn it. You're freezing."

At home, she wore skintight leather pants and T-shirts that might've been painted on. Her dark hair was always tousled. Her midnight-blue eyes danced, always laughing. But right then, her clothes were tactical and tattered. She looked pale and exhausted.

A pang of concern pushed against his chest. He'd always been protective of his team and of those loyal to him. And even as pissed off as she was at him—and God only knew why—Jared wanted to do more than the usual. He wanted to protect her from the elements, from the Taliban, and from whatever the fallout would be from the ongoing manhunt for a likely never-to-be-seen-again child.

Her e-mail, which he still had tucked in his back pocket, was on his mind. It bounced around with confused ideas of Sugar as an ATF agent and as an operative who'd been trapped and left behind by her GSI partner, then by Titan. Jared struggled with that identity and reality, as well as his awareness that he was interested in her in a way that differed from his concern for other women. Other women he fucked, but fucking Sugar would mess up everything. She was a cool chick one day and a pain in his ass the next.

She'd always been a pain in the ass—like she was right then. "Sugar, take my damn shirt. Exposure isn't taking you out on my watch."

She snagged it and pulled it over her knotted hair. She raised her eyebrows and threw him a tight nod. That was it. *Hell, what did I expect? Her to say thanks?* He chuckled. *Not a chance.*

"What's so funny?" She tilted her head, and her voice sounded stronger than he'd expected.

Never expect anything with this one. "I've been to this mountain twice in a week. Of all the places I've had to double-hit, this wouldn't be on my list."

Her eyebrows came crashing down in a line that crinkled above her nose. "That was you before?"

"Sure was, baby cakes."

"Screw you, Jared."

He laughed again and wondered if their bickering was a game or a defense. "Mind telling me why you're pissed at me for saving your stubborn ass?"

Even without daylight, her midnight eyes shone as though they were unaware of the elements. If she shivered again, it would take strong will more than training to keep from holding her. Then again, transferring heat body to body was operating procedure under certain circumstances.

She shivered.

If the air were a few degrees colder, he could make the argument that they had fallen under those *certain circumstances.* "Look, Sugar. Didn't know you were here before. So forgive me. Okay? We better now?"

She didn't look at him. "I didn't want you here."

"Because you had everything *so* under control here? Christ."

"Jared, you're a dick." She tried to elbow her exit. Hard. Where did she think she was going? He gripped her bicep, holding her in place against him. She was stronger than she looked, which sent another ripple of awareness straight to his toes.

"Explain the attitude," he growled against her ear. Her soft skin teased him.

"No."

"Explain why the hell you're in Afghanistan."

She pulled her ear from his lips and sliced a glare at him. "Because I was bored."

"Liar." His voice rasped, and he tightened his grip on her.

"I needed to get away from a headache."

Closer to the truth. He was a headache? "Fair enough." They locked in an unexplained moment, and he could feel the thump of her heartbeat through all the layers of gear.

"Let me go." She tried unsuccessfully to shrug away.

"You'll run away, for whatever stupid ass reason."

"I won't." She gave a thin smile. "I'll stay. I need a ride home."

He loosened his grip on her, but neither moved back. The pounding in his chest reverberated into his throat. The tips of his fingers pulsed. "Good."

"Good," she whispered.

A piece of dark hair dangled over her eye, and he brushed it back, dragging his finger into its tangled softness. *Fuck, I didn't need to do that.* He dropped his hand and let his fingers slide down the slope of her neck, tracing a path to her bicep. *Goddamn. Didn't need to do that, either.* But he couldn't stop.

She sucked in a breath and held it for a two-count. "You shouldn't do that."

"Why not?"

"Because we're on the side of a mountain. Because you're you, and I'm me."

She apparently had the same concern he did—that it would ruin everything. "Not good enough reasons."

Her eyes sparkled, then she looked into the darkness, biting her lips. "Because we're in the middle of an op, waiting on news that could go either way."

"It'll be good news." Maybe, maybe not. But she needed to have faith.

"I'm not so sure."

He caressed her arm with his thumb. "That's why you're pissed?"

She blinked, and he could've sworn he spotted resolve. "Keep your hands to yourself. People are waiting, working, so if you're done trying to get into my head, let's help find Asal and bug on home."

Bug on home? She was cute when she threw down field lingo. And that made him want into her head as much as her pants, though maybe he hadn't realized either desire burned as strongly as it did until that moment. Talk about killer timing. There she stood, pretending this tension wasn't going to play out. Someday, someway, it would. "Such a tough girl."

"Don't placate me, J-dawg."

He held in a laugh. "Wouldn't dare."

Roman beeped into his earpiece, signaling they had found the girl—alive. He gave Sugar a thumbs-up. Her tension melted away, and relief radiated from her bright eyes. She released an exhausted breath as her stance softened.

That was his in. "I'm getting you out of here."

He pulled her close to his body as they scooted from their alcove. The ledge was tight. Harsh wind could push an unsteady Sugar toward the valley. Even if it hadn't been so crucial to hold her close, his protective gut said he might have anyway.

They made quick work of the trip to the rendezvous spot, but came up short at the sight of his men. They surrounded a small girl, wrapping around her like an outer ring of guns and glory. Sugar took off running toward them and barreled through the strapped muscle heads.

Jared wasn't far behind. Brock pulled out of their formation. "A kid? What's the deal?"

"No idea."

They both stared. "What are we supposed to do with her?"

Jared paused, with no plan in mind. "Where did you find her?"

"Housed up in the rocks. Looks like she had a tree-house thing going on, except it was filled with knives and sticks. She's the only live thing out here, except for the goats."

"She's coming with us." There. That was the start of a plan. It made sense. Maybe.

Brock cocked a brow. "To Abu Dhabi?"

"What are we supposed to do?" Jared glared. "Leave a damn kid exposed to the elements, to freeze to death?"

"There's going to be a lot of red tape on this one. Laws on top of laws."

"Roger that. We'll hit up the Red Cross or a UN attaché. They'll know how to handle this. She's got to be an orphan. They'll find her an adoptive family. Right?"

"Right." Brock shrugged. "Until then, we're the best armed babysitters money can buy."

He wasn't about to tell his rule-following second in command that this was an out-of-pocket trip or that GSI, technically, still had the contract. That their trip was the operative equivalent of pro bono.

A chopper appeared over the side of the cliff. No jumping to rappelling ropes with this cargo. The helo passed them, signaling they were behind schedule. Not good.

"Move boots."

They had to cover fifty yards to the rendezvous spot, where it was level and the chopper could hover near the ground so they could hoist themselves up. Getting to that spot required the team to traverse a sheer part of the mountain. The plan worked fine when the pickup was for only Sugar. But the kid? That was too risky.

The men were on the move, guns out, pivoting, on the lookout for the unexpected. Sugar and the kid stepped in line, and he had the rear.

Over rocks, through brush, everyone did fine. They made good time, and he could hear the helo waiting. Once they were over the sheer part, they would be out of there.

Pht, pht, pht. Cash was in the helicopter, and sputtered bullets weren't saying, "Hi, nice to see ya." The team had spent too much time on the ground looking for the kid, and someone had come to pay them a visit. They couldn't go back and get out the way they had arrived.

"Go!" Jared gave the directive to move forward.

They reached the steep surface. Flat. Like a sliding board of death. Damn near a seventy-five degree angle. Rocco moved across, clawing his way into foot holes and using a tool to dig out handgrips. He secured a rope and tossed it to Roman, who tied the line taut, creating the one safety net they could construct.

Winters went first, tying on a carabineer and testing the line. Success. He was safely on the other side. Roman secured the kid with a carabineer and belt, then urged her to cross. His arms chopped and gestured like a New York City traffic cop. "Follow him. Do that." He repeated twice.

If the angle weren't so steep, Roman would probably have crawled out there with the kid. But it wasn't an area that two people could cross at the same time.

"Go, Asal," Sugar urged.

Asal. The kid had a name, and it meant "honey." *Small world that Sugar and Honey found each other.*

Rocco and Winters beckoned from the other side, waving and smiling as best they knew how. Winters had a kid at home, so his good-guy face was more practiced.

Gunfire thundered again in the background. Then a blast fell from above. Cash loved to pick off the enemy. If he was throwing grenades, there were more tangoes than he had time for. It was a clear signal to get a move on. Pronto.

Asal looked at Sugar, who gave a reassuring nod. Newly confident, the girl took a step out, then another. She got her bearings and scooted farther, halfway across. Then she was two-thirds there. Gravel gave out, and skidding rocks sheared off the cliff as a child's scream echoed into the night, and her feet struggled for footing.

"Asal!" Sugar yelled to her, stepping to the ledge. Jared threw a hard arm around her waist, holding her back.

"Hang tight." Quickly but cautiously, Jared crawled onto the incline. The girl had been saved by a few yards of tactical rope and belt, and he would get her to the other side. The seconds passed in slow-mo until he reached Asal. With an arm looped around her shaking torso, he used the rope as their lifeline.

They inched up the vertical slide. Wind gusted and howled. Fabric flapped hard. Dirt jumped into the air. Asal whispered, but Jared didn't know the translation. He guessed it was along the lines of, "Let's not die today."

After a few more feet, they finally summited the safe side after a tenuous climb.

He put the girl down. There were no tears across her face, just a big grin. The panic from falling was long gone. *I'll be damned.* She waved to Sugar.

"Good job, kid."

Asal repeated, "Good job kid." And it made Jared smile.

Cash buzzed in his ear. "Tangoes everywhere. I'm holding them back, but you guys need to move."

"Roger that." Jared looked at Sugar. "Ready?"

She nodded, clipped on her carabineer, wrapped her hand around the rope, and took a step. Gravel shifted. His stomach dropped, but he didn't stop her. She stepped again. More gravel fell to the ravine below.

"Wait. Sugar, hold up." He studied the surface and couldn't see the slipping stones. They were loose, but how loose?

Determination painted her face. A thin smile said she was moving forward again. Another step scattered more gravel, which cascaded down the mountainside. Again, she stepped, loosening gravel. Her footing faltered, but she caught herself.

"Get back there," he ordered, looking into the black abyss below.

She didn't look over her shoulders but wrapped her hands in the rope, balancing precariously on the slope. The wind carried her voice. "No other way out."

"There's always another way. Get back there."

"I'm tied to this rope. I'm fine."

She was closer to him than she was to the other side. Another grenade blew in the distance. She stepped forward.

"Goddamn it, Sugar. Stop." His heart chugged uncontrollably, like an out-of-control freight train. Bad feelings needled him, tingled in his palms, and put pressure on his chest.

Her foot inched forward. Rocks that were much larger than gravel slipped. The ground was giving out beneath her.

"Get the kid out of here!" Jared ordered. If Sugar was going down, the kid wasn't going to bear witness. "All of you, go."

Winters grabbed the girl, turning her around. Her cry for Sugar's safety bounced into the night. His men fell out into the darkness, heading toward the chopper.

"Don't move," he said to Sugar.

She looked at him, flashing a tight smile. He clipped on a carabineer and stepped onto the slope. Walking the absurd angle was like walking on a wall.

As still as a statue, Sugar stayed. The gravel and rocks around her didn't. "Well, this sucks."

"Stay put."

"Not moving."

"Your lips are, baby cakes."

More rocks fell, and he launched himself in her direction. The rope went taut, and his hand met her rigid arm. Rocks slipped around them. Pulling her to him, he backed them toward safety. The groundcover gave way. His hip hit rock, jamming his shoulder into boulder. Sugar was locked against his chest, and they slid with the falling dirt until they snapped to a stop. The rope stretched to capacity and held their weight.

"You shouldn't have done this," she hissed.

Too damn bad. "You needed help."

Together, they found footholds and pushed up. His fingers were frozen, and his muscles burned as he pulled their weight. Blasts of cold air were a constant. Reaching a safe surface, Sugar crawled over to a boulder, leaned against it, and dropped her head back. He did the same, catching his breath. The scent of smoke drifted in the air. Gunfire popped in the background.

As the moon appeared from behind clouds, Jared looked at Sugar. The milky moonlight bathed her beauty. Jared ran his hand through his close-cropped hair. That was too close. "You okay?"

"Never better."

"Right. Remind me to help you out again. You're so appreciative."

"Just forget it." She rubbed her eyes and then threaded her fingers into her hair, smoothing it. Then she moved them down to her lips, where she blew on them, rubbing them together.

"How cold are you?"

"Not very."

Yeah, right. It was in the thirties, maybe colder. With the wind chill factored in, brisk temps were assumed dangerous. Freezing was more like it. She ignored him, shivering.

Cash interrupted Jared's thoughts. "We're too hot. Pulling out." In the distance, the chopper rose. His earpiece buzzed in and out of range. Static again, then Cash's voice carried into his ear. "You two good for a couple hours?"

"Roger that," he said, nodding to Sugar. He mouthed, "Few hours. No problem."

She nodded.

Cash's voice crackled as the chopper receded. "Oh four hundred, pick up at the bottom of base camp."

"Affirmative," Jared replied, knowing Sugar would enjoy the rappelling-rope take-off as much as he did.

Static filled in his ear, then silence. He pulled out the earpiece. Sugar's hands were tucked under her arms, in her armpits, as she huddled against herself. Her body shook. His healing gunshot wounds ached, and the cold was beginning to seep deep into his body.

"Take my gloves," he offered, taking them off.

She shook her head, her teeth chattering. "You'll freeze."

That made him laugh. "I'll survive."

"So will I. I'm fine." Her teeth chattered.

"Goddamn, woman. You're stubborn." Without thinking, Jared dropped to the ground next to her, wrapped her in a bear hug. She fought his hold, maybe just enough to be able to say that she did. But the struggle was an exhausted token gesture.

Then all stilled. The brightest of stars shone like diamonds in the black sky. The night was silent once again, but that didn't mean much. Tangoes were ready to tussle not far from their shelter. Forgetting it all, he held Sugar close, and the closeness felt... significant.

Flickers of desire bled through him. Not in a familiar, wanna-jump-her-bones way. *At least not right now.* It was more torrid heat and carnal realization. Her shivers slowed, and her chattering teeth stopped, making the pressure in his lungs feel like he couldn't take a deep breath if he wanted.

She sighed, and as if by reflex, he pulled her tighter to him. A thrill soared from his head into his chest. His pulse went erratic. It didn't make sense. Everything in his life, from work to women, was as structured as it was wild, and that warm buzz bouncing in his brain wasn't on the schedule.

He'd jumped out of planes into explosions, sunk to the bottom of oceans to battle riptides. But this rush was like what addicts must feel when drugs first hit their veins, why they went searching for another hit.

In her lax position, she burrowed against him, and without his control, his eyelids slowly shut. Savoring it, he could only feel, only be in that moment, refusing to understand how or why he felt the way he did.

Her head was tucked under his chin, and her hair pushed in his face, tickling his neck. Her bottom curved against his groin, and they lay as one in the frozen night against a boulder.

Jared took a breath, trying to quell the eager anticipation of something more than he'd experienced before, though he didn't know what to call it. He focused on the act of heat transference. This was a tactical act—a physical deliverance of heat to a woman who'd been held against her will in sub-freezing temps.

"Better?" he asked.

Sugar barely nodded. She didn't act like a rescue victim, but she wasn't the same badass with the Teflon exterior from GUNS. Maybe it was the moment, not the girl.

"If you let your guard down with me, Sugar, and drop the tough-girl act, I won't tell a soul."

She nodded again.

Maybe it was both the moment and the girl. "Okay, then. Get some sleep, and we'll get the hell out of here in a few." And for some goddamn reason, he nuzzled into her hair and pressed his lips to the back of her head. *A fucking kiss.*

She didn't move. She didn't respond, yell, or throw him an elbow. He threw his leg over hers with the silent excuse of staying warm and let her drift off to sleep.

CHAPTER SIX

Intense muscle fatigue. It was the first thing Sugar noticed before her eyes cracked open. The next was a semblance of warmth. Not that she was warm. No, her feet were numb. Her cheeks wind chapped. But a stronghold of arms and legs had her cocooned. *Jared.*

She tested her parched lips and tried to swallow away the dryness in her throat. A headache was kicking in full force. All in all, she felt like crap, and she had big problems to work out. The catalyst for her running away had wrapped his solid, muscled arms around her. She couldn't be strong around the jerk. *Her* jerk.

Her radar attracted the bad boys. It always had, but she'd been damned good at staying unattached and unaffiliated. Until Jared. His presence was enough to make her tongue-tied, warm, and bothered. Staying away from him had been the best course of action. Too bad the few thousand miles she'd put between had been reduced to inches, and here he was, tangled up with her under the edge of a giant boulder.

Forgetting being dehydrated and exhausted, her blood flash-flooded, intent on making sure she noticed Mr. GI Joe. An explosion of goose bumps cascaded down her back. *Noticed* was the PG-rated version of how her body responded to him.

She shook the horned-up thoughts from her head. They were buds who worked together. If she'd seen him in a bar, she would say, "Hey, let's grab a beer." Hell, she'd dated, for lack of a better word, one of the men who worked for him.

But then their dancing-on-the-edge flirtation spiraled out of control and got real. She'd broken cover to help Jared, making the decision to think about someone besides *numero uno*.

Whether or not he'd realized it, he had needed her help. Hell, whether he realized it or not, the look in his eyes hadn't said thanks, it'd said DTF. Down to fuck.

That wasn't the road she wanted to go down, but she was certainly all about coasting on the shoulder, having a little fun. *Nothing wrong with working with hot Mr. Grumpy Pants.* And it would be a hell of a challenge.

Look, but don't touch. Flirt, but don't give in. Seduce, but not really.

Jared was a sport. He would never cross the line. Too rigid. Too many rules. But everything had changed again, and she didn't know why. He had kissed the back of her head. That wasn't flirty, fun, or DTF. *It was freakin' sweet.* And she liked it. Too much. Disasters were made out of this type of hookup.

Jared wasn't the relationship type, and she respected him for knowing it. For flaunting it. He was an all-American hero mixed with rugged good looks. A man like Jared Westin wasn't meant to be tied down.

And a girl like her... No one could flirt better. She could sway her hips just right. She knew when to pause, drop her gaze, or smile. Sugar could work a man over without getting caught up. She'd perfected it for undercover work, for avoiding relationships, and for having a good time, with no strings attached. But a Jared-and-Sugar combo felt like it had a lot of strings—all of them loose ends and knots.

"You awake?" The gravelly, morning timbre of his voice raked from the shell of her ear straight to her stomach.

She nodded. All she'd been doing around him was nodding. Gestures worked best when she didn't trust her voice or the words that might pour out of her mouth.

He tightened his arms around her, causing her empty stomach to somersault. "We've got thirty-five minutes. You hungry? I have a protein bar."

Hungry? Try starved. But acknowledging that might require some talking. And maybe a little manners. "Very."

Sitting them up, he opened a zipper and produced the bar. It could've been filet mignon. Nothing had ever looked so appetizing.

"Here." He tore open the package and handed it over.

"Want some?"

"Nah. I'll eat later."

Do I look that hungry? Hm-mm. Guess so. It was gone in four bites.

Jared cleared his throat, rubbing his hands together. His gloves were covering her hands. They were too big, but they did the job.

She stripped them off her hands. "Take these back. I'm good."

Protesting, he tried to push them back on her, then stared at her palm. She'd cut it on that rusty knife. A nasty infection had turned the skin red and yellow. *Perfect.*

"Why didn't you tell me?" His voice was disapproving. Maybe annoyed.

"What do you want? A line by line of everything that hurts? My hand, my head. My throat is dry—"

"How'd you split your hand like that?"

She shrugged. "Rusted knife, no handle."

"Asal gave you the knife?" His face was tight. His dark eyes were expressive, and his brows were furrowed. "Why? You were trying to escape, or…"

"I needed to fend off my suitors. It worked. The cut was a by-product." She smirked at the wound. "I wasn't the only one cut by the thing, so two wrongs made a right in that case."

The muscles in his cheeks twitched. A deadly rage burned in his eyes. "Did they…" He cleared his throat again. "Did they hurt you?"

"No." She closed her fist to keep from staring at the cut. "Actually, you came just in time. So, thank you." She tilted her head, showing as much gratitude as she could with what little energy she had.

Anger radiated from Jared. He gave a grunt and nod. "We were going to helo out of here on rappel lines, but your hand is jacked."

A spike of adrenaline rushed through her. "Nice. No, I want in. I'm fine." She opened and closed her hand, making a show of being fine, ignoring that it hurt.

"Not a chance, baby cakes. I should've thought about potential injuries. Plus, you're fatigued. I don't need you dangling off a line."

"What are you going to do, Jared? Carry me back to America? Every obstacle that's come up, you've backed away like I'm some glass figurine. I'm not going to break. I'm sure as hell not going to die. I already made that decision."

He chuckled. "You've been making a lot of *decisions,* haven't you?"

Confused, she stared at him. "We don't have a choice, and I'm not waiting around any longer. Help me wrap my hand." She paused as he rubbed his forehead. "Look, Jared, I'm not here because I'm bad at my job. I'm no weakling. I'm more than ready for this."

"You're here because Kip Pearson screwed you."

"Yeah, I think so." The icy tone to her voice matched the temperature.

"I know so."

"Then good. You know so. I'd planned on finding the fucker and taking him down. Maybe you want to help me."

"There's something bigger going on," he said.

"Always is. I just want to finish what he started."

"Kip's on the take." He cracked his knuckles. "All goddamn GSI is corrupt, and I'm gonna shut 'em down. You want in?"

"Kip Pearson's mine."

Jared didn't look at her. "We'll see about that."

"No deal. I get Pearson. Do what you want with GSI, but he and I have our issues to work out."

He refocused on her. "What happened out there?"

She sighed, almost too exhausted to explain everything she'd seen. "The outpost police were corrupt. They worked with Taliban forces. GSI turned a blind eye, training both OP *and* Taliban. The money and guns aren't missing. GSI's working the system. Making loot. Training the enemy for big payouts."

Jared rubbed his chin, but he didn't look surprised. He checked his watch, then tore a piece of fabric from his shirt. "We gotta go." Little by little, that man was losing all his clothes to her. "Give me your hand."

She complied. It looked tiny compared to his larger, rougher ones, which made quick work of the bandage. Her cheeks flushed as she tried to ignore his touch.

After tucking in the end of the bandage, he held her fingers in his. "You sure this will do?"

Sparks shot up her arm, and she snatched away her hand. "Yes. It's fine."

"Jesus, Sugar. Did that hurt?"

"No. I just want to get out of here. Can we go already?"

He watched her. Every emotion she had was surely plastered on her face. Interest. Lust. Uncertainty. She couldn't hide it. *Why can't I keep anything from this man?*

"You know what? Something's going on between us," he said, deep in concentration.

"Nothing's going on between us." *Because I won't let it. Because you think I'm a fun time, and for the first time, it scares me.* "That's insane."

They stared, silent. She waited, feeling the electric charge that pulled them closer.

"Insane?" He leaned over and let his lips hover near her earlobe. "Something's going on. I like a challenge, and you scream, 'Just try me.' That, Sugar, is *something*." He didn't touch her. He didn't have to. Tingles exploded down her neck, shooting toward her navel. Jared drew back, again locking eyes with her. "You're a cool chick. I'm just worried fuckin's gonna ruin everything."

The pounding in her heart reverberated into her throat. The tips of her fingers tingled. *Everything* tingled.

He righted himself. "Nothing to say?"

She took a breath, regaining her composure. "Easy fix. I'm not interested."

"Like hell."

"I'm. Not. Interested. Get it through your thick head, big boy." She pushed on his chest and was reminded once again how stout and solid he was.

A smile that made her dizzy teased across his face. He snatched her hand pressing against his chest and held it in his grip.

Keep your head, girl.

"You mind backing off me? Or do I need to push against this brick wall again?" With her other hand, she flicked her finger against a tactical-shirt-covered pectoral muscle.

He laughed, clearly enjoying the tension she denied. "Baby cakes, you're the most fun I've ever had on the side of an Afghani mountain. Let's go."

Danger never made itself known. But Jared's gut said they were GTG. Good to go. With Sugar hot on his six, he forged a path down the mountain. Right on time, the helo came into sight. He turned back to Sugar. An adrenaline jump-started smile crossed her face. Wrapped hand or not, she was stoked for this. So was he.

Never thought I'd do this extraction twice. Although this time, he wasn't jumping off a cliff into the black night.

Never thought I'd be waxing poetic or whatever with Sugar in a cave. Telling her shit like, "Something's abrewing." *Christ.* He thought he might as well cut off his nuts after a sentiment like that.

Dawn split the sky, and the enemy was nowhere to be seen. Their chopper came in fast and hovered low, just long enough to drop the ropes. They dangled for only a few seconds before being pulled on board the helo, but it was better than a roller coaster ride. The chopper pulled up, swinging the ropes, and he looked at Sugar, who was hanging in the air.

Now that was a cool chick.

Cash and Roman helped pull her in while Jared admired her form, how she wrapped a leg around the rope and hefted herself toward the hatch. Minutes later, he was by her side.

Brock was manning the aircraft, and Cash and Roman served as lookouts, their trigger fingers at the ready. But Brock had an A-10 cannon at his command that housed a big kaboom and could decimate a building or two in a single blast.

Jared and Sugar pulled on headsets, and he pulled down the mic. "Where's Winters?"

Roman and Cash laughed, throwing them bottles of water spiked with electrolytes. They tasted like crap, but did a body good. He cracked his open. Warm and fizzy, it was gone in three gulps. Sugar handled hers with a little more finesse, but it disappeared, too. *Good girl.*

She wiped her mouth. "I hate that stuff. Got another?"

Damn, she fits in well.

Roman tossed them each another bottle.

"Winters?" Jared asked again.

Brock shook his head at the front. "Baby Winters decided today was go day. Mia pulled the emergency button, and his ass went home. Mach speed."

"No shit?"

Mia Winters was a firecracker. Jared could only imagine the phone call that Winters got. "Thought that wasn't supposed to be for another week or two."

"She hit him up on the sat phone, said to get his ass home. Contractions were coming hard and heavy. She called during the middle of one. Threatened to kill him."

"Nicola's on her way to replace him," Cash added.

"You know she speaks all kinds of Persian?" Brock asked, sounding impressed. "She speaks everything."

"You surprised?" Roman rolled his eyes at his sister's reputation.

"Can't help that you didn't get the brains in that family," Cash said to Roman. "Or the good looks. Man did you lose out."

Cash chucked them protein bars. *Cinnamon Raisin? Great.* He looked to see what Sugar had. Same thing. Jared made a mental note to get rid of anything with raisins in it.

Sugar eyed Jared. Maybe she wondered about Nicola. Or maybe she wondered why he was trying to look at her bar.

"She speaks twenty languages or so," he told her.

"Add in the dialects," Roman offered.

"And she can talk to anyone on earth," Cash finished.

"She's going to help us with Asal?" Sugar asked, toying with the wrapper without opening it.

"You bet. And I want all my men ready. Winters's punk ass is excused. I'm tired of GSI. I want them gone. Down. *Finito.*

And if you want in on Kip Pearson," he offered to Sugar, and she nodded. "Then maybe you'll have to partner with Titan. Think you can handle more than just selling us our guns, baby cakes?"

She scowled, probably at his calling her "baby cakes" in front of others. "As long as you promise me Kip, then count me in. Where's Asal anyway?"

Brock crackled into the headphones. "With a friend."

"She's safe." Jared wanted to reassure her and make her understand that he realized how important the kid was to her. The kid had given Sugar a knife, and on his list of things that earned points in his book, the kid had done her a solid, earning a lot of points.

He ripped open his bar and finished it. *Disgusting raisins.* Sugar hadn't touched hers. "You need to eat. Now."

"I will."

"My chopper, my rules. Open it. Finish it."

"Pushy bastard."

"You know it now, if you didn't before. Eat."

She smirked at him, unwrapped it, and took a big bite. "Hate stupid raisins."

"No one likes raisins. That's not the point."

Cash rummaged around. "I might have—"

"Shut it, Cash." Jared crossed his arms over his chest.

Shaking his head, Roman looked at Cash. "That's got nothing to do with raisins."

Cash glanced at them. "Total vibe-age. You can't take these two anywhere."

Sugar nailed him with a gird-your-loins glare. "Watch yourself, cowboy."

Cash wasn't wearing his cowboy hat, but it was Sugar's go-to name for him. Suited him well. Sounded good in a threat.

His men cracked up. Sugar chucked a bottle at Cash. They fell apart, laughing harder. Jared pinched his eyes shut, listening to the team whoop and holler. Sugar blended in with the boys, just as smoothly as Nicola and Mia did.

Maybe he *was* feeling her in a pull-her-ponytail kind of way. But vibing? Maybe he understood why she'd hightailed it away   from   their   headache.

CHAPTER SEVEN

Air conditioning poured over Sugar as her hotel room door clicked closed. She took a deep breath, and the smell of a fresh, clean room almost overpowered her. The trip to Abu Dhabi had been a long one, what with stinky men and obnoxious banter along for the ride.

Far past exhausted, she didn't think she could sleep, but she had an hour and a half until she could meet Asal and Nicola. That free time could be killed with a long, hot shower.

Sugar spun on the marble floor, taking in the chandeliers and artwork in her suite. It must've been designed for royalty, and the walls had to have been gold plated. It was extravagant. The Titan boys lived well when they made pit stops in Abu Dhabi.

She walked farther in and… *Oh my God.* The building wasn't just a skyscraper hotel. It was a castle in the sky. Gorgeous furniture. One-of-a-kind art and décor. Floor-to-ceiling windows looking out from the sixty-third floor.

"Excuse me, miss." A uniformed man appeared out of nowhere. His exotic accent sounded beautiful. "I shall serve as your butler."

Sugar's mouth hinged open.

"If there is anything you need, please call for me." He gestured with the remote in his hand, then placed it on a carved table. Nodding, he backed out.

A butler? She'd heard that even the worst tourist hotels in Abu Dhabi dripped money, but this was world-view blowing.

The room phone rang. Finding the cordless on a table, Sugar wondered if it was the hotel staff or Titan. "Hello?"

"Everything okay in your room?" It was both, in the form of Jared acting like hotel staff. "Need anything? Nicola should've talked to the concierge and had some clothes delivered."

"I have a butler." It was all she could say.

"Comes with the Titan package, baby cakes. Anything else to complain about, or you handling yourself okay?"

Jared the prick was back in force, and it was oddly comforting. They'd barely said a word after she'd choked down her protein bar.

"All good, J-dawg. Thanks for asking."

They held the line, neither hanging up. Jared mumbled something more gruff than inaudible.

"What?"

"I'm coming to see you."

"I have to take a shower." She paced over to the closet. "Then I want to see Asal, check in with Nicola, meet the person from the United Nations watching—"

"They've been delayed. Everything's fine, but legal red tape on this one is complicated. You have no idea the favors I'm calling in so you can watch out for this kid." He grumbled again. "She'll end up in a safe place, though."

"Got it. Thanks." Sugar walked through the expansive living room, over ornate rugs, and into the bedroom. That bed was larger than a king-sized mattress. With a look around at the closed doors, she eyed the potential closet.

"Take a shower and throw on some new rags."

Holy Versace! The closet was filled with high-end, to-die-for stuff. She checked the tag. *In my size!* She liked Nicola better and better the more the two of them crossed ops. "I might get dressed, J-dawg. But, trust me, it won't be in rags."

He grunted. "Chop, chop."

The call ended, leaving the dial tone ringing in her ear. *Chop, chop?* More like ka-ching. She knew Titan was well-funded and the boys lived the high life when they weren't in the trenches. But butlered hotel rooms and designer civilian wear was enough to make her give them a harder time about working   tough   jobs.

She looked at her finger, which was still holding the tag. Grime coated. Caked with dirt. Disgusting. On a mission, she spun, tossing each layer of her clothes off as she walked to the bathroom.

Surprise, surprise. It was bigger than her entire bedroom at home.

Sugar eyed the shower and the Jacuzzi. *Might as well live like the locals.* She smiled and turned them both on. The shower would scrub away the layers of gross. The hot tub would soak away everything else.

Glancing at his watch, Jared tapped his boot. The elevator was taking too long, and the thing was the fastest one in the world. He had a million things going on, but he needed to talk to Sugar. Emphasis on the *need*, like it was a requirement, when it was most certainly not.

Just like he hadn't needed to hit the hotel gift shop and send every stuffed animal, bags of snacks, and a pad of paper to draw on to Asal's room. He'd spoken to Asal's United Nations babysitter, but she had issued a warning—chill out on the gifts, something about not wanting to overwhelm the kid. Seriously? If he'd grown up on the side of a desolate mountain and suddenly found himself in one of the poshest hotels in the world, stuffed animals and candy wouldn't be what shocked him. The running water and electricity would.

But he wasn't going to fight with the UN lady, not after all the strings he'd pulled. Nor was he going to listen. If the hotel gift shop received any new kid crap, then Asal was going to get it.

Back to his bigger headache. Sugar.

He reached her door and knocked hello with the toe of his boot. No answer. After another kick-and-wait, he let himself in. One of the perks of owning an equity stake in the place and housing his team there any time they swung by the United Arab Emirates: he could show up whenever he wanted, no invitation necessary.

The UAE Hotel *room* was a joke. All the suites were more like luxury apartments. Indulgence was one of the many benefits of having offices in Abu Dhabi and Dubai. They didn't spend much time there, but the time they did balanced the time they spent in swamps, deserts, and jungles while their enemies tried to kill them.

He'd found that people in Abu Dhabi treated caviar the way Americans did butter. There might have been more Ferraris and Lambos pacing the streets there than there were in Los Angeles. Too bad a few miles away, in hundred-degree desert heat, the ugly side of life existed. But the ugly side of life kept him in business. Despots. Tyrants. Arms. Drugs. Sex trade. This hotel was a bubble, and for the moment, he was okay with that.

He walked through the living room. No Sugar. Then he rounded the corner.

Bam! Strike to his throat.

Her fast hands retreated, and she moved to knee him. He spun them around the corner, slamming Sugar's hand to the wall, disarming the 9mm in her other hand.

"Easy there, killer."

"What the fuck? You can't just walk in here, creeping around."

He stilled against her. Her wet hair was tied up on top of her head, and her damp skin was wrapped in a towel. "I knocked."

"I didn't hear you." Her face was scrubbed clean of makeup. *Au naturale and too goddamn gorgeous.*

"Not my problem."

"So you just walk in?" She pursed her lips disapprovingly. "Poor form, J-dawg."

He loosened the grip on her wrist and drew back. Sugar dropped an elbow above his collarbone and went for his goods again. He blocked her knee.

"What the hell, baby cakes?"

"I'm sick of you showing up places."

Her hair had fallen. Wet stands were strung across her face. The white towel barely covered the swell of her breasts. The rise and fall of her chest. The look in her eyes. The blood rushing through his body. It all pushed him to her again.

Deep within his chest, a growl vibrated up. "You want me to leave?"

She said nothing.

Slowly, he placed one forearm, then his other against the wall, caging her to him. His chest pressed against the towel. This was a good way to get her to run. Again. But he couldn't walk away.

"Say you want me out, and I'm gone." The scent of flowery, feminine shampoo beckoned him. He breathed her in. "But I don't think you will."

"You're a cocky son of a bitch."

He itched to touch her warm skin, to slide over its silkiness. "Not an answer."

"Too bad." She wasn't pushing away and hadn't kneed him again.

"I'm cocky. I see something I want, and I go after it. But you can have any guy you look at, so why you looking at me like that?"

"I'm not," she whispered.

His mouth nuzzled past her hair, to a delicate spot under her ear. The scruff on his cheek scratched over her soft skin. She was too gentle to have been on a mountain, weathering the elements.

"Now this is the second time I'm going to call you a liar." His teeth teased her earlobe. A staggered breath escaped her mouth. At the flick of his tongue, she tilted the angle of her head just a degree. He savored the kiss. "God, you taste good."

His hands slid down the wall until he felt the damp hair hanging over her bare shoulders. His fingers feathered into the wet strands, and his lips traced along her jaw, to her chin, then hovered over the fullness of her pink lips.

Her breath tickled him, and he closed the distance, covering her mouth. Electricity rolled down his spine, jackknifing his gut. Her fingers knotted into his shirt, pulling him in to deepen the kiss. Their tongues danced. She tasted as sweet as her name.

A furious need to hold her tight, to possess her, took over. It cleared away any thoughts like, *Let's fuck and get it over with.* In its wake, it left a confusion and anticipation that made him more determined to lose their towel barrier.

He ripped off his shirt, then ravaged her mouth. The plush towel brushed against his skin, teasing and enticing him. Sugar's hands caressed his biceps. Her fingertips scratched down his arms to where his hands wrapped around her waist.

She bit his lip, he opened his eyes. Midnight blue met his gaze as her lips smiled under his.

"Don't say anything that will ruin this, J-dawg."

Would you stop with the J—

She loosened the towel with a flick of her finger, letting the white cloth fall open like a curtain. Gravity tugged the towel, and he'd never seen a more perfect body. He drank her in, his eyes slowly burning a path from her chin to her shins, memorizing the perfection in between.

Sugar grasped his belt, unclasped it, and then pulled it loose. It dragged and caught on every belt loop before it came free and clanged to the ground. His pants hung on his hip bones, and she smoothed her hand over his hard-on, testing the zipper.

"Condom?" she asked.

He nodded. "Condom."

Reaching to his back pocket, he pulled out his wallet, and she slipped his pants and briefs down. Both her hands took him as he toed off his boots and socks. She slithered her fingers up, over his abs, into the smattering of his chest hair.

"Bedroom?" He kissed her lips, biting and exploring her sinful mouth.

She shook her head. "Not a chance."

Sugar never broke the kiss as she pulled him down to the rug. The landing was soft, and the fibers brushed over his back as she lay on top of him. His fingers entwined with hers. Everything moved quickly, releasing all the pent up *should they, shouldn't they*? But her curves begged for attention. He wanted to kiss and caress, bite and suck. He wanted her moaning because of him.

She took a breath and locked her eyes on his. "Condom. Now."

Hell, why try to change the course of a Sugar storm? The woman was on a mission. Who was he to slow things down?

He ripped open the foil, and in his gut, he was ready for more than a fuck. Something stronger. Something more intense. His brain had gone haywire. It was a dream come true, but the naked hurricane above him made it cloudy. "Sugar?"

"Please shut up."

What's your problem, Jared? Christ. Had he ever second-guessed a fast-and-furious? No. This couldn't get any hotter, and he couldn't want the woman any more.

Jared flipped them over, positioning himself between her legs. A groan purred from her lips.

"Please," she begged him, breathy and moaning. She writhed under his weight. "I need this. You."

His hips flexed, meeting heated flesh. Her eyes shut, a moan escaped her, and he kissed her, to catch it vibrating against his lips.

"Goddamn, Sugar." As he inched into her, she met his cadence, and they moved in sync. *Perfect fuckin' precision.*

She pulled her knees back, wrapping her ankles around his back. He had the all-clear to drive them both to heaven. With each thrust, she wound tighter on his cock. More wild. More in control of her fate. Her breaths went erratic, mirroring the one-two punch in his lungs.

Sugar called out his name as she climaxed, loud and guttural, stroking his stud gene and making him feel invincible. Her muscles pulsed, and she used him. God, how she used him, milking her explosion. He loved it. *Use me, baby. Any and every way possible.*

Her deep-blue eyes opened, churning like rough seas. The body that was always stronger than it looked made a move, righting herself on top. Her crazy brown hair was tousled. He looked down at her creamy, pink skin and rosy-tipped, full breasts that he could palm. He clasped her waist and slid his hands to the solid weight of her breasts.

She rocked her hips, smiling as she watched him thumb her nipples. Her hands snaked over his, up her neck, and into her hair. Sugar was on display. The view was magnificent.

Jared met her pace. Her devilish grin dared him to more. It was their battle of dominance, and damn if she didn't try to win. *Not going to happen.*

She dropped her head back. Moans told Jared another pleasure bomb loomed, that she would climax again with each thrust and sway. He pushed her toward it, needing to see her release astride him. His hands caught around her waist, moving her and rewarding himself.

"Jared."

She called out his name again, then called out to God. Her body bucked and arched. He held her in place, dragging it out, making her cry out all over again. She opened her eyes. Unexpected innocence, desire, and emotion catapulted him to release. Every muscle tightened. Everything he didn't understand between them culminated then. All his energy and want poured into her.

His name fell from her lips as she bent over and kissed him deeply. Muscles going lax, his mind going empty, he could do nothing but feel her draped over him.

The kiss ended. Their cheeks and chests clung together. Sugar slid off him, and he wrapped an arm around her, giving her a pillow. They lay in silence, letting their breathing regulate.

He turned to her, unsure of the words after their intensity. Chalk one up to Sugar. She knew how to make his insides explode.

She sat up and snagged her towel. "That was fun. Glad we got it over with."

What? He choked back, *What just happened?* Her words reverberated in his brain. He'd heard what she said, but... *Yeah, no.* He propped himself on his elbows. "Got it over with?"

As she stood up and wrapped her towel around herself, Jared stared at the transformation.

She pulled her hair away from her shoulders. "I'll see you around," she said and spun on a bare heel.

"Are you serious?" He jumped up and spun her back to him.

She raked a gaze over him. "You're still naked."

"'Cause we fucked thirty seconds ago."

"So pull your pants up, big boy." She gave him a fake smile and turned around again. "You should take that as a compliment, by the way."

"Sugar."

She stopped, looked over her shoulder, and shook her head. "I get it. Used to throwing women out, maybe they beg for a little cuddle time? Not me. Don't worry."

Jared pitched the condom in the trash, walked over, and kicked his pants and briefs into his hand. He laughed, shaking his head, then slid into his pants. Socks and boots went on next. He left the shirt off, tossing it over his shoulder.

He walked past her and went to the sink to wash his hands and throw water on his face. He rubbed a hand through his buzz cut and turned back to her.

Even in a towel, she could exude her typical badassery. He dawdled a minute more to piss her off, then said, "You're kicking me out. Classic."

"I'm not saying, 'Don't let the door hit you on the way out, Jared.' I'm saying, 'Glad we did that.' Maybe now we can work together and not *vibe*. All that sexual tension, we had to knock it out of our systems."

"Ah, so you did me a favor. Let me guess. You've *decided* one-and-done. Maybe it's even your *motto*."

Her eyes narrowed. "What?"

"We should talk about this later." Pulling his wallet from his pocket, he extracted the folded e-mail and tossed it to her, then turned his back and made his way toward the door. He heard her unfold the paper, followed by a sharp gasp.

"Fuck you, Jared."

"Too late. You already did."

The hotel room door closed behind him, sounding finite, even though he could pull a key card out and open it again.

He stood in the hallway, pissed off... and tense. He had no idea why he was so angry. *Screw that 'it was fun, see ya later' bullshit.*

He took a deep breath and turned to the door, having no clue what his next move should be. Screwing Sugar had messed it all up. He had known it would. Every damn thing would go bad. The last hour of his life needed to be deep-sixed. Turning away from the door, he pulled on the shirt and punched the elevator call button.

CHAPTER EIGHT

Back in the tub, Sugar propped her head on a pillow of towels and stared at the creased copy of her e-mail. Jared had known her feelings the entire time. She wished they would just go away—the feelings and the man. Her on-the-fly plan to screw away her interest was a big fat fail.

Should have stuck with your avoid-Jared-Westin plan.

When she closed her eyes, the shock on his face played over and over again. *I'll bet that man has never been thrown out of a bedroom, certainly not after showing off his moves.* His muscles had muscles. His scruff. His chest hair. His hands. She shook her head, but the images kept coming. Jared was... substantial, in every conceivable way.

Her X-rated thoughts were knocked clear across the bathroom by another round of aches in her chest. And she had a *substantial* thing for him. No one else should touch him, kiss him, or do him. She'd just found out that she didn't have one jealous bone in her body, but rather, her entire skeletal system simmered with jealousy.

Jared wasn't a one-girl guy, and she didn't desire to be that pathetic lady trying to change a man.

"I hate you, Jared Westin," she said to the empty bathroom. *Shut up.* Playing pretend all alone was a bad habit. The only time she'd ever felt like this was when she'd almost lost GUNS. Other than her sister, that gun range was the closest thing she had to a significant relationship. It'd been there her whole life. Her dad had lost it in a poker game, the thieving bastard. And her lying mother had never been strong enough, or around enough, to tell him to get his ass in line.

It was a miracle Sugar had rescued GUNS. Really, it was a miracle neither she nor Jenny had morphed into their mother.

So GUNS was her home-life substitute. Her safety and security. After she used Titan to help her exact revenge on Kip, she would go back to her comfort zone.

The bath water had cooled. Sugar got out, dried off for the second time that day, and slipped on designer pajamas. The pink, silky fabric was freshly laundered and smelled like flowers. She made another mental note to thank Nicola.

Her doorbell rang. *Hotel rooms have doorbells? Only in Titan land.*

Sugar padded to the door and checked the peephole. *Nicola.* She threw the door open. "Asal!"

The little girl jumped into her arms.

Nicola smiled. "Hey, girl."

Asal planted a wet kiss on Sugar's cheek and wrapped her arms around her neck.

"Hey, Nic." She hugged Asal back. "Hi, you. I missed ya."

Nicola walked into the foyer. "This little girl's had a lot to say. Some things about the hellhole you guys pulled her out of, but mostly about you. Think she thinks you're some kind of angel."

Sugar laughed. "Hardly."

"Yup, that's what I said. She keeps insisting, though. The UN attaché might think you're a hallucination or an imaginary friend."

Sugar set her down, then patted her head.

Asal said something to Nicola, who nodded. "Asal's English is pretty good, considering. But she's been working on this for you."

The little girl beamed. "Thank you, Sugar. You saved me."

"Of course, sweetheart." Sugar knelt, smoothing Asal's combed hair and tucking it behind her ears. The little girl beamed, and Sugar's heart exploded with pride and hope. Then she stood and focused on Nicola. "Were you able to find out anything   about   *the*   *husband*?"

Nodding, Nic said, "Hadn't touched. Actually, never met her. Her brothers had died in an explosion, mother in childbirth, father in the field. An uncle shouldered the responsibility of raising her, but wanted her gone. Traded her, like a dowry, for some grain and a goat." She looked at Asal. "Earmuffs."

Asal wrapped her hands over her ears.

"I figured being around Titan, we needed to watch out for what she hears." Nicola scrunched her shoulders. "Anyway, I want to kill the motherfucker. A goat?"

A quick gesture, and the earmuffs were dismissed. They walked into the living room. Asal babbled in another language, and Sugar loved the sound. Letters and words, soft and lyrical, twirled through the air.

Nicola coughed, suppressing a giggle, and nonchalantly tossed her head the direction of the floor.

Goddamn condom wrapper. Sugar's cheeks flushed, and if Asal weren't nearby, she would've cursed Jared's name.

"I see Jared's stopped by."

Sugar saw no point in lying. The ride from Afghanistan had more than clued her in to the topic du jour. Everyone thought they were knocking boots. Why deny it now that they had?

Nicola said something Sugar didn't understand, followed by a slow English version, complete with hand motions. "Wash your hands. We will eat soon." Asal ran down the hall, and Nicola pierced Sugar with a stare. "I knew it. And I *so* want the details."

"Nothing to say." Sugar picked at a cuticle.

"Bull-flippin'-shit." Nicola snorted, her hands on her hips. "There's a condom—in your living room."

Sugar stepped over the metallic wrapper, as if hiding it with her foot would make the conversation disappear, as well.

"Spill, Sugar."

She rubbed her temples. Jared was her headache even when he wasn't the problem. The foil scratched the sole of her foot. If he hadn't left that there, the conversation would be a non-starter. It was his fault. She rubbed her temples again. "First and last time. Fun and done. Nothing to say other than that."

"First time..." Nicola's nose wrinkled in thought. "On the floor of your living room?"

"We weren't going for the most romantic of moments."

"I'd say." Nicola did a piss-poor job at hiding her grin.

Sugar bent over, grabbed the wrapper, and pitched it. "Thanks for the clothes. They're—"

"Oh no, no. You're not getting out of this convo that easy."

She shrugged, feigning a bored expression. "Seriously, nothing to spill."

"Details. Give me at least one juicy detail. Don't make me beg." She steepled her hands in prayer.

Shit. Shit. Shit. "I don't know."

Nicola wasn't letting it go, and she prompted, "The man who considers himself the *master of everything* was... Work with me here, Sugar. I'm dying."

"Master of everything?" Sugar rolled her eyes. "Of course he does."

"And does he live up to the self-titled moniker? He's..." She rolled her hands, urging Sugar to continue.

Before she could stop, her cheeks flushed again. "He's impressive. I'll leave it at that. Good enough?"

"Hell no." Nicola pouted.

"What do you want?"

"A onetime afternoon romp? That's it? What did he say? What'd you do?"

Sugar chewed on her lip, wondering how she could put it. "I politely said thanks and asked him to leave."

Nicola's jaw hung open. Her eyes didn't blink. She didn't make a sound.

Sugar tugged at the hem of her pajama shirt. "Come on, Nicola. Don't be so shocked."

Her jaw closed, then dropped again. With a shake of the head, she clasped a hand over her mouth. "*You* kicked *him* out. Oh my God. I want every last detail."

"That sounds harsh, and don't you think this is a little personal?"

"Are you kidding me? You've slept with Cash. We're beyond that."

"Nic! That's not fair. We ended before he knew you. Met you again. Whatever. Cheap shot, Nicola, cheap shot."

Asal came out of the bathroom, displaying freshly scrubbed hands. She was adorable in her clean clothes, and she'd tied her hair into a ponytail.

Nicola gave another foreign-tongued spiel and then its English translation. "Go to the kitchen. Find a snack." She looked at Sugar. "You have food in there, right?"

"I don't know."

Asal was in and out with two bags of dried fruit and nuts.

"Guess so."

She skipped to the couches, grabbed a remote, and found cartoons on the flat screen. "Kid adapts fast."

Nodding, Nicola got back to it. "Rewind back to where you kicked his tight ass out of the room, and *go*. God, I would have sold my guns off to see that."

"He's a manipulative bastard."

"Not a news flash."

"Well, he wasn't one hundred percent upfront on some things."

Nicola shrugged. "Nature of everyone's favorite prick."

"You're not helping."

"You're not spilling, but tell me how I can help."

Sugar wanted to scream. "I meant you're making this complicated. There's nothing to help. It's done. It was fun. And I don't want to do it again."

"Then why are your eyes bloodshot?"

Maybe she should've checked the bathroom for Visine. It had everything else she could want. If Nicola Garrison knew she'd had a cry-fest in the Jacuzzi, Sugar would never live it down—or forgive herself for being unable to control her emotions.

Nicola softened. "Look, Sugar. I don't have many girlfriends. Just one at the CIA. Hazard of the job, I guess. We don't work with a lot of women. I could use a second friend. Hell, you might need a first."

"I don't have friends. They're baggage." *Though I do have a sister and never should have e-mailed her about Jared.* She had wanted to call her sister after Jared left, but she'd opted for a bath and avoided an explanation of the all-alpha idiosyncrasies that made up the Master of the Universe.

Ignoring the jab, Nicola continued, "You don't have... typical relationships. But I think Boss Man's doing a number on you, in a good way. It might help you figure it out if you talked about it, like, chick to chick."

Sugar crossed her arms, her defenses going into high gear. Battle guards up. Shields at the ready.

Nicola tried again. "Impressive, huh? Somehow, I had no doubt, but don't tell Cash I said that."

Sugar tried to imagine gossiping about Jared, a man who thought he was God. After all, on the floor, she'd moaned both, "God" and "Jared." *Guess it'd be easy enough to get confused.*

Unfolding her arms, Sugar mumbled, "I'll try the friend thing on a trial run."

"Trial run." Nicola's laughter bubbled. "There's a club downstairs. I think you're in need of a couple drinks. Asal has to spend the night with the UN attaché tonight, so it's game on for us."

Sugar studied the woman who was volunteering to be her friend. It wasn't that she couldn't make friends. She had plenty of GUNS gals to kick back with, but none she trusted. Still, she walked to the counter, took the folded paper, and handed it to Nicola.

Nicola glanced at the paper, then her. "This is..."

"An e-mail between me and my sister. She's watching GUNS for me while I'm gone."

The paper crinkled as Nicola unfolded it. In the background, Asal was on her feet, singing the *SpongeBob SquarePants* theme song in English. *Smart kid.*

Nicola read the e-mail and then folded it, shaking her head. "*Nosy*. They act like they're not. But those men couldn't keep their noses out of private crap if it killed them." She bit her lip in thought. "But if it were my guess, Parker hacked into your e-mail to pull details on the GSI project, saw this, and decided Boss Man needed a kick in his *impressive* ass."

Sugar flinched at the invasion of her privacy. "I don't even know Parker, and he's up in my business."

"Parker's the most well behaved of the bunch. That's not saying much, but he's discreet. He's the tech guy. Can hack into any system, phone, computer, whatever, if you gave him the right tools. But Jared had this on him? That says a lot."

"Yeah, that he's a dick. Which I already knew. So no new revelations. The sex was hot, and hopefully, we got it out of our system."

"You're lying."

"Christ, everyone keeps calling me a liar."

"Don't lie, and maybe that'll stop."

Sugar walked over to a barstool and leaned on it. *The truth blows.* Her feelings were written in that e-mail, and she'd teared up after Jared had left and she had kicked over a chair.

She cleared her throat. "Jared needs to be a one-time rodeo. He and I... we think the same. Or at least we did. Then something happened up here." She tapped her temple. "And I wanted more."

"Actually, it may've happened here." Nicola tapped her chest. "What if he wants more, too?"

"Impossible." That wasn't the Jared she knew.

"Then why'd he run across the globe with that e-mail?" Nicola asked.

"No idea."

"You should have seen him when he found out you were captive number two."

Sugar shook her head. "He was—"

"There was a clear transition from Jane Doe to Lilly Chase. He threw a phone. Threatened to call the White House. May've stockpiled nuclear weapons. The man was... a beast. Possessive, protective. Hell, he went all primal. For you."

For me? No way. She had a strong urge to sit down.

Both their phones buzzed at the same time. Sugar almost didn't recognize the ring since she'd had her phone for only a few hours.

Nicola pulled hers from next to her hip piece. "Staff meeting in Jared's suite. One hour." Her smile went from earring to earring. "I can't wait."

An anxious punch made Sugar consider calling in sick. "This is going to be awful."

Asal walked over with empty bags.

Nicola tossed her hand. "Nah. Entertaining maybe, but not awful. Besides, no one's thinking about you two right now. They're on Titan baby watch. Now that's funny. Let's grab food with Asal before we win an award for worst custodians of the year."

That's right. Baby Winters. Boy or girl? And what would a Titan guy name his kid?

Spike. Killer. Blade. Guessing the name would've been fun, but baby hoopla wasn't her thing. Besides, the nervous need to throw up surpassed her curiosity. She had sixty minutes until she faced off with Jared again.

CHAPTER NINE

Sugar and Nicola dropped Asal with her UN babysitter and made the walk of doom to Jared's suite. Nicola raced to the door, tugging her along while Sugar bit her freshly glossed lip. Avoiding Jared was high on her agenda, but since that mission was impossible, she at least wanted to look like she could care less. A cherry shine on her kisser and another swipe of mascara did that.

Still, the carpet was quicksand, and her every step was weighted, bringing her closer to what should be no big deal. The churning in her gut had nothing to do with dinner. She entered at her own risk, knowing that acting casual would be unbearable after their roll on the floor.

The door was propped open, and the whole crew was there, minus Winters and Jared.

Brock, Rocco, Roman, and Cash sprawled over a couch. Nicola beelined to Cash, who grabbed her by a belt loop and toppled her onto his lap. Brock said something about getting a room. Rocco and Roman groaned, and Nic whispered into Cash's ear.

Jared walked in from the kitchen, beer in hand. "Princess," he said, nodding to Nicola. "Nice of you to join us."

Sugar smirked. *Whatever, we weren't late.*

Nicola's smile was too big and too telling. "Boss Man."

He grunted, eyeing Nicola's toothy grin, then stiffly turned to her. "Sugar."

"Jared." She sounded as rigid as he looked. *Alrighty. That wasn't uncomfortable or anything.* Her heart beat a drum line in her ears. Loud enough everyone should've heard. But they didn't. The awkward silence lingered, until Rocco burped. *Thank the Lord.*

She sat next to Brock, who, as far as she could tell, hadn't done the Jared-Sugar double take.

Jared cleared his throat and started the briefing, which was standard stuff—a recap of why Sugar and Kip Pearson were sent to check up on the outpost police. He gave them her update on GSI's intermixing of Afghani police and Taliban forces.

Turning from the group, Jared asked, "What else you got for us, Parker?"

Parker? Her cheeks felt warm. Parker had gone through her personal items. He knew more than he should. Even if she weren't hyper-private, which she was, he'd crossed a big hairy line.

A voice from her blind spot startled her. She turned to a flat screen. A man who looked like he should've been lumped on the couch beside the other Ramboes chewed on the end of a pen. Big muscles. Chiseled jawline. Not what she thought of when she thought *hacker.*

He pulled the pen from his mouth. "Satellite images showed GSI arrived about six hours after Sugar was pulled out. They loaded up some shit and firebombed the place. Looks like they had a daisy-cutter do a flyby. Nothing left but rocks and smoke."

Jared walked toward the flat screen, taking a long swig of beer. "Makes sense. Destroy the evidence. Nothing to report back."

Parker cocked a half-grin. "Except what I can dig up."

"Then dig, my man. I want enough GSI-coated evidence to start a goddamn Congressional hearing." He finished his beer, then rubbed the bottle in his palms.

Sugar could see the wheels turning behind his hardened face. The same scruff from earlier covered his cheeks. He wore the same uniform—a tight black shirt and tactical pants. It poured over his chest, melted to his package, and cupped his buttocks. She had a soft spot for looks that could, would, and had   killed.

"Sugar," Jared snapped.

No way does he know what I'm thinking. No freakin' way. Right? She tried to stay stonefaced. "Yeah?"

The intensity of his black eyes almost knocked her out of her seat. They raked over her, making his scrutiny obvious to everyone in the room, and he certainly wasn't assessing her in any professional capacity. *Score one for the cherry-red lip gloss.*

"GSI's gonna want you dead." The certainty in his voice would've shaken her if she hadn't already known she was marked for six feet under.

"I know." She attempted an unconcerned shrug. "If they're all on the take, then I'm collateral damage."

"Not yet, you ain't, baby cakes."

She narrowed her eyes, again, not thrilled with him using the nickname in front of his team. "No shit, *J-dawg*. I don't intend to be." The Titan team watched them like a tennis match going back and forth. *How about this for a point?* "Tell us your plan to take down GSI, and I'll tell you mine to kill Kip."

His eyes crinkled with what she suspected was amusement. "Not very ATF of you."

"Maybe Parker didn't read enough of my e-mails. Right before I left, ATF unceremoniously booted my ass to the curb."

Onscreen, Parker threw his hands up. "Shit, I didn't read *everything*. I was on a search-term mission. Not to find out about the details of Sugar's life."

But you certainly found enough, didn't you, Parker?

Jared's jaw ticked. "You're telling me they fired you? Because you helped Titan?"

"More or less."

"Trust me, you'll have your job back." He crossed his thick arms over his black-cotton-clad chest. The man couldn't have looked any more serious, and it made her insides tingle. "Hell, Sugar, might as well count on a raise. If not, ATF's got another thing coming to them."

She rolled her eyes. "Not looking for a fix-it. Thanks, anyway."

"What the fuck are you going to do? Send out resumes?" If he'd seemed pissed before, he'd ratcheted up to irate. "Skill set—can fieldstrip a rifle, build an AR, and has a decent throat punch."

"I don't know, J-dawg. My throat punches are more than decent. I'd call them effective, given what I was after." And it had worked. She lashed out at him, he pinned her, and then they jumped on each other in her hotel room. Absolutely effective.

"Everyone out," he snarled, and she knew to sit still.

The screen went black. The knowing looks on the guys and the nosy look on Nicola meant this was just him and her. Their come-to-Jesus discussion was coming way earlier than she'd expected. *Fine. Bring it on, big boy.*

Nicola flashed a wink before she shut the door.

Alone with Jared Westin. Again. She shivered, and the temp had zilch to do with it. Her only excuse for that was fine-tuned feminine awareness. She could've done a girly-parts roll call just then, because they'd all shown up for duty, jumping to attention.

"Sugar."

This again? "Jared." She tried for a casual deep breath, but her lungs laughed at the idea. Not happening. She was dive-bombing into this convo oxygen deprived.

Jared ran a hand over his cheek, making a rough noise. He'd trimmed back his scruff since she'd touched him last, leaving just enough prickle. Her fingertips itched to test its abrasion.

"You can't talk about murdering someone," he said.

"I can do whatever I want. It's retribution." Sugar pouted her lips and loved how his gaze zeroed in on them.

"There are rules of engagement." He surveyed her, perhaps choosing his words for maximum impact. "Kip Pearson was in the wrong, and you're better than him."

Sugar curled her lip. "You don't know that."

"The hell I don't, baby cakes."

He sat down on the couch, dipping her cushion toward him. Jared smelled like soap, spice, and everything so deliciously nice. "That's not why you kicked everyone out of here."

"No shit. You have two minutes to explain yourself. Avoiding and Afghanistan? That's bullshit. The attitude problem in your hotel room? Start talking."

She looked out the window. His room had a better view than hers did, and she needed to focus on it instead of the brawny vision of tactical magnificence in front of her. "Don't feel like it."

He took her chin between his finger and thumb, then turned her to face him. His thumb brushed her cheek, and her stomach shot up and exploded like a Roman candle. "Try again."

She swatted his hand away. "Why are you pushing me on this, Jared? Leave it be."

"I don't want to."

"Why?" Exasperation poured off her. She needed to push him, shake him, and kiss him like crazy. And that was the problem. Couldn't he get that through his thick head without a step-by-step?

Jared let the silence suffocate her long enough that she should've run for the door. But she wasn't going to go down like that.

When she couldn't stand it anymore, he continued. "I already told you, Sugar. Something's burning up between us. Even if there wasn't, holy hell, woman. Why run from sex like that?" He whistled. "That was some legendary stuff."

"There's nothing to talk about." *This isn't working.* Heat crawled up her neck, toward her face. Embarrassment made her crave the fetal position.

"I can get to the truth. There's not an interrogation subject I can't break. And with you, baby cakes, I'll take my time." His voice was so low that she felt its vibrations. "Imagine the ways I'll make you talk."

She could tell he knew what he was doing. In another couple of minutes, she would want to be in his arms so bad it hurt—more than it already did. She had to go. *Now.* Sugar stood up. "Would you leave me alone—"

Back on the couch. Flat on her back. Sex on her brain.

Jared perched over her, and she had no idea how it'd happened. All she knew was that the scent of soap and spice was making her mouth water. His broad chest and arms caged her to a La-Z-Boy prison.

"What the fuck is your problem, Lilly Chase?" he growled.

Lilly Chase. Her name stole her breath, knocking shut her eyes. She tried to regain even a slice of composure, then opened her eyes to stare into Jared's sinfully piercing gaze. The tornado swirling deep within her belly served as an alarm, sobering her. "I don't have time for games, Jared. Stop playing on my weakness. I'm getting tired of it." She shoved. "Get off of me."

"I'm your weakness?"

"As if you haven't figured that out. Stop toying with me." She knocked him again. "Seriously, move all this muscle."

"Toying?" A slow smile curled into his cheeks. "You think I'm not interested?"

"I think we both know how to play the game. But I can't hold up my end of the deal. Okay? White flag. I'm surrendering. Find another playmate."

"I don't want to, Sugar, and we haven't made any deals."

"You know me. I know you. We *know* the deal. Don't kid yourself. I'm certainly not."

"Explain the deal. What you *think* you know."

"No strings. All fun. Zero feelings."

He belly-laughed without releasing her. "You think I'd be lying on top of you, asking you all this crap if that was the case?"

"Yeah." She tried to elbow out but failed. "I think you're having a fucking great time."

"Oh, Sugar. Fucking you *was* a great time. I plan on doing it again."

She plowed a fist into his chest. He laughed again.

"God, Jared—" She tried to pull from under him. No luck. "You want to know my problem? I hate the way I feel about you. I don't like it, and I don't want it." She shook her head against the cushion, angry that things had come to this point. He'd won, like he always did.

"Why the hell not?"

She stopped thrashing. "Simple. I don't trust it."

He narrowed his eyes and tilted his head. "*It* or me?"

"Both."

Dissolving the distance, Jared covered her mouth with his. Slow and sensual, the licks and kisses defined bliss. Her head swam; she'd never been kissed like that before. He was communicating his feelings and his desires. He rolled his warm body against hers, and everything spun. The room. Her mind. All scrambling her stronghold against him.

Her senses were alive, and she loved the touch of his corded muscles and growing hard-on. A tangible quality inhabited their kiss.

Words weren't necessary. The hot spear of his tongue conveyed his thoughts and emotions. If he wanted to pass along his interest in her, then he could mark that item with a red checkmark. Job well done. Applause for Boss Man.

Jared delved his tongue again, sending a wave of need through her. Her nipples tightened. Her legs melted, allowing him to nestle closer.

The man could kiss like he wrote the how-to book. Maybe the kiss would never end. Her fingers knotted into his shirt. If she held him close enough, maybe her fears would float away, and reality would never set in.

His lips closed over hers, extinguishing her impossible wish. "Nothing about that kiss said stop." The deep baritone of his words flittered over her skin.

"Let's not do that again," Sugar whispered. Her mind and heart were at war, and she needed to escape. She couldn't give in to him. Her heart would break within a second, and she would be a fool. She didn't believe in monogamy. Neither did he. She didn't understand why her body and mind were betraying what she knew at an instinctual level.

Jared sat up, giving her distance. Cool air rushed over her, and the awful abandonment hurt. *What?* She was a basket case. She had all the makings of a crazy, needy woman. At least she'd been kind enough to warn him. Thank God he was smart enough to heed caution.

The look of a champion crossed his face. He was used to getting his way. "I'll give you space. I'll even let you run away. But, Sugar baby, I'm hot on your trail. You won't know what hit you."

He whistled for the second time and walked away. Wiping her smeared lip gloss, she sat up quickly and collected herself. *Hot on my trail?* What about when he was done with her? That was the problem. He would be done, and she would be a sad excuse for an old flame.

Hours had passed since Sugar had sought refuge in her hotel suite, and now she was being forced out. She was allowed a moment to fortify herself with liquid courage.

She slammed her shot glass onto the kitchenette's granite counter at the same time as Nicola did. They both reached for their lemons. The bitterness made Sugar squint, but that was the point—the sour burn of distraction.

"Nice." Nicola smacked her lips, tossing her lemon into the trash can. "Can we go now?"

Sugar grabbed her gloss and applied a fresh coat. Right about then, she would've gone anywhere Nicola suggested, so long as it was a diversion from her day. "Yup. Let's do this."

Sugar's outfit said not only that she wanted a distraction but that she was one. Their ladies' night would be fun, and she could care less who was in the club. Jared surely wouldn't be. That would be like storing a warhead at a playground. The two didn't mix.

There was a small chance that he would be around, brooding in a hallway somewhere, ready to screw with her head. But while she was wearing her club getup, he was likely to pin her to a wall, and that involved a whole different type of screwing with her. *One could always dream… Hell, stop that*!

"Sugar?" Nicola narrowed her eyes. "What'd you say?"

Lord knows what she'd said. "Nothing worth repeating."

"Ha. I bet."

Glossy lips and a sexy outfit were in order. Just in case they did a walk-by and found Jared smoldering in some corner. She would keep walking, even if her Louboutins suddenly became concrete blocks.

They headed out. Hallway, clear. Elevator, clear. No Jared anywhere in sight.

"You look disappointed." As she and Sugar exited the elevator, Nicola smiled like she knew the carousel of craziness that was Sugar's brain on Jared. "Forget him. Let's go dance."

"I'm not—"

"Uh-huh. And I'm ready for a night by the fire with a book." Nicola shot her a half-cocked grin. "Come on. We'll grab a cocktail, scope the scene, and forget about our men."

"You have a man. I have a headache."

"Shit, girl. Cash is a constant headache. Doesn't mean we don't—"

"Finish that sentence, and this trial friendship is over."

Nicola laughed, shaking her head. They walked into the hotel's club, where the bouncers waved them in without as much as a glance. They were pretty girls heading into a room full of partying billionaires. Letting them waltz in was probably part of the bouncers' job duties.

"Jared and Sugar, sitting in a tree..." Nicola spun on her heels, letting the music drown her out.

Sugar grabbed her arm and beelined to the bar. A gaggle of uber-rich men parted, eyeing her like fresh meat, despite their current arm candy.

Maybe she wasn't into this scene, after all. She could be upstairs, talking that UN babysitter into more time with Asal. They could chill out to SpongeBob or whatever the kid was feeling. But it was probably close to bedtime. *Dang, what do I know about kids?* She could figure out kids if she wanted to. She shrugged to herself, still intent on reaching a bartender.

Once she got the bartender's attention, she ordered. "Two shots. Make 'em burn."

"Awesome." Nicola nudged a guy out of her personal space. "Thanking you in advance for my hangover tomorrow."

Sugar rolled her eyes. "I'll take yours if you don't want it, *princess.*"

"Oh, there it is! Just like Jared."

The bartender slid over two shot glasses filled with amber-colored who-knew-what. "You two are cute. Really."

"Grab your shot, *friend.*" Sugar pushed it toward her.

"With pleasure." Nicola laughed. Then they each downed a shot.

Whoa. Burn all right. Christ. Sugar breathed out. Her eyes watered.

Nicola slapped the bar.

"That's what I needed." Not some silly notion of her and—

"Jared." Nicola smiled.

Exactly. Wait. "What?"

"You get this screwed up look on your face at the oddest moments. It's gotta be Boss Man. What happened after we left?"

"He threatened to make my life miserable."

"He said that, huh?" Nicola flicked her empty glass and let it slide down the bar. "Probably his equivalent to, 'Let's go to dinner. Here are some roses. Can I hold your hand?'"

The pack of men around them grew tighter. The scorch from the liquor felt great, but the tight quarters made her want to knock a few faces. "Let's dance."

Nicola nodded and shoved a guy who had stepped too close. "Timely change of subject."

Feigning innocence, Sugar "accidentally" let an elbow stab at an overly friendly bystander.

They pushed out of the human testosterone knot and toward the dance floor. Pulsing music. X-ed out dancers with glow sticks. The place wasn't her definition of party central, but it would get the job done. She could blow off the extra tension, then eventually pass out. With the shots coursing through her blood, surrounded by the thumping of music and the bodies, her body demanded to dance.

"Over here." Nicola grabbed her arm, pulling her toward the center, where there was open space.

Better to be here and not with Asal. She was growing seriously attached to that kid, hard and fast. The same was happening with Jared. She had two people to guard her heart against.

Hands wrapped around her waist. Probably some oil baron or gulf prince. A jerk of her shoulder caught his chin, and her message that she wanted to be left alone got across as loudly as the awful music. She laughed, and Nicola smiled, blowing a goodbye kiss.

Sugar laughed. Nicola was a cool chick. She fit with Titan. Maybe Sugar needed more downtime. Who cared that she wasn't with ATF anymore? After she was home, she could run GUNS and try for something more stable—like not flying to Afghanistan. *What was I thinking with that move? Oh, yeah. Avoid J-dawg.*

Until she was home, a few dances, a couple of shots, and off to bed would have to treat her right.

"This night just got *so* good." Nicola grinned from ear to ear. "You'll never guess who just walked in."

CHAPTER TEN

Games weren't his thing, but Sugar was. The sooner he admitted it, the sooner he could deal with it. *Whatever that means.*

Jared looked around the club. Dark walls. Flashing lights. Thumping Euro-bass giving him an ugly headache. Russian mobsters chilled on couches with leggy supermodels. Middle Eastern playboys held court over gaggles of beauty-queen look-a-likes begging for sex. He saw Nicola, and then Sugar.

No one compared to her. She was a trussed-up brunette working the dance floor, displaying too much flesh for public viewing. *And those moves.* A girl who could work a dance floor like that would be even better in bed. Though Jared was more than aware of Sugar's talent. He'd had a taste and wanted more.

With a twist of her neck, her thick hair slid over a bare shoulder. She was daring some sexy moves, ignoring the men feasting on the view. Sugar and Nicola had men circling them. Jared was comforted by the knowledge that either woman could knock a guy out and not miss a beat on the floor.

Possessive need clenched his chest. What he wouldn't do to break a few faces. Then no one would stare at his girls. *Shit, where is Cash? Princess doesn't need to be eyeball-fucked like that.*

But instead of breaking up their party, he savored the visual. Sugar's skirt clung to a curvy backside that he wanted to sink his teeth into. After that party parade, it needed a solid slap. His palm could almost feel it.

A Euro-trash-wannabe stud took a step too close to Sugar. Then another. *Fuck that.* Jared put down his drink.

Sugar popped her fist back, connecting with the bastard's nose, and deep in Jared's gut, pride swelled. She hadn't even turned around. The strobe light flashed, and Nicola flicked the air as the man staggered backward, covering his face and hollering. *Fuckin' A. Good girls.*

Content to watch, he settled back onto his barstool, then Nicola caught his eye. She snaked her finger at him. *Come hither? That'd be a 'fuck no.' But thanks for the invite. Christ.*

Nicola leaned to Sugar, who turned, nodding. And that gave him a much better look at her getup. The dark tank top was melted over her curves. It would've been a plain-Jane club-going staple on some chicks, but on Sugar, the way it covered her bombshell breasts, it was an invitation to a fantasy league.

Grabbing Sugar's hand, Nicola pulled her toward the bar. Toward him.

He was transfixed by Sugar's shirt. If he tore it off, it would do nicely to tie her to the bed with. Her leather boots worked her legs, cupping at her kneecaps—it was only a matter of time before he slid those off and ran his hands straight up under that skirt.

In Nicola's blind spot, Douchebag McGee made a move, his hands outstretched. A growl bubbled, and Jared's instinct to slaughter the dude took over. He was up, on the move, and on them in a heartbeat. Before Jared could inflict punishment, Nicola captured the other man's wayward wrist in a joint lock and twisted. *Goddamn, my girls are good.*

"Princess. Sugar." Jared watched them feign innocence. Douchebag McGee cowered on his knees, with Nicola's thumb pressed firmly into his pressure point. Just to make sure the message was clear, Jared leaned down. "Look at them again, you won't see tomorrow."

He led the ladies to a private area. A waitress appeared as if on command, handing the women champagne and him a bourbon.

"So protective, Boss Man." Nicola giggled.

"Princess,   if   Cash   saw   you—"

"He'd have given us high-fives. 'Cause we fuckin' rock." She and Sugar bumped knuckles, then made them explode.

Patience. Deep breath and fuckin' patience.

A shadow moved. Cash the sniper was on the move, ghosting it like he was on the job. Jared didn't say a word. Cash wrapped an arm around Nicola and pulled her tight. She melted into him. How she knew it was Cash and not Douchebag McGee, Jared had no idea.

"How long've you been here?" Nicola fawned over Cash, her hands splayed over his chest.

Cash nodded hello to Jared and pulled his wife close. "Long enough to know you girls were pushing the line."

Nicola rolled her eyes, Sugar shook her head, and Jared wanted to go someplace else.

"Let's go, Nic."

Nicola agreed, toying with Cash's shirt. Then the ladies did some gossipy girly giggle that left Nicola laughing aloud and Sugar pushing her away.

Cash and Nic were all over each other as they left. For two people who could flip the switch to serious whenever they were on the job, they could flip to honeymoon mode just as quickly. It was nauseating. Jared shook his head. That left just him and a silent Sugar, who was the animated life of the party, except when she was within striking distance of him. He wished that hadn't changed.

She smirked. "Don't you have a line to throw down?"

"Nope."

The quickest of wounded looks flashed across Sugar's face then disappeared. "Why the hell not? I thought you were 'hot on my trail.'"

He took a sip of his bourbon. "I've recalibrated my approach."

She crossed her arms, unintentionally making her breasts fuller. "Whatever. I'll see you around."

Sugar turned, and the view of her backside was heart-attack material. She swayed it in a soft side-to-side action that could've hypnotized him. Her dark-brown hair swished to the same cadence. Fisting his hands into pockets, he ignored the guttural need to knot his fingers into that silky mess.

She marched to the bar, fending off suitors, and ordered shots. One. Two. Three of them.

Great, Sugar's on a kamikaze mission. That was not the kind of behavior he wanted to see up in this joint.

She gave a listless flick of her wrist, and the bartender pulled out the bottle.

Hell no. He'd had enough. She wasn't drinking herself vulnerable in Abu Dhabi. The club might've turned a blind eye to two chicks knocking around guys on the dance floor. But it would also look the other way if any man pushed his luck with her. Willing or not, drunk or sober, Sugar was on the short list of a few men who were eyeing her. If she was leaving unwillingly, it was going to be with him.

Jared swallowed the rest of his drink and embraced the burn. He slammed the glass down, got up, and shoved imbeciles out of his way.

From behind her, he clasped her bicep. Their gaze connected on the mirrored wall in front of her. He nuzzled into her hair. The scent of vanilla and flowers filled his nose. And he flexed his grip on her muscle, letting his thumb caress the underside of her arm. "We're going."

She didn't turn around. "I'm not."

"Make a scene if you want." He grabbed hold of her other arm. He rejected the urge to slide his palms over her skin. "No one will care."

"I'm not going to bed with you."

"Didn't ask you to." He breathed her in again and inched closer. "Move your ass, Sugar. Before I move it for you."

He would wait a three-count. After that, she would be slung over his shoulder. That wasn't his best course of action, considering he didn't know how much that too-short skirt would cover—or what was under that skirt. He groaned. *One, two...* Jared held his breath, willing her to slide off the barstool. *And three.*

She stood up, elbowing him away.

Thank fuck.

"Fine." She put her arms out to assure her balance.

He grabbed her hand, lacing his fingers into hers. It was small. Delicate. Innocent and feminine. *Surely, you've held a chick's hand before. Right?* It was an unfamiliar feeling. *So, eh… maybe not.*

Her fingers tensed against his knuckles. Other than the knife cut on her palm, her hands were unbelievably smooth. How could she work on AR-15's and have survived an Afghani mountain without getting so much as calloused fingertips? He had no idea. The only explanation was that she was a champ.

They exited the club, and he guided her toward the row of elevators. His hand, still interlocked with hers, balanced out her slight wobble while they waited.

Ding. The brass doors opened. They were alone on the elevator. He punched the button for floor sixty-three, with a solid plan to secure her in her room and somehow lock it from the outside. The numbers flew by, knocking through the forties, then the fifties.

It should've slowed. They hit sixty-one, sixty-two, and then sixty-three. And the elevator blew past it. Jared punched the button again as the elevator shot into the seventies. The penthouse capped out at ninety-nine.

"Jared?" Sugar's voice wavered.

He let go of her hand and pulled the emergency-stop button. The elevator slammed to a stop. Sugar hit her knees, cussing. His shoulder slammed the wall, taking the jarring hit. The lights flickered off, then cut to emergency lights.

"What the fuck?" he growled, hitting the operator button. He stared toward the security camera and jammed the button again. "Hello?"

An American voice poured through a speaker. "Our apologies for the problem. You're between floors. Maintenance should arrive soon."

Owning an equity stake in the hotel just paid off. The loyal staff knew Jared by name, but the man over the speaker hadn't addressed him directly. The hotel was well aware of who Titan was and made certain allowances for them, like his suite that doubled as an armored apartment and security measures that made Fort Knox look like it was protected by mall security.

Besides, anyone speaking through the speaker would've had a foreign accent. "Not a problem. Thanks for the update."

Sugar's eyes were wide. Despite the liquor, she was smart enough to stay mum.

"Come here, woman." He pulled Sugar tight to him, then slammed them against the wall. His lips trailed up her neck, to her ear. "Don't say a word. We're in trouble."

She moaned an understanding. He ran his hands down her back and cupped her behind.

Jared nudged her earlobe. "I'm going to toss you up. Punch out that grate and pull yourself out. Don't look over the edge, and hang on if another elevator passes. I'll be right behind you."

A noise echoed in the elevator shaft below—the sound of voices, mechanical clanging, and climbing.

She repositioned her head, dragging a breath across his skin, the same as he'd done. When her lips tickled the shell of his ear, he groaned. *Get your head in the game, man.*

Sugar murmured. "I've been drinking. I don't know if—"

"You'll be fine. You're a pro, and that's not a maintenance crew coming for us." A loud clang echoed in the shaft again. They were getting closer. "Ready?"

She didn't answer, just closed the distance, sliding her lips over his.

If that isn't the best damn good-to-go I've ever had... He kissed her a second longer than he should've and then catapulted her toward the ceiling. The grate busted free, and Sugar deadlifted her body up and over, short skirt, tall boots, and all. *Mystery solved on what was under that skirt. Not fuckin' much.*

Using the handrail, he pulled up and kicked in. The elevator swayed. Thick cables and wiring held the elevator in place. Shouts came from below. Other elevators rose and fell nearby. Their elevator shook as the cords swayed. He pointed to a metal ladder. "Move."

She was on it, climbing, with him hot on her six. The elevator shaft smelled like grease and rubber. Everything was dark, dirty, and dingy.

Above them, doors opened. Florescent light illuminated the shaft at what must've been ten floors up. Jared grabbed Sugar's legs to still her. They flattened against the ladder. *Crack.* A handful of neon glow sticks fell past them, then rolled on the roof of the elevator.

Male voices carried down the shaft. "Do you see them? Did they get out? Find her."

Jared squeezed Sugar's legs twice, hoping she knew to stay in place. Their ladder was narrow, and he needed to move above her to get them out of the shaft. He reached around Sugar, stepping carefully to the side, and shimmied up the side of the ladder until they were face-to-face.

"They can't see us. Fuckin' morons. Are you okay?"

"Little dizzy," she whispered.

"Focus on the ladder. I want you on me. When I take a step, you take a step. When I stop, I'm going to open the door, get us out. I need you to hang on. Can you do it?"

She nodded.

"Gotta say it for me, baby cakes. I need to know."

Her voice whimpered, "I shouldn't have drunk tonight."

"Least of our concerns. If you can hold your balance, I'll get you safe. Got me?"

She took a sobering breath. "I'm good. Go."

He wrapped a hand around her head, sliding his fingers into her hair. "Nothing's gonna hurt you. Ever. Not me. Not these fucks. Let's move."

He pulled ahead of her, hating to leave her without a safety net. But he saw no other choice. They moved to the next floor's opening. He looked down, and she concentrated on the ladder rung. *Good girl.* Below, boots stomped into their elevator, and faces peered into the dark shaft. He could see them, but they couldn't see him—until he opened the doors. Then it was game on.

Jared reached over to their exit, which was an elevator door. His toe reached the lip of a small overhang. The rushing sound of another elevator approaching worried him. He hissed, "Hang on, Sugar."

He flattened against the door, clawing his fingers into holds, waiting out the wind from the flying elevator. Sugar's hair flew around. Her gaze never strayed from the ladder.

The elevator passed them, paused, then dropped with the same gale-force winds. As it passed, he shout-whispered to her, "Come on up, until you parallel me. I'll pull you over."

She didn't say a word, but climbed the five rungs. The nearby elevators were on the move. Cables bounced, and the closest elevator came to a stop. Assuming people got on and off, then selected their floors, Jared figured he had a solid thirty seconds of inactivity.

He pried open the doors. Light flooded their location. Gunfire rang out from above and from below. He reached for Sugar's hand and yanked. She flew to his side, rolling on top of him into the hotel hallway.

Jared jumped to her and ran his hands from her cheeks to her hips, looking for signs of injury. No blood. No tears. No problems.

Pulling the concealed weapon from his back, he ducked into the shaft, looked up then down, and fired back. "Don't shoot at my fuckin'"—*girl*—"team."

Ping, ping. Bullets ricocheted around him. They would kill innocents if they kept up this game. *Enough of this.*

He jumped up and slid his weapon into its holster. Sugar balanced in her high heels, looking down the hallway. No one came out to investigate the noise. Smart. But he would've bet his AmEx Black Card that a dozen-plus callers had reported gunfire. He also bet that not a single one of them had been connected to real help. If GSI had a guy shutting down the elevators, they definitely had someone intercepting outgoing calls.

Jared snagged his phone in one hand and grabbed Sugar with his other. He blasted an emergency code via text to the team, but if they'd heard gunfire, they were already on the move.

Switching the phone for his gun, Jared kicked open the staircase door without letting go of his girl.

"This way." He pulled her down a flight of stairs.

Sugar didn't complain as they took the steps three at a time. He spied a service door and made a move. Checking once, then twice, for GSI, he shoved her in and shielded her, just in case. They tucked in behind industrial carts piled with dirty linens. Jared pulled out his cell and hit direct connect to Brock. "GSI's on the move. Botched elevator hit. Center elevator. Bag and tag." He ended the call and looked at Sugar.

"I shouldn't have had so much tequila. I should've known this was coming." She rubbed her temple. "Look, I've been a bitch. I'm sorry for this, for earlier. For getting you shot at."

"I get shot at all the time. Not a big deal."

"But not because of me. I'm sorry, okay? I feel like crap, and not because of the Patron."

Her big blue eyes shone. He didn't know if she was overwhelmed or emotional. That didn't matter—it was a knee to the nuts. "Shit, Sugar. My primary responsibility is you. Figure that out. Keeping you safe. Making sure you make it from point A to point B."

Why did that feel heavier than I meant it?

Her bare shoulders looked cold. That flimsy shirt wasn't one he would've recommended for a game of evade-and-run. She had black smudges from her breasts to her boots and marring her hands and face. A primal compulsion beat deep in his chest, like King Kong. Gather her up. Whisk her away. Just the two of them. There was no safer place than in his arms.

His throat tightened. Her outfit was having too strong an effect. He turned away.

"Jared?" She touched his shoulder. "Wait."

He turned. Without thinking, he wiped at a black smudge on her collar bone, but he only made it worse. "Yeah, babe."

Her cheeks went pink. He'd never seen shy play on her before. Sugar bit her lip. "If you're honestly.... hell, I don't know what I'm doing. But I'm willing to take away the booty call embargo." She took a breath, and the vulnerability disappeared. Sugar flicked him in the chest. "But if you hurt my feelings, I'll cut off your balls and leave you to bleed out."

He laughed and took a step closer. *This is the kind of girl I'm falling for? Wait... am I falling for her?*

He shook his head and kneaded his knuckles into his eyes. He opened them and stared at the vamped-up knockout who'd threatened his manhood. For this chick, he would take a risk. If nothing else, he would go down having fun.

CHAPTER ELEVEN

Sugar's throat was Sahara dry, and her head was swimming. She felt sober, but that was only the adrenaline. Too much tequila was still burning through her veins. The hotel service room was hot and humid. Piles of linens, humming pipes, and industrial gadgets that did Lord knows what cramped the already-small space.

Jared stepped away from her, hushing orders into his cell phone. He didn't have to whisper. The humdrum of the equipment kept his call confidential. She couldn't hear a word, yet she could guess every word. Sugar needed help. She couldn't handle herself. *Screw that.* Irrational and irritated, she couldn't calm her annoyance. Titan didn't need to swoop in at every occasion.

She gambled a step forward and felt her leg tremble. The stiletto boot teetered on its heel until she leaned back to the wall. *Maybe they did, and maybe I'll stay put for another minute.* Her hands shook, and her head pounded. *Freakin' adrenaline-tequila shakes. Coming down's gonna be a bitch.*

"You okay?"

She glanced up to see Jared watching her stare at her vibrating fingers. *Great. Never better. Fan-freakin'-tastic.* "You can stop asking me that."

He smiled as if this were the most fun he'd had since choppering out of Afghanistan.

Good for him.

"Well, all right then, Sugar. For a minute, I thought you'd gone all woozy-stumbly on me. Guess that wasn't you about to take a noser into a hot-water pipe."

"Oh, kiss my ass, Jared."

He chuckled, and she wanted to smack away his grin. Cockiness poured off him, as if he might lean her across his knees at any moment. "Don't think I won't, baby cakes."

Her skin flushed. Knowing what was on his mind, knowing how good it had been before... He was a roller derby of distraction. Around and around they went. A little violent, a little fun. Lots of games and strategy. She was hungrier for him than she'd realized.

As though he could read her mind, in two long strides, he was at her side, snagging her hand. She didn't fight him because she was already fighting with herself. *Don't crawl into his arms, rub his chest, or plead for a kiss.*

As he led her back to the stairwell, her body buzzed. His hyper-vigilant king-of-the-operatives hat was still firmly in place. All his talk and those soulful looks were little more than foreplay to him. He could toss them out and forget. Too bad she was still on fire.

The protective act worked for Jared in a major way. He was sexy in his own style. Not even decked out in tactical gear, he looked as if he ate his Wheaties every morning, then bench pressed his Expedition.

His gaze swept from side to side, on the lookout for bad dudes to kill. *My vigilante white knight.* He was smooth about it; she would give him credit for that much. At every turn of the stairwell corner, the man knew what was on the other side before she did. *Such a badass.*

They passed her floor and kept moving, probably to his suite, which was definitely the safer option. Hers would have enemy eyes on it. She was still a target, even if Titan had decimated whatever GSI ops were on site.

He opened the door onto his floor, ready to kill, and walked them to the door farthest away from the elevator and closest to the other set of stairs.

"Home sweet home." He inserted his key card and toed open   the   door.

She tried for a deep breath, which didn't work out so well. Who knew why this time? She'd already been in his suite. They'd already done the down and dirty. Nothing else came to mind that could take her breath away. But, still, it was gone.

The weight of the room strangled her. Its tension and apprehension were smothering, except to Mr. Unflappable. Jared moseyed past her, not remarking about how she clung to the entryway like a wallflower at a high school dance.

Unable to step forward, Sugar wrestled with an internal battle. *Alone with him again—I want him. I don't want him.*

"Hungry?" he called from the kitchen, rummaging around. The rest of his grumbles were inaudible, probably about her and their situation.

"Here." He threw her a large bottle of water. His towering frame stretched against the doorway. "Drink."

Always in charge. Always flexing his muscles. And why was that man always forcing food and drink on her? *So irritating*. But she *was* thirsty. "Okay."

She twisted the top and followed him into the living room. He was so pushy. Although, he seemed to only push when necessary, like when she was dehydrated or drunk. Sugar bit her lip. Maybe *he* wasn't the ass.

His brooding, intense gaze was hot. *Lord help me.*

"Drink faster, Sugar."

She stifled a *yes, sir* and a flip of her favorite finger. "Fine." Tipping the water back, she drank as she'd been ordered. *Seriously, I can take care of myself without J-dawg telling me how to behave.*

"Mr. Westin?"

Sugar screamed, spurting and spinning. The butler stood behind her. She took a choking breath. Water dribbled down her shirt, and she choked again. *What—are all butlers on stealth mode?* Of course they were; they'd been trained by Jared Westin, operative extraordinaire. "Sorry, my bad."

She wiped at her shirt, again noticing how greasy her hands were. *Oh, that's hot.* A shower was high on her priority list.

His expression unreadable, Jared crossed his arms. The butler appeared unfazed. After all, he did work in a hotel that had just been the scene of a gunfight, and as far Sugar could tell, the Abu Dhabi's version of the cops hadn't shown up.

The theme song to *Cops* played in her head, uninvited. Sugar took a long chug of water. She definitely needed to sober up more than she'd thought.

Jared shared a knowing glance with the butler. "A little help in the kitchen, my man. Black coffee and food that'll soak up Jose."

"Patron," Sugar corrected.

"Patron," he said to her, none too thrilled at her correction. Then he turned his attention back to the butler. "Maybe some breakfast. Pancakes. Waffles. Something. No raisins."

She raised her eyebrows, but he nodded to the butler and walked away while dialing his phone.

No raisins? So now the bastard has a sliver of a heart, and *he pulls a thoughtful moment out of his well-shaped ass.*

"I'm going to wash my hands." She found a washroom in the hallway, where the décor was masculine. Very Titan and very lived in. She wondered how often he stayed there. How many other women had his butler made breakfast for? She knew she shouldn't care, but her mind wandered anyway.

After only enough time for her to speculate on the inner workings of Jared's head, the butler knocked on the ajar washroom door and invited her to the dining table. Heavenly aromas drifted out the kitchen before she could say *Top Chef: Abu Dhabi.*

Jared came back with a mug of coffee and flipped a chair around so that he could straddle it. He nodded to her empty water bottle. "You need some coffee?"

"No. Thanks, though." Her sobering was in full effect. So was exhaustion. She needed to sleep, but that wouldn't be happening any time soon. Not while people were trying to kill her. Not when she wondered about how she was falling for a man who, to the best of her knowledge, had never had a single long-term relationship. Just like her.

Plus, caffeine would make her jittery, and that wouldn't help anyone. Staying awake and being exhausted was the best plan. "What's on our agenda? I can't stay squirrelled away in a hotel room forever."

The butler appeared with an orange juice for her and two plates of pancakes. Jared's fingers flexed around the mug, and he remained mum. A twinge in her stomach said he was holding back. He tapped a finger on the lip of the cup, drumming through the steam. He was holding back. Big time.

"Jared?"

He put the coffee down and cracked his knuckles, one at a time. "You think this is your fight, Sugar." His cadence was slow, thought out. The tone was patriarchal.

"It is." Her speculation was right on. Something was up. The worst seemed likely. Her stomach twisting, she nodded him on, willing him to understand what she needed. Maybe not all of the fight was hers, but she definitely owned a good portion of it.

"You'll hate me, and that's fine. I don't care. GSI's out of your league. At least when they're rappelling elevator shafts. You and Kip, one-on-one, I'd bet on you. You're smart, know your weapons. But you versus all of them—I'd rather have you somewhere safe."

What? Not a chance. "Jared—"

"No discussion." He took a long sip from his mug. "Until this hotel is clear, you stay within my eyesight. The boys will line up whoever they find, interrogate them, and we can leave. I'd guess mid-morning."

"Leave? Like go home."

"Yeah, you know a different definition, baby cakes?"

"We can't just leave."

"Why the hell not?" He put his mug down, pinched his brow, then dug into his pancakes while still straddling the backward-facing chair.

"I'm not leaving Asal."

The fork stopped midway to his mouth. His head dropped forward. She had no doubt that he'd forgotten about the girl. *Well, to hell with him.*

He took his bite and chewed like he was gnawing on cement. "Sugar, what do you expect me to do with her? You pulled her out of a bad situation. Feel good about that. She'd have died on the mountain. Now let the UN gal do her thing. Put Asal in a safe home."

"You mean orphanage?" she spat, slapping her hand on the table. The silverware rattled. The tiny flicker of her appetite was long gone.

He took another bite, then another. "I don't know what you want from me. What did you think you could do, just hang out with her in this hotel for the rest of your lives? Shit."

She shrugged. The future seemed far away. She hadn't thought about what she wanted—or what Asal needed. Her thoughts were running faster than she could keep up. "Well, no. Not a hotel necessarily…"

"Wait. What?" Jared dropped his fork. The clatter echoed like the chaos in her life. Loud and obnoxious. "Where did you think you and Asal might hang out?"

"I don't know. I hadn't thought about it until right now."

"And now you're thinking… what, Sugar?"

"Maybe she could come home with me." It was a whisper. A revelation. An oh-my-God moment when she realized something life-changing had just clicked. She cleared the cobwebs from her voice and narrowed her eyes, willing him to understand how strongly she felt. "I want her to come home with me."

"Do you have any idea what kind of paperwork and time commitment you're talking about? The red tape alone—"

"You're an ass. For a second, I thought you weren't a cold heartless bastard." A harsh laugh bubbled from deep within her chest, catching her off guard and reiterating her feelings. This would happen, with or without the great Jared Westin. "I need your help. I don't ask for help. Ever. Here's me, doing a first. Help."

"Sugar—"

"Jared. You're talking about an orphaned kid as though she was a package to be declared at customs. She's going to go to an Afghani orphanage. You get that? You know what that's like out here? Hundreds of kids, waiting for a lotto ticket. It never happens. So fuck you. She's coming home with me. You're the goddamn doer and fixer of everything. Master of the fuckin' universe. Fix this. Figure it out."

She slapped the table, and her hands stung. She hadn't realized that tears brimmed and were sliding down her cheeks.

Needy and helpless, she was showing Jared... herself, not the façade she presented to the world. On display, she was vulnerable and wanting something she didn't know how to get. Asal, not Jared. Maybe both. "Screw this. I have to go."

Sugar had been a burden as a child, and it was awful. To feel unwanted... she shook her head, needing to escape from her thoughts, but she couldn't. An unwanted child in an unwanted marriage was hard enough in working class America. But to be an unwanted kid in a third world orphanage? *Hell no. Not going to happen.* Her mind catapulted through everything her mother and father had made her feel. Abandoned. Obnoxious. Useless. She could do better than they had. She could provide Asal something much better than an orphanage.

She shoved herself away from the table, not noticing Jared standing over her, and slammed into a brick wall of warm muscle. She wondered how long ago she had slipped into her memory daze.

He wrapped his arms around her and petted the back of her head. He was hugging her. *Hugging.* It made the tears fall faster, and she buried her face in his embrace.

"It's okay. You're fine," he soothed. The deep timbre of his voice didn't sound like the mechanical lines Titan recited to rescued victims. It sounded heartfelt. A new swell of tears fell.

"It's not." She sniffled. "Nothing's all right. Everything I want is just out of my reach."

He pulled back. *How appropriate.*

Then he palmed her hand, rubbing his other hand over her knuckles. "Sugar, we'll get it figured out. Let me grab you some clothes, and you can take my bed. Catch some z's, and it'll be okay."

He pulled her tight again. She should've leaned away. She needed to shield her heart. But she couldn't. Her muscles melted into his. He smelled amazing. All natural and male. A hint of gunpowder and coffee.

"Sugar?"

"Yes?"

"Every man in that club wanted you to look his way tonight. And I wanted to kill each one. I need you to know that. If

Asal's that important to you, I'll figure it out. You believe me?"

"About which part?"

"Lord, woman. You drive me crazy." He tilted her chin up, wiping the tears away. "I don't like to see you cry. I don't want to see you upset, and I don't want some dickhead eyeball-fucking you."

She smiled, feeling, for the moment, cared for, and ignored the niggling temptation to run away. "I need a shower."

"No invite? Thought you lifted the embargo."

"I need to *shower* and get some clean clothes."

"An objective I can handle." Placing his palms on her cheeks, he held her gaze. "I'm glad you're here, and not because it's safe. I like you here with me."

He leaned over, brushing his lips over her bottom one, sucking it into his mouth and stealing her heart. Her eyes fell shut. For that second, she lived in the present, when neither of them had battles to fight. The soft slash of his probing tongue pushed her lips apart. She flexed her fingers into his shirt, clawing her nails against cloth-covered skin. Her heart raced, and arousal pulsed deep inside.

She fought for the kiss. His lips burned her alive. Soft and hard. Sensual and domineering. He walked her backward, until they collapsed against the wall. His teeth raked down her cheek, then her neck. A moan erupted past her lips as he devoured her skin, teasing her collarbone, tearing the strap of her tank.

"Sugar, baby, you deserve better than me. But I think we both want to see where this goes." He threaded his fingers into her hair. Twisting. Tugging. Teasing. His tongue continued its torture.

"Yes." The word sounded as aroused as she was. She was still covered in grease and smelled like an elevator shaft. "I really need a shower."

"I can't promise," he said, husky and low, "that I'll keep my hands off you tonight, but I will make sure you get enough rest to survive until we're home. Shower, and I'll be waiting for you."

CHAPTER TWELVE

With the water turned off, Sugar watched the droplets flow down her arms and off her fingertips. She didn't know what to do with herself as Jared's words tumbled in her subconscious. *I'll be waiting for you.*

The bathroom was like a sauna. Steam clouds rolled through the large room. Surrounded by foggy mirrors and steam, she shivered. Goosebumps raced down her arms and legs as though his words were tangible, stroking over her damp skin. Conflicted and confused, she didn't understand why his one-liners squeezed her heart. They couldn't be meant to penetrate as deeply as they did. He was a playboy. His lines were his tools. She wasn't stupid. Or maybe she was, and denying that his sentiments held truth was simply moronic.

The solid-wood bathroom door separated them. Jared wouldn't barnstorm the bathroom and tangle with her like they had in her hotel suite earlier. She knew it in her bones. He would wait her out because he had said this could be different and that he cared. And he'd promised not to hurt her.

She was naked and hidden by a wall. She considered wrapping herself in a towel. *Not like that stopped him before.* But in her suite, it'd been all freestyle sex. This would be different. The register of his voice and the strength in his hold had said so.

"What are you waiting for?" she whispered to her fogged reflection in the mirror.

Her nerves were popping like fizzy champagne. The booty embargo lift was in full effect. Even her emotional veil had inched back. Before, it'd been playtime. Now, Jared had strong words and serious looks.

Chaos and emotion reigned in her brain. Her palms felt ready to detonate the second she walked out the door. And that had nothing to do with sex.

Go time. She grabbed a robe, tied it snugly, and cracked the door. Across from the bathroom, Jared was propped against the wall, brooding.

Bulging, bare muscles crossed his chiseled chest. Gray sweatpants hung dangerously low on his hips. A dark trail of hair smattered from below his belly button to the teasing waistband.

Her throat ached. Her stomach somersaulted. "You've been waiting long?"

"Longer than I realized." He stepped toward her on bare feet. They locked in a trance as the heat of the steamy bathroom enveloped them.

With a flick of her wrists, she displayed her hands. "Had to scrub all that grease off my fingernails."

"Not what I meant." His words came out in a guttural growl, making her muscles clench. He took another step closer. "You're unbelievable."

Jared unfolded his arms. Rippled muscles and skin pulled taut across his broad chest. He closed the space between them before she could say something to ruin the magic.

She hesitated. "What if GSI shows up? Firebombs the door. Catches us... not paying attention."

"Impossible."

"Nothing's impossible." Case in point, she was standing with the half-naked Boss Man in his hotel bathroom.

"Then improbable."

"Oh, you got lines." A joke. A jab. Justification for her distrust. But it didn't feel like typical alpha stuff. It felt intense. Hot. Needy. When he talked, her body quaked. Her mind listened.

"The only thing I've got tonight is you."

And *that*, she heard. His fingers floated down the fabric of her robe, gliding from her shoulders to the sash, and toyed with the knot. "You need a change of clothes?"

"Eventually."

Arousal flashed deep in his black eyes. "Eventually. Noted."

She could've pulled up her protective shields. Relationships should be defined as *disasters*. Some couples could pull them off; most couples couldn't. Not that Jared was offering coupledom.

Sugar would never chase a man after he'd lost interest. No way would she turn a spineless blind eye like her mother had.

The more entangled she and Jared became, the harder she would fall, and the more it would hurt when he walked away. She would keep her pride, and he would never look back. Whatever Jared's current interest was with their spark, it would smolder and eventually die.

"Sugar?" Jared melted his body against hers, hands moving to her hips. "Lost you for a sec'."

"No. I'm here."

"Bullshit, woman. One second, you're all..." He purposely raked his gaze over her, studying her curves as though they hid his promised land. "But now you're closed off."

"Imagining things, J-dawg."

"*J-dawg?* The nickname of defense mechanisms. Now, I know I was right." He nipped her earlobe. "Lilly."

She flinched in his arms and turned to face him. Nose-to-nose with him, her eyes flared. "My name's Sugar. I don't go by Lilly." That was the name her parents gave her. That was a weak name. The name didn't hide the softer side that she'd decided to bury long ago.

A heaven-sent smile made her knees shake. "It suits you."

"The names aren't interchangeable." She wanted to wrap the robe tighter, to run away from the bruised nerve that he had no idea he'd stomped upon. But she wasn't going anywhere, not when he smiled and looked and smelled the way he did. He was all suave alpha male on a mission, and his spiel was straight truth serum.

"I like *Lilly*, Lilly. You can't make up rules and expect everyone to play by them." He loosened the sash and slid a hand under the robe to her barely damp hip. Rough and strong, the contact was simple and erotic. A wave of shivers rioted across her skin, from her breasts to belly and beyond. The pads of his fingers flexed into her skin. "I play by my own rules. Thought you'd know that by now."

She knew. Sighing, she let his hand explore her stomach. *Sweet mercy, we'll never make it into his bedroom.* She would be a puddle of mush. Jell-O legs and spaghetti arms. Pulling it together was more than necessary. The embargo might've been trashed, but her heart still needed swaddling. He was a damn visceral vice that hulked half-naked in front of her, but she could survive this obsession.

"I like control." She tried to sound convincing, but it came out a whisper. "Rules. Mottos. Mantras. Have them for a reason."

He pulled the sash loose and let the ends fall free to dangle by her sides. His palms slipped over her nipples. *Traitorous tits.* They'd been begging for his attention, and he noticed, teasing each mound with a massage that would make her climax if he wasn't careful.

"You think I don't have a code? Fuck it. Let's forget my T-and-A tenets and your guard-your-heart statutes." His thumbs and forefingers teased until her eyes closed and her body went soft against his.

Guard my heart? Her bottom lip quivered, and she didn't try to stop it. "I'm not in a good place to negotiate."

"So don't. Give me the sincere Sugar. I like to play with the ball-bustin' Sugar, but bench her tonight. I want the real deal."

"I'm—"

"Nope. Don't lie to me." He brushed his lips down her neck. His teeth dragged, ordering lightning bolts to rappel down her spine. "Don't hold anything back with me. Ever."

"Ever?" She rolled her neck, allowing him full access. He was asking for a lot. But she could trust him.

She could... right? Yes. She could. She would.

"Ever," he growled. The authority in the word and the iron-clad strength in his tone made it a commitment that she could agree to.

"Okay." A weight in her chest lightened. *Wait.* The foggy mirror reflected a fresh scar on his shoulder. Sugar stalled, turning for a better look. "This is recent."

"Shrapnel. Doc got it all out." He went back to her neck. "Won't say it doesn't still hurt."

"You were injured when you came back for me?" She batted his mouth away. "Jared?"

"Got an ugly freshie on the back of my leg if you want to gawk at that, too." He brushed a wet strand of hair away from her cheek. "Nothing could stop me from bringing you home."

"Oh." Nothing? *Maybe I can do this with Jared. Maybe.*

She grasped his cheeks and kissed him hard, needing to convey what "Oh" meant without uttering a word. She could feel all of him. His hard-on strained into his sweatpants as her robe acted as a curtain, framing her naked body for him.

Their tongues tangoed, dancing to the tempo of a symphony progression, entwining and caressing. It was an overture, a prelude to his delectable devouring of her, completely and totally, leaving an undying need for more.

"No more games." Jared scooped her into his arms.

"Agreed." Her fingernails grazed his stubble, scratching his chiseled jaw. "No more."

Gone was the steamy bathroom. He carried her into the dimly lit bedroom, placing her in the middle of a luxurious down comforter. Satin and silk surrounded her body. The bed dipped as he came closer. His large frame steeled above her.

"Every time I close my eyes, Sugar, this is what I see. You. Naked. And all mine."

She almost choked. She wanted that, needed to hear it, and would take whatever temporary basis he offered. For this moment, she could justify his ill-guided confession.

Sugar pushed her arms out of the robe and offered a crystal-clear invitation. Her. Him. Now. "You're the one wearing pants. What should I think about that?"

He captured her lip with a bite, groaning into her smile when she flexed her hips. "Such a bad girl. Always pushing me."

"That's how you like me."

"You know me too well."

Their mouths clashed. Her tongue grazed his, challenging and chasing. Heat rioted within her belly, swelling behind her breasts. Constricting in her throat. Saturating the area between her legs. Every sensitive zone was on a high alert, waiting impatiently for Jared to kiss, bite, and tease.

He found her nipple, freezing her breath. Mind-numbing, arousal-decreeing licks and flicks of his tongue caused her back to arch. Each suck and pinch elicited tiny bucks that she couldn't control.

God, how he made her feel and how her body responded... and he hadn't even *really* touched her. Not yet.

But he would. The vivid memory of their romp on the floor had given her a sneak preview of what she could expect. Great things. Monumental things. And that had nothing to do with the size of the heat he packed. *Heaven help me.*

"Enough," she ordered. "Lose the pants. Now, Jared."

He chuckled against her skin. "Not yet."

"You want me to beg?"

"No, sweetheart." He gave her a harsh kiss. "I need this as much as you do. Taking my time."

His hand trailed down her stomach, then between her legs. She was ready for him, slick enough for more than a tease. "Please."

"I want you burning for me."

She trembled against his barely there touch. Fast and furious was long over with. He was giving her a slow death, and she needed more. "That's just cruel."

"I'm a bastard doling out torture," he murmured, trailing the tips of his fingers across her folds.

Her head fell back, pushing deep into the feather comforter. He nudged and stroked, opening her to him. Variations of his name rolled off her tongue as she savored his fingers dancing against her flesh. Insane emotion built with their skin-on-skin collision.

"Fuckin' beautiful, Sugar. Love the sounds you make. Love how sweet you are."

Oh, God. He moved down to her stomach and dipped his tongue into her belly-button, then wrapped his free hand around her waist, pinning her still. She moaned his name again. No wonder he had a God complex. She couldn't stop from crying out. She didn't want to. *Jared. Jared. Jared. Ruler of the bedroom, Jared.*

His tongue trailed from one hip bone… lower and lower. He stopped.

"I'm dying." She couldn't hold back the begging any longer. "Put me out of my misery."

He smiled, laughing against her skin, then lavished her with sinful kisses while on his mission to her other hip bone. "I could do this all day."

"No, you can't." Her voice was hoarse. "You won't. We need this. Together."

He bit her flesh and speared a blunt finger into her wetness. She jackknifed. "True."

"Again," she moaned. She would beg again—anything to move along from anguish to apex.

He pressed into her again and circled his thumb against her most sensitive spot. His finger voyaged deeper against muscles that'd barely recovered from his previous entry.

"That good for you, baby?" Watching her face, he encircled her bud of nerves with his thumb. All she managed was a throaty sigh and a nod. A *please continue, whatever happens, don't stop.* "So expressive. Show me more. Show me the real Sugar."

Two fingers penetrated, slamming her eyes shut. Her head fell to the side, and her breaths erratically pounded their own beat. She drew her ankles back and bent her knees against his broad shoulders. He lowered his head, poised at the center of her heat.

"Jared…"

And he kissed.

"Yes." She swallowed the word, failing to breathe and speak simultaneously. "I need you."

That honesty spiraled her mind. His fingers and tongue found a staggering cadence, and she fell apart, not caring if the pieces never fit back together again.

Writhing against his onslaught, her legs wanted to snap closed, but his forearms wrapped around her thighs made it impossible. He licked as if dousing her in hot flames. Rapture filled her body. Pleasurable sensations and revelations overpowered her.

"Fall apart for me, Sugar." It was a directive, a command that roared for her attention. The vibrations between them reached to her soul, fueling the fervor. "Now, baby."

She unraveled, bucking into his mouth. He gripped her hips, holding her in place, drinking her in. His velvet tongue rode each pulse. Her hands ripped through his cropped hair. Unable to grasp strands, she gave up. Her hands smacked onto the bed with a mind of their own, gathering the comforter into her fists. Stars exploded in her head. Bright, shiny bolts of electricity zipped about the room.

He let her come down from her high. Slowly. She savored the wave of euphoria, soaking in the wonderfulness that was them.

"Perfect." He sat up, pulling her tight to him. In a voice gravelly and deep, he told her, "I've never tasted anything as perfect as you. Sweet fuckin' nectar, Sugar. I'm addicted."

Addicted? They should form a two-person support group to survive their high together. Her limbs shook. Her brain couldn't connect thoughts to words, so she said nothing. Jared rolled to the nightstand, shucked his pants, and slid on a condom.

He leaned over and kissed her. Lightly and lovingly, he started the path to a blistering explosion all over again. It held the hidden promise of a mind-scrambling release. That man always had a plan. An objective. Thank the gun gods above, it was her pleasure.

His wicked mouth did what she'd learned it did best— ravage her with kisses, turning their connection into something better. Nothing had ever been as good as Jared. Nothing ever would be.

The deep, brooding shadows on his face and the primal possessiveness that poured off him clutched her heart, stealing all logic. Like a tango target, she had nowhere to go, and the fallout would be catastrophic.

"Can't wait to have you again." He crawled toward her. "You're in my head, girl. In my blood. I can't stay away."

Interlacing their fingers, Sugar pulled him on top of her. She locked her legs around him, positioning his shaft, which was poised for unimaginable ecstasy.

"You said… don't hold anything back?" Her mouth readied to bare her innermost secrets before her uncertainty had a chance to say, "Shut the hell up." But the uncertain, lucid part of her brain remained mum, conveying an unquestionable belief. *Jared won't hurt me.*

"Never." He tightened his grasp on her hands, squeezing tight. "Never hold back from me."

"I don't want to just…" *No looking back.* "I want this to be more. Make love to me. I need all of you. Even if it's just this once. Just tonight. Let me be all yours."

A flash of something crossed his face. A pause. A moment.

Pin, pulled and tossed. The grenade was in his backyard now.

He kissed her gently, nudging her lips open, then he touched his forehead to hers. "For you, Lilly Chase, I'd do anything."

Her heart and her very soul sighed. Relief made her want him all the more. Jared flexed his hips, pressing his erection against her. Sore and needing more, she released a moan. He captured it with a mesmerizing kiss. That kiss didn't seem possible from a man as impenetrable and inflexible as the battle-hardened warrior between her thighs. But for some crazy reason, it made perfect sense for them.

Splitting her from the inside, he thrust. Huge and hot. Pleasurable pain and dangerous desire. Their pace worked to incredible, indelible. He held her, soothing and stroking. Promising the world without a word, he filled her, pushing her to a shattering realization. She'd tied herself to him. His wild, jagged barbs ensnarled her heart.

Arching her back, she absorbed his drive. Cries craving release carried through their kisses. A tornado of tension swirled. Her insides throbbed, building a tempest of intensity. She couldn't breathe or see. She could only feel the deep connection.

"Yes, Lilly. Come for me." His words were a carnal command.

Lilly? He was with *her*, not the Sugar she presented to the world. She nodded, understanding and needing release, needing to ride the wave that neared crest.

His hips rode into overdrive. Panting and perspiring, Jared owned her. She'd climax because of him, for him—

And again. She felt a release unlike any she'd known. Tensing and tightening, throbbing for her master of everything, Sugar combusted. Lights and stars burst in the eye of their hurricane. She tried for a breath, then another, before failing. She found the ability only after staring into the force of his gaze. It steadied her amid their swirling storm.

Torment painted his face. "You're destroying me, baby."

"I'm already ruined," she whispered. At least the devastating truth was out there.

Pounding into her, capturing every sound she offered, Jared surged toward his zenith. Sensation ripped through them, his release rocketing into her as he strained, his muscles tight. His howl of her name sounded primal.

Watching him come, feeling him through the godforsaken condom, ignited her all over again. They struggled wildly. Tight in his embrace, Sugar felt as if she were holding on to a supernova. Her tears threatened to fall.

He collapsed against her, creating a tangled heap of their bodies. Gasps raced one another, alternating like pulses clamoring to a barbaric beat. His mouth was still connected to hers. Not a kiss. Not a lick. Just a hold. From lips to legs, they were flesh on flesh. No space. No secrets. Just Jared and Lilly.

If she'd fallen asleep in his arms, she didn't know. Time stilled. Danger disappeared. They weren't in Abu Dhabi. They weren't anywhere.

He whispered against her ear, ensuring she was awake. "I'm in uncharted territory. And the only goddamn thing I've got in my arsenal is you."

Pulling him impossibly closer, she let her heart escape, along with a sigh. "Jared—"

His cell beeped like an alarm. He reacted immediately, barreling over her, grabbing it as if a man had gone down. "Fuck me."

Maybe one had. Terror struck her, and his tenderness was gone. The hardened bastard was back, and her stomach sank— not because she didn't love his commando routine, but because it meant something had gone wrong. Titan had a casualty? Because of her? She couldn't live with that guilt.

His eyes narrowed, and a knot travelled the length of his throat.

"What's wrong?"

His hands flexed on the cell.

Sugar sat up, pulling the comforter around her to fend off a sudden chill. "Goddamn it. Tell me."

He paused a beat, steeling strength into his features. "Asal's gone."

CHAPTER THIRTEEN

Jared's gut tensed trigger tight. A missing Asal meant a war-ready Sugar. The anger and apprehension was visceral and tangible. He had to stop her emotional bleed out. However, he had no idea how to pull off a maneuver like. He couldn't Ace-bandage her worry or splint her rage.

"Sugar. Take a breath. It'll be fine." Yeah, they both knew his words were textbook response. He needed a plan.

"Who was that?" Her lips were red and swollen, reminding him of their tangled-sheet blowout. "I need to know everything."

"Rocco. My team's all over the hotel, finishing up GSI." Any plan he could draft involved his number two, Brock, getting everyone in line.

Sugar scowled, pouring venom. "They missed something." She jumped up, taking the covers with her.

"Easy there, baby cakes."

"What did he say?" Her body leaned forward like she was liable to attack if he made the wrong move.

The situation was serious, and no amount of sugarcoating would make it better. "He said—"

"Spit it out, Jared."

"The UN chick's dead. Asal's nowhere to be found."

Sugar gasped. "What the fuck? What if Asal's dead, too? God. I bring her to this fancy hotel when all she's known is rocks and caves. Fucking goats—"

"She's alive. She has to be." His heart pounded. Taking the kid? Asal was strong, a spitfire who'd shimmied across a mountain with his special forces team. She would survive, and he would make sure Sugar knew it. "They wouldn't have left one body if they were going to kill Asal. It's better that she was here then on a devastated mountain. We'll find her. Bring her back."

That kid had etched a place in his heart, and he wouldn't fail her or Sugar.

"To me." Resolve burned in her eyes. It was an order, and he wasn't one to take them from anyone—except her.

Jared nodded. "Yes, to you." His phone rang again. *Brock.* "Tell me something good."

Sugar wrapped the covers tighter around her body and paced his bedroom.

Snagging his sweatpants off the floor, he pulled them on and matched her paces. This wasn't how the night was supposed to end.

The status update was grim and to the point. Professional hit. Clean sweep. Asal was still missing, and his team was ruthless on its recovery objective.

Sugar cracked her knuckles. "GSI's going to use her to lure me out."

How is this possible? No one knew about Asal. Just Titan and his counterpart who'd arranged for the UN attaché. Jared trusted everyone who was in the know. Nothing added up.

"Brock, have someone sweep Sugar's room for bugs. Hell, every room we have, including mine." Even though his was swept daily and monitored constantly.

With a grunt from Brock as a response, Jared ended the call. Brock would issue the orders to the team, and Jared could stay with Sugar, at least until it was time to fix the situation, and keep her from going nuclear. GSI couldn't have gone too far with Asal. They couldn't have...

Bullshit. Why would he lie to himself? GSI had access to just as many planes, trains, and for-hire ex-military forces as Titan did. The problem with GSI was they were dirty. Snatching a kid for bait? Buck Baer would do it in a hot second.

A vein protruded on her temple. Her neck strained. "My room was bugged. This is my fault. I'm gonna—"

"Sugar, stop."

His phone rang. Rocco's name scrolled on the screen. "Yeah, Roc?"

"Swept all the room but yours. They're clean. Brock's headed to you now."

No bugs? Why would GSI remove them? That would be pointless.

"Get dressed." He threw sweatpants and a shirt to Sugar. "Unless this building is bombed and crumbles, there's no safer place than in this room. Brock will stay with you after he sweeps my suite."

She pulled the shirt over her head, then shimmied into the pants. "Where are you going? I'm coming—"

"To have a conversation with GSI. To stick my foot up Buck Baer's ass until he chokes on my fuckin' bootlaces."

She rolled the waist on the pants in choppy, spastic moves. "I'm not going to sit here like some—"

"Yes, you will. You'll do as ordered. I don't care what just happened in this room between me and you."

Her face didn't fall. *Thank fuck.* What he'd said was habit, but what he felt… that said he should've toned it down.

She nodded. "Got it."

If that reaction didn't make his heart pound a little stronger. "Sugar—"

"I won't sit long," she said through closed teeth. "Do your job, Jared. And when the time comes, I expect you to turn me loose."

He gave his word. *Now for showtime.* Parker could find Buck anywhere in the world, but chances were, he was sitting on his pompous ass in a fancy chair. *The prick.* The call to Parker rang once before he answered.

"Yo, Boss." Parker was obviously expecting him. His team ran liked a well-oiled machine. Smooth and deadly, each part did what it was supposed to. "Feeding the surveillance video to Rocco now. Brock's already been in touch."

"Get Buck Baer on my television screen. Now."

"Yes, sir. Give me five."

The line disconnected. No pause. No doubt. That was a good employee.

Jared snagged a shirt. Stalking to the living room, he pulled it on. Buck Baer was a piece of shit on the lowest of levels. After that night's disaster, Jared would tear him apart. Piece by piece.

He paced in front of the television, mentally counting down the five minutes he'd promised Parker. The screen flipped on to a gray, static-showered picture. It blinked.

Once.

Then twice.

Finally, Buck Baer appeared.

"Jared Westin. To what do I owe this unceremonious request to chat face-to-face? An emergency, as I understand it?" The ruddy-faced jerk smirked. The audio was clear enough to make Ma Bell proud.

Restraining his inner grizzly, Jared took a breath. "I want the girl."

"To the point. I always liked that about you, Jared. Oh, wait. I meant to say, whatever do you mean?"

"Your team's here. You went after my mark. You took a kid. Very far outside our rules of engagement, Baer."

"I don't play by rules."

"Fuck your games. I don't give a shit what you siphon from the government, foreign nationals, or the damn Taliban. I'm giving you one chance to produce the child. One hour, or I promise you, GSI will collapse. You'll deal with me. A fate far worse than going to Leavenworth."

"Don't know—"

"Fifty-nine minutes." The poise in his voice surprised even him. Jared would take out Baer and GSI anyway, even if Asal showed up bearing Girl Scout cookies. "Clock's ticking. Don't sign your death warrant."

"Goodbye, Jared." And the connection was cut.

What the hell? No ransom? No request for Sugar? His phone rang a split second after the screen turned off. He grabbed it. *Parker.* "Speak."

"Not good."

"No goddamn commentary. Update me, now."

The mechanical locks on his door began to wind. Very few people had the ability to enter his suite, but he didn't care. Given the three-second window of security enhancements, Jared readied for a kill. He leaned under the couch, removing a stashed 9mm, and leveled it at the door. It cracked. Slowly. *Brock.*

"Announce yourself next time." Jared stashed the weapon back in place and made a mental note to tag all the guns hidden around his suite once Asal was safely in his custody.

He pointed down the hall. "Sugar's in the back room. Eyes on her at all times." Bringing the phone back to his ear, he paused. "Wait. Knock first."

Brock laughed but kept moving.

"Parker. Intel?"

"Surveillance feeds were scrambled. Working on that. No eyes on GSI, though. Don't know who or how many we're looking for."

Damn it, Parker. "You aren't earning your paycheck."

"But I can tell you that I've identified every vehicle in the parking garage, with exception of two Range Rovers. I'd say we're looking at a team of no more than eight. Ballpark, three below your elevator, three above. Leaves two to man the security station and handle hiccups."

That sounded about right. "What else?"

"Nicola processed the UN scene. Got no clue how they knew about the kid."

"I want that intel breach figured out—"

The television screened blipped back on. All static. Parker whispered in his ear as if someone might overhear. "GSI's trying for a connection. I can block it."

"Let it through."

Beep. Buck Baer appeared, and Jared almost ripped the screen from the wall. "What the fuck do you want, Baer?"

"Turns out, I know where your girl is. Imagine that."

"I'm not playing games with you."

Buck laughed, leaning back in his chair. "Sure you are."

"He's not, but I will," Sugar said as she stepped into the room.

Goddamn it! He turned on his heels to see her. Gorgeous and insubordinate. "Sugar, stand down."

Buck's laughter poured through the sound system. Jared turned back to the monitor, wishing he could strangle a man through the television screen.

"No." Buck pressed his fingertips together. "This is perfect. Just the lady I want."

Brock stepped in front of Sugar. *Brock had better have a damn good excuse as to how she got around him, otherwise he's benched. Indefinitely.*

"Simple offer. A trade. Lilly Chase for the girl."

"No." The word roared from deep in Jared's chest. "I don't negotiate with imbeciles."

"Fine," Sugar said. "Not a problem. When and where, Buck-o? I have some choice words for you."

Sugar's propensity for not following rules was legendary. The spectacle shouldn't have been a surprise to Jared.

Buck Baer clapped. "Nicely done, Jared. Gorgeous girl, just fucked hair, wearing your clothes. I'd heard you kept your team and your jobs close, but I can tell you take serious care when showing your *appreciation*."

"Watch your ass, Baer."

"Of course. The kid's already on the way to me. Bring Miss Chase back to the States. I'll give you further instructions later." The screen went black.

Jared spun to Sugar and Brock. "What the hell was that?"

Brock shifted blame while rubbing his jaw. "She's got a good sucker punch and knee action."

"I forgot you asked me to behave." She shrugged one shoulder and gave a half-cocked grin.

"Goddamn it, Sugar. We plan and concur. Not react and show our weaknesses." He scrubbed his hands through his hair. "Find a way to confirm Asal is with GSI, heading to Baer. Airport security or something. And have Parker track that plane. If all looks good, we're heading home within the hour. I want to take down GSI from the inside, hand Asal to Sugar, and tie up this ridiculous op with a damn bow."

Brock didn't miss a beat and walked to the door. "I'll round everyone up."

Sugar started in the same direction. "I'm headed to my room."

"Like hell. Stay put."

She waved a hand down to the curve of her hip and back up. "I'm in your jammies, big boy. No way am I jumping on a jet with Team Titan until I get my own clothes. So *escort* me there, or turn me loose. Preferably with a loaded weapon."

Holy mother of... What the hell am I going to do with her? Jared snagged her hand and tugged her to the couch. "Here, nine millimeter. Give me a minute. I need to grab my shit, then I'm coming with you."

Twenty seconds later, he had his go-bag and returned to an empty living room. Sugar would be the death of him, and it had nothing to do with guns and ammo.

CHAPTER FOURTEEN

Distrustful of the elevators, Sugar hit the stairs. The dirty tile was cold on her bare feet. The walls were generic and whitewashed, which was surprising for a place so plush.

After everything that had happened in the hotel over the last few hours, she'd expected people to be running for their lives and armed guards on every floor, at every door. But nope. Nothing.

Black letters painted across the wall read sixty-third floor. Her floor. She shoved open the door and peered around the corner, looking for anyone else with a gun. Or a bomb. Or some other way to kill her.

All clear and so quiet. Almost too quiet. She shook her head. Her mind was playing tricks. But still, her hand wrapped the 9mm in a death grip. Normally, she was calm under pressure, but given the last few hours, a stranglehold on her piece could be forgiven.

She padded down the hall. Her room had been checked for whatever GSI might've rung up. She had no reason for nerves, but the jitterbug act was still swirling in her stomach.

GSI wasn't there. Asal wasn't there. There was a better chance that Jared would come flying down the hall, ticked because she'd left without a goodbye. Sometimes, she couldn't help but want to piss the guy off. It was so much fun—even when someone could fall from the rafters and take her out.

Her lips curled into a smile. Jared was *cute* when he was mad. Now there's a word for Jared—cute. She laughed. He wasn't in a million years, yet somehow it *so* fit. She loved the way his lips got all pouty and his brow furrowed. He did that Mr. Clean-arms-across-his-chest thing that made every muscle flex. Well, that wasn't cute. That was downright smoking. But the cute thing would be her secret.

Fast footsteps tickled her hearing. She spun, flicking the safety off, and smacked into a man. "Jesus Christ, Brock."

He took a step back, ignoring the gun. "You know how mad Boss Man is?"

"Don't care. Couldn't be too mad if you showed up and not him." Flipping the safety back on, she dropped the 9mm to her side.

Brock rubbed his eyes. "I was closer."

"I hate waiting and didn't need a babysitter."

"You're just as ornery as he is."

Her lips twitched into a proud smile. "Maybe more so."

"Look." Brock took a step forward. "You gotta come with me. We need to go."

She turned on a bare heel. "I just need a few things out of my room. Give me a minute."

"Sugar, let's go."

His hand landed on her bicep, and she spun back.

"Get your paws off me, big guy."

His fingers tightened.

"Seriously, Brock. I won't take it from Jared, and I won't take it from you."

"I don't want to—"

"Then don't. Tell him you didn't find me. Tell him you found me *after* I changed my clothes." Pissed his fingers might leave a bruise, she shrugged out of his tight grip. "It's like you guys just expect us to handle everything that comes with Titan. Rules and orders and edicts. Well, newsflash, Brock. I want my own damn clothes."

"The rules are there for a reason." He took another step forward, sounding angry that she was pushing him. "If you listened, if everyone just listened, nothing would be so damn complicated right now."

"Thirty more feet. You're fighting with me about thirty flipping feet." She started walking. "I'm almost to my room. If you're going to force me back to Jared, do it now. Otherwise, I'm changing."

He started after her, rumbling, "Do you have any idea what kind of danger you're in, Sugar? I could've been GSI. I could be—"

"But you weren't. You're the second in command at Titan. The number two to Mr. Loyalty himself." She stopped at her door. "Just like I know this room is safe, just like I know you won't hurt me. Nothing will happen to me right now. Not with you standing there. Come in or stay out. I need to change."

His phone rang once, and he cursed before answering. *Great, Jared's checking on me. Just what I need.*

Brock ran a hand over his face. "Nope. Nothing on the target." He clicked off the phone. "Change. Make it fast."

"That Jared asking about me?" She put the keycard in the slot, and it unlocked.

"No."

She laughed. "Damn, Brock. How many projects do you guys work on?"

He dropped his head back and stared at the ceiling as she held open the door. "One too many."

"You coming in?" Why the seconds with him took forever, she didn't know. He was slowing them down. "Brock? You coming in, or you have some *target* to take care of?"

Stepping through the threshold, he straightened his shoulders. He let the door close behind him. "Yes. To both."

Every pair of Titan eyes were on Sugar for the duration of the flight home. She could feel them. Well, less on her and more on Jared's iron grip on her hand. His team watched, no one saying a word. And that said more than anything. *Seriously, when was the last time any of the Titan boys could keep their mouths shut? Never.*

Too bad his death grip had zip to do with anything hearts-a-flutter. He was pissed. In a major way. The handholding was no claim on her as a woman. He was simply a free agent holding an assignment in place.

Tsk, tsk, J-dawg. Should've known I'd have something to say to Buck Baer. Controlling her attitude wasn't a talent she could boast. Neither was staying put. He shouldn't have been too surprised that she'd walked out of his suite.

The wheels hit the runway, and the jet flaps went up, relieving some of the tension in the cabin. The braking engines roared until the jet made a turn and stopped.

Almost free.

"Think she's safe now, Boss Man." Cash laughed. "You can let go of her."

"Shut it, cowboy," Sugar snapped.

Jared squeezed her hand, and she didn't know if he was telling her to be quiet or if the motion was a testosterone-heavy version of, "I can fight my own battles."

One by one, the rest of the team disembarked the plane as Sugar and Jared sat in place. Jared didn't move and didn't seem to notice they were alone.

Enough. "All right. This was fun. You gonna give me a ride to GUNS, or do I need to get a taxi?" She looked out the window, at the private airstrip. No taxis. *Of course.*

"Let's head to Titan." Jared stood and tugged her behind, the handhold firmly in place.

She pulled back. "Cash was right, ya know. I'm fine. Safe and on my home turf." *Almost.* "We'll do our dance with Buck and kick his ass later. For now, I want to go home."

"GUNS and home are two separate places."

She shrugged as her eyes adjusted to the sunlight. "Might as well be the same. I feel more at home at GUNS."

"Not sure I should drop you off at a weapons depot."

"Nobody's coming after me. Not yet, anyway. I'm not going to grab my guns and knock on GSI's door."

"No one's coming after you?" He stopped midway down the airplane stairs, glaring. "I know you're not that stupid."

"And I know you can't drag me everywhere, acting like my personal bodyguard."

They started walking again. He kept a secure grip on her as they crossed the empty runway. "There's a hit out on you. You need me."

"Wrong, Jared. I need no one. Never have and never will. But I do like you, so this whole white knight act isn't unbearable. The handholding thing, kinda cute in a grumpy-bastard kinda way—"

He pulled her tight, his lips finding hers. A rough, needy kiss silenced her mind, her mouth, and her comebacks. The crush of their lips and tongues brought everything to a stuttered stop. Everything except the wild beat of her heart.

Jared growled against her lips. "You make me so fuckin' hard, I can't think straight."

Holy hell. Tummy flip, meet brain freeze.

His mouth devoured hers, nipping at her tongue and stroking it with his. *Dying.* She was dying for him to touch her. Have her. She would settle for on the tarmac if they couldn't make it anywhere. "Please. Let's do something about it." Despite his attitude, she hadn't forgotten what he did to her. How her body moaned and craved every inch of him.

"My truck. Let's go."

Hell yes. She nodded, her body plastering to him as he moved them quickly toward the parking lot. His fingers flexed into her flesh and kneaded. Zips of fire burned from her lips, spiraling to her toes and washing away jet lag and their quarrels.

A lone Expedition waited in an otherwise-empty parking lot. No crew. No airport staff to be seen. They were there in a second, falling against the SUV, which was cold and hard against her back. Bracing his hands on either side of her head, he trailed kisses down her neck. Rough. Teeth scratching. An impressive bulge in his pants nudged the soft spot between her legs.

Beep, beep. The doors unlocked.

"You want me, baby cakes?"

"Absolutely." *Maybe more than ever.*

He grasped the backdoor handle, opened it up, and lifted her inside. In such a tight space, Jared loomed over her, somehow closing the door behind them. She wasn't sure his hands had ever left her body. A million sensations covered her body, but she couldn't tell what he was doing or where he was. It was just hot and needy. Uncontrollable. Unstoppable. Just like the man.

His eyes burned black. "You know what you do to me?"

"This." She palmed him, stroking over the zipper. He was hard and on a mission.

"Not sure I'll ever get enough of you, Sugar."

"That's my problem." Her breath was ragged. Her chest arched into him as if he'd commanded it. "Find your own."

"I need more of you than a quickie in my truck."

"Amen to that." She clasped his buckle. "But it'll do for now."

He popped the button on her jeans with nimble fingers, then tugged her pants and thong down her hips. "For now—"

A loud knock stunned her into stillness. For all his concern over her safety, neither of them had been watching for trouble. Fury crossed Jared's face as he un-holstered his sidearm and turned to look out the tinted window.

"Mr. Westin, you okay in there?" a voice called from the outside. "Saw your car. Everyone else left."

Jared's dropped his head, chuckling. "Security. Cock-blockin' security."

Sugar pulled herself upright, adjusting her shirt. Jared holstered his weapon and opened the door. Blushing, she followed his lead and opened the opposite door. They'd been caught making out by an oblivious man wearing a reflector vest.

"We're all good. Thanks."

Realization colored the guy's face scarlet, and he scooted to his waiting security truck, which had yellow rotating lights on its roof. *How'd we miss that thing driving up?*

Jared clicked his seatbelt into place and, with a slap, put the Expedition in drive. "Buzz kill."

⁂

This day could not get any weirder. That morning, he and Sugar had been busted for making out in the backseat of his Expedition. Lunchtime came and went, and they had made good use of their time at GUNS with a nooner in her office. That afternoon, as Jared stood in Colby Winters's familiar living room, a sense of dread made it hard to get comfortable.

An adoring Winters walked into the room with a little bundle of blue blankets wrapped protectively in his arms. The man beamed, never taking his eyes off his son. "This is Ace."

The all-points bulletin had already gone out to Titan. Andrew Reese "Ace" Winters. Ten fingers. Ten toes. All good news.

Jared took a step forward, tiptoeing so as not to disturb the little thing.

He'd never seen a newborn before. *Little* was right. What was the kid? Five, six days old? Ace snoozed quietly, his eyes sealed shut. The goofy grin on Winters's face screamed proud papa. So did the tired eyes. That wasn't the face of the warrior Jared knew. It warmed his heart a little to know his guys weren't just gun-slinging machines.

"Want to hold him?" Winters extended his arms a little, offering Ace.

"Oh, hell no." Jared's hands flew up as if the baby was TNT with a short charge. His boots moved him back on instinct. "I mean, *heck* no." Right? He shouldn't curse around a kid.

Winters chuckled, and Mia walked in. She had the same tired eyes as her husband, but was just as happy and proud. *Good for them.*

"Jared Westin." Mia put her hands on her hips. "I *know* you didn't just say no to holding Ace."

"Uh—"

"Big toughie like you is actually scared of a sleeping infant?" She shook her head.

"But—"

"Colby, don't hog the baby." Mia flicked her husband's shoulder. "Give Jared a chance."

There was no negotiating with Mia. "I don't—"

"Clara, in here please." Mia looked down the hall, beckoning the torture he'd signed up for.

In blurred the toddler, running full blast. Blonde pigtails bounced with each erratic footfall.

Onto the couch. *Bounce, bounce, bounce.*

Over the side.

Onto a chair. *Holy hell, get down!*

Then to the floor. And she was off and running.

Jared lifted a hand to wave or something, and then realized his mouth was hanging open. This couldn't be little Clara he'd seen stumbling around a few weeks before, clinging to the couches to move about. This was the roadrunner of children.

"You sure you got this, man?" Winters handed the baby to Mia, who shook her head at Jared. "I could stay home. I knew it was short notice, and not like I'm calling some random babysitter just 'cause my mom can't do it."

"No. I got this." He could handle a toddler. He knew Clara. *Never been alone with her…* But he had to-do list from Mia, which he'd studied… and Googled, because who really knew what a tri-ci-coo was? *When did people stop saying tricycle?*

Clara ran through, running a circle between the living room and the kitchen. The hallways were like a toddler-sized track. This time, tucked under an arm, she had a red stuffed animal with bulging eyes.

"Clara." Winters stepped toward her, removed her from the ottoman, and placed her in front of Jared. "You remember our friend Jared?"

"Hi!" she shouted, waving the ugly red animal.

Jared crouched. "Hey, Clara."

"Give her a high five," Winters urged him. "Works every time."

Uh. Okay. He put up his hand. "High five?"

Clara ran forward, smacking his hand and giggling.

"That's Elmo." Winters pointed. "Know where he is at all times, and you'll be fine."

A drumroll replaced the normal beat of Jared's heart. A red stuffed animal was the key to his survival? Surely, he would survive this with or without Elmo. "Got it."

"So, we're leaving." Winters met Mia at the door.

She waved like this was an everyday thing. Jared and Clara. Alone. No big deal. "Bye, guys. We'll be back."

"Bye!" Clara hollered then ran down the hall. "Bye, bye, bye."

Using her voice like sonar, Jared raced to find her. *She moves so damn fast.* Then all was quiet. *Damn. No wonder Sugar wants an older kid like Asal.* She could skip the whole terrible twos, not that Clara was even two yet. He should've called Sugar, but it hadn't occurred to him that babysitting would be a two-person project.

Where was Clara? His heart double-timed. *Has to be the kitchen.* He did another lap around the toddler track. Thirty seconds into Operation Keep the Kid Alive, his mission was looking bleak.

A chair scratched across the floor. Jared spun and dropped to his knees. Clara was crawling, weaving under the chair legs, dragging Elmo. *Christ almighty, I should've brought a homing device. Could've just attached it to her shirt as a precaution.*

His cell phone rang. Nope. No time for distraction. He went for the ignore button and saw that Sugar was calling. "Hello?"

"You okay?"

"No. Yes. Why?" He dropped to the floor to keep a better eye on Clara.

"You sound like you've been huffing helium. All high pitched."

"Are you okay?" *Feeling like this was life or death right now...* "If you're good, I have to go."

Clara shimmied from underneath the table and ran toward the stairs. Fast on her trail, he got there before she did. *Okay. Big white gate. Not a death trap.*

Sugar sighed. "I'm fine—"

"Okay. Bye. I'll explain later."

She sighed again. "I'm worried about Asal. I hate waiting for Baer and feel like I need to do something."

Clara hit the living room again, bouncing on a seat cushion. He hovered so she wouldn't tumble to the floor and break her neck. "You agreed to meet Baer. That was a game changer. But we got this. It'll be okay. Two more days, she's yours—"

"What are you doing?" Sugar asked.

Yeah, good question. Good fuckin' question. Fencing in a chair with his arm span. Crawling on the floor. Wondering how many teeth a toddler could knock out with a fall to the floor. "I'm... babysitting."

She snorted into the phone, laughing. "Excuse me?"

"Ace had a doctor's appointment. Winters's mom got sick, couldn't watch Clara. Mia asked if I could, so she and Winters could go to the appointment. Here I am."

Sugar clapped in the background. "And he's good with kids, ladies and gentlemen. What can't Jared Westin do?" She laughed again. "This is priceless. I'd pay to see this."

Clara ran down the hall, screaming, holding Elmo high over her head. He was in fast pursuit. "Sugar, I have to go."

"I didn't think you were the kid type."

God, seriously. This conversation is happening now? "I'm not. I am. I don't—hadn't thought about it." But had he thought about it? Asal and Sugar and—"Clara, wait!"

Clara made a sharp right, coming to a stop at the back door. That might be good—a big open space without too much to hide under or climb on. He could see her in all directions and could get to her quicker than she could get into Winters's lake. *Okay, good idea, kid.*

He opened the door. If he thought Clara could run before, she was on fire as soon as the door opened. Her little legs ran track-star style. Her trajectory was all off. If she stood up a bit more, it would be better. She would be less likely to—

Wipeout. Oh shit.

Jared ran to Clara while Sugar blabbered in his ear. Clara popped up faster than he could ask her if she was okay. *Running again? Tough kid. Okay. All right.* The kid was okay. He took a breath.

He sunk to his haunches, watching Clara run in circles. "Christ."

"What?"

"Kid's got energy. A lot of it." He watched their surroundings for any signs of danger. Ditches. Branches. Sinkholes. Whatever. "She runs, constantly unbalanced. Climbs up stuff that isn't stable. Under stuff that could fall. The kid's fearless."

"Ha! Sounds like you."

"No joke. She could train the guys. Jump first, ask questions later."

"You'd make a good dad."

The words tied his stomach into a knot. That had never occurred to him. Not the good part, but the dad. That'd never been in the plans—not that he made plans like that. It was all Titan, all the time. But before Sugar, it'd been all women, all the time. And right then, he wasn't interested in letting Sugar get too far from him.

Whatever that means...

Keeping an eye on Clara, he held the phone to his ear with his shoulder and cracked his knuckles. "I want to see you tonight."

"You just saw me."

Nothing was ever easy with Sugar. "You got a problem that I want to see you again?"

"Have to work. Lot of stuff to catch up on."

"Our deal was you'd stay home after we left GUNS."

"Oh, now, Jared." Her voice purred, and if he hadn't had a laser focus on the kid in front of him, his mind would've wandered. "You know I didn't get much done there. You kept me far too occupied."

Goddamn if that isn't the truth.

Clara stopped running and froze in place like she'd seen an enemy running straight for her. Her hands went up, then down, and then she wailed.

Every fiber of his muscle went on high alert. His mind hyper-analyzed the perimeter. "Where the fuck is Elmo?"

Sugar exploded with laughter. "Elmo?"

Clara hit the ground, then rolled on her back and screamed. He spun left, then right. Elmo. Where was the stupid bright-red doll?

He saw it—a dozen yards away—and sprinted for it. Snagging it on the move, he hightailed it back to red-faced, tear-streaked Clara. He grabbed a little fist, inserting Elmo in between her tiny fingers. Like he'd hit the off switch, she smiled, sat up, and started *singing*.

"You're too distracting, Sugar. Elmo went AWOL, and things almost got bad. I gotta go."

"All right, J-dawg. Have fun babysitting. I might stay home and think of ways to drive you crazy. My new favorite pastime."

I'll give you a new favorite pastime. He shook his head. Not the time. Not when Elmo was on the run. "Later, baby cakes."

The kid type and a good dad. She was already screwing with his brain. He tapped his fingers on his thigh. What he wanted, what he was good at, was all things Titan, which was very much like Sugar's push to make GUNS her world. But she was making room for Asal. Was she making room for him, too?

Clara ran over to him and held up her hand. *High five.* He gave her hand a tap, and she giggled, running off at top toddler speed. *Yeah, I could handle kids. I'm good with them.* They certainly weren't an easy gig. But so what? That didn't give him permission to start questioning himself. The trouble was Sugar. Getting wrapped up in her equated to complications.

Winters's dog came out of nowhere, and Clara squealed, breaking his concentration. He had no time to think about anything other than what was right in front of his nose.

Sugar was armed and had the start of a plan. She would make up the rest along the way. The weight of the gun balanced perfectly in her hand. Her touch warmed its cold metal. Measuring every step, ensuring each was the quietest one possible, she inched closer to the mark.

The room was dark. The air conditioner hummed. Adrenaline pumped through her veins. God, she loved a good game. *Tonight's might be the best. Ever.*

She crept closer, scaled the bed, then straddled the snoring man. The move was pure power.

She nuzzled the business end of the gun against his lips. The snoring stuttered, then stopped. He blinked. Brain waves and synapses fired. His body stiffened.

"Wakey, wakey, you sly motherfucker." She dragged the barrel over his teeth, watching his face in the dim light coming through the window. "Kip Pearson, we meet again."

He opened his mouth, but nothing came out.

"That's right. Think very carefully before you speak." Rage and vengeance coursed through her blood.

Scratchy-throated, he murmured, "If you're going to kill me, do it."

"Nah, I'm here for two reasons. First, where's Asal? Second, you'll deliver my message."

He laughed into the barrel. "Not a chance."

She reared back and pistol-whipped him. Kip gave a satisfying sound of pain. Blood trickled out a nostril. "I have no problem killing you, Kip. Like you had no problem killing me. But you serve a greater purpose. For the time being." His torso shifted under her, and Sugar pulled the slide on the gun, then shoved the barrel under his chin. "Careful. I'm easy to underestimate, apparently. One slip of the finger, and well, you can guess."

"You'll kill me anyway."

"I won't." She tapped the gun against the soft fleshy spot under his jaw. "I told you. I have a message you need to deliver. Be a good sport, Kippo. Tell mama where her girl's at."

"Hell, whatever. Doesn't matter." The wheels were turning behind his dimly lit face. "He's expecting you anyway. Buck Baer has a place outside Charlottesville. In the mountains. The kid's there. That's all I know."

She pushed the gun into his throat. "Do you know how much will power it takes to not pull this trigger? Give me a reason not to pull the trigger."

A light sweat broke out across Kip's forehead. "There's more than one kid. Consider it a peace offering." He licked his lips nervously. "Come on, Sugar. You know it was just business in Afghanistan. Nothing personal. There's another kid or two with Buck. That kind of intel's worth giving me a break."

Another kid or two? Why would GSI have children? "Not sure I believe you, but it's a start."

"Like I said, he's expecting you. With or without Titan. Good luck."

"I don't need luck, Kip." She pulled a pair of handcuffs from her waist and slapped his hands together. "I just needed you to know that I could get in here and that we're not finished."

"Oh, come on."

"Someone'll come looking for you, I'm sure." She slid off the bed, grabbed a second set of cuffs, and shackled his ankles to the bedpost. "You'll be okay, until you aren't. Don't forget to tell Buck Baer he fucked with the wrong gal. I'm gunnin' for him."

CHAPTER FIFTEEN

Her hands tight around the leather steering wheel, Sugar slid her car into her driveway, with the radio blaring. Her high beams caught a mass of man, all anger and crossed arms, standing in her way.

Shaking her head, she put the car in park and pocketed the keys. *Why am I surprised? Why wouldn't Jared be waiting for me?* It was the middle of the night, and he hadn't been there when she'd left. Sugar sighed and climbed from the driver's seat. Slowly, for good measure. Just to make her favorite brooder wait.

"Fancy seeing you." Her boots crunched in the silent night as she walked past him toward her front door. A growl rumbled behind her. She guessed he wasn't in the mood for the old blow off. "I'd invite you in, but it's late. I'm tired." *And I don't want to play twenty questions.* She had too much research to do to find Buck's place. She was sure she would need a couple of hours to drive there. Never one to wait for the fight, she thought it seemed like a decent idea to bring the fight to Buck. She could take Asal and make sure he knew she was in the mood to stay alive.

"Where have you been?"

The coldness in his voice would've stopped a lesser woman. "Running errands."

"Sugar—"

"Jared." She turned, smirking beside her front door. His face was pinched tight. "Gotta get my beauty sleep. I promised we'd talk about Buck tomorrow after he's contacted you."

He took a step forward. Enraged energy poured into the night. "I can tell when you're lying."

"But I'm not. We'll talk about Buck *tomorrow*. I swear." She made a cross over her heart, then blew him a kiss.

"You're up to something."

Well, hello, Captain Obvious. What gave it away? The one foot in the door, the other kicking away a man who makes my heart pound double-time? Good job, J-dawg. "Always am. If you want any future relationship between us, that's a mantra you should come to terms with, real quick."

He rubbed his hands together and unsuccessfully tried for an unaffected look. He relaxed his shoulders, and removed the upset snarl across his face.

Such a plotter. A negotiator.

"Two heads are better than one." He took another step forward.

Oh, bullshit. He only wanted to know what she'd been up to, but it was true enough—two of them working on a Buck plan was better than her working alone. Mr. Master of Everything was good at tactics and strategies. Basically, all she had was: load up on explosives, find Buck, then go home with Asal. Her plan had holes.

"I'm good." She bit the inside of her lip. Really, that should've been: "I'm stubborn."

He took a step forward. At that rate, he would have inched inside her door sometime just before dawn. "Then let me in. We'll sleep on it."

Even when he was all motives and persuasion, he made her throat constrict and her blood pound in her neck. The idea of him in her private domain gave her shivers. "I don't think you have any intention of sleeping."

"You don't know that." He took another step forward in his kill-me-slowly ambush.

Exhaustion and the start of self-doubt screwed with her the longer she remained outside. Tucking her arms across her chest, she sucked in a slow breath and prayed he didn't notice her internal battles. "I know you better than you think, Jared. I know that you're worried about me. I do crazy shit without thinking. I get it." She inhaled another cold breath to strengthen her assessment. "I know you're pissed that I'm out in the middle of the night."

His demeanor shifted. A knowing look creased his brow, and his eyes narrowed like he'd sighted his target. "I know you smell like gunpowder."

Unconsciously, she stepped back. The back of her heel hit the porch lip. He had her cornered. Jared was good. But so was she. "Back off. I always smell like gunpowder. Hazards of being a gunsmith."

"You're an ATF agent. GUNS was your cover."

"I *was* an ATF agent." Sugar unlocked the door, readying to give him a final boot. "GUNS was a bonus, and it'll be around for a long time. Can't say I care about losing my badge. Can we continue this discussion tomorrow? I've got a lot—" Two hundred pounds of muscle pushed past her. "Well come on in, asshole."

He walked down the hall, eyeing her place. "Nice digs. Different feel than GUNS."

Did I expect anything different? Her head dropped back, staring at the ceiling. "Since you weren't invited—"

"Show me around, or I'll give myself the tour."

"You can't stay long."

"Got something to do tonight, baby cakes?"

Frustration poured into her fists, and her nails dug into her palms. "Maybe I do. So if you wouldn't mind. Let's wrap this up and say our goodnights."

He spun to stare at her, then kept walking. "Not used to a woman kicking me out."

"Get used to me." She tossed her purse on a table. "Or get over me. Two easy options."

He flipped on a light, then another. "I'm going to ask you one more time. Where were you?"

"Time for you to go." She kicked off her boots and wiggled her toes on the cold floor.

"You went looking for Asal?" He tilted his head, and his eyes shone in the darkness as he studied her.

"Looking for Asal? Not quite. So, if that's all, you can go anytime now. I'm saying my goodbyes and goodnights. Not sure I can paint a better picture. Maybe I need a Titan map and a mission objective?"

"You'll go out again." He folded his arms across his distractingly broad chest. "Soon as I'm gone."

"Maybe." That wasn't a lie. He didn't need all the details. "If you don't mind, I'll check in with you tomorrow."

"No go, Lilly Chase." He plopped onto the couch. "You have three choices. First, you go to sleep. Most reasonable of the choices. I'll assume you'll ignore this one. Second, we forget it all and head to your bedroom. You'll nix that plan, too, but there's my vote. And third, you tell me what you did, what you're doing, and we'll hash something out together. I hate lone ranger shit, so cut it."

Fine. He wants to know. Let him handle it like a big boy. "I cuffed Kip Pearson to his bed. He told me where Asal and Buck are."

A wave of shock crossed Jared's face. She could've bet on that reaction, and it made her smile. Surprising him was fun.

Jared scrubbed his hands over his face. "Goddamn, woman." He blew out a long breath. "Fuck me."

She tapped her bare foot on the ground. "I chose option three. Are you going to use that giant Titan brain of yours and concoct a plan for me, or should I slip out after fucking you senseless?"

A low rumble of a laugh erupted, and he rubbed his temples. "Let's combine the best of those suggestions."

The foot tapping stopped. The nails-into-palms digging ceased, and she slammed her hands to her hips. "I'm serious, Jared. I'm after my girl—"

"And GSI's after mine!" He strode forward. "What are you going to do? Threaten Baer? Tell him to back off?"

She shrugged, trying to ignore his possessive outburst. "Not if you come up with something better."

"You're killing me." He cracked his knuckles, then his neck. "How about a compromise? Can you handle that?"

His expression wasn't as much annoyed as...

What the shit is he feeling over there? Concern? "Maybe." She followed him farther into her house and ignored the tingle that she got from the idea that he cared.

"*Maybe* doesn't work. Either yes or no. Otherwise, you'll be tied to the bed if I don't think you'll behave. Let's try again. Are you capable of compromise?"

"If that's what it takes to get tied to my bed…"

"Sugar," he growled.

She was exhausted and losing steam quickly. And if there was a chance he could come up with a plan better than her non-existent one… "Explain the terms of a compromise, then I'll consider."

"Sleep on your attack-dog approach. We'll catch some z's and head in before Baer contacts us. You and I will bring the fight to him. Just let me figure out the logistics, get the team ready, and gather your back-up."

"I dunno…" She needed him, and she hated needing anyone. Maybe that was the problem.

"Look, Sugar. You've got me by the gut strings. I'll protect you, whether you like it or not. Let me do my job. Stand down for a goddamn minute, and then you'll have one of those happily-ever-after endings. You'll get the kid. No bull's-eye on your head. Every day, you can run GUNS. Whatever your dreams about the future are, you'll have it if we play by my rules."

He began checking her windows and investigating her security measures without waiting for an answer, looking confident in her response. A tremor of rejection prickled up her arms, tightening in her throat. He'd made no mention of himself in the future. But what had she expected? Outwardly, she tried to make everything about sex, constantly kicking him out or evading him.

As if she could ball up and choke off any emotion, Sugar reflexively threw her arms across her chest again. "Fine."

He stopped and turned. "Now what's wrong?"

Great question. Her waffling emotions had to be exhaustion. Feelings like those shouldn't crop up in her thinking. "Tired. Fine. You win." She tried to act relaxed and put on a show of being reasonable. "Sleep, then kill."

Jared laughed. "Sleep, then kill? Something like that." He paced to her, then dragged her toward the couch. "Sugar, wasn't that long ago a woman joined my team, and I quickly learned that the word *fine* means anything but."

"Wise counsel you've got from Nicola."

"Wanna tell me—"

"What's the deal with you and Buck? GSI's personal." She pushed his chest, knocking him easily back onto the couch as if that'd been his plan. "It's not just me."

"Old history."

"All history is old." She stood awkwardly above him as he leaned back, relaxed. All her muscles were tight. Her mind was anxious, bouncing from one thought to the next.

Jared looked positively comfy, sprawled on her couch like he was about to watch a game. "Agree to a compromise, then I'll answer your questions."

"That's blackmail."

"More like coercion." He tapped the cushion next to him on the couch, inviting her to sit. If she sat, her guard would be gone. Maybe that would be good. Clearing his throat, he brought her back to the moment. "Which neither of us has a problem with, Sugar. Agree or not?"

She took a deep breath, momentarily sidelining her night's plans. He was right. "Fine, yes. I agree. Coerce away."

"Sit with me, and I'll tell you all about old history."

She collapsed onto the leather couch. Her arms hung limply from her slouched shoulders. "Okay."

"Baer and I were Rangers together. The dickhead couldn't be trusted, but he was good at the job. Almost on par with me. We complemented each other in the field."

"Egos got too big? You guys got out and started rival firms?"

"Little deeper than that." He took a deep breath. "We were in southeastern Africa, some village, doing Lord knows what. Whatever political bull-crap we were sent to do. Intelligence under the cover of lending a helping hand from Uncle Sam." Jared pushed his head back on the couch. His brow furrowed, and his dark eyes filled with hatred. Uncharacteristic lines appeared on his forehead. Maybe the memory she'd asked him to dig up should've stayed buried.

"You don't have to tell me. It's okay."

"There was a local punk. Maybe nineteen, twenty years old. Leader of a rebellion army. The US was turning a blind eye to him. His army—all kids, child soldiers—were systematically killing off villagers who didn't tow his load of shit. But not before the fucker would take their possessions, what little those people had."

This wasn't what she'd expected him to say. Bad news tinged his voice, and it was already an awful story. "That's terrible."

"That's just the reality out there. Nothing the news ever reports." He sighed and stared at a wall. Silence hung for seconds, but it could've been hours. "The rebel leader would march families to giant graves. Line them up and use his child army to mow 'em down. The next round of disobedient villagers would have to shovel a dry layer of red dirt over the bodies and stand in line, starting the process again. The African village version of fuckin' Hitler. Goddamn genocide."

Her stomach soured. This wasn't a memory she should've asked for. She didn't deserve it after how she'd behaved. He didn't need to tear off a Band-Aid for her. "Christ. I'm sorry."

"The guys had to pull me back." Cold, hard anger burned in his words. The temperature of the room seemed to drop a dozen degrees. "I wanted to tear that rebellion apart with my bare hands. But orders were strict. Do not engage. Watch and report." He sneered. "Buck Baer not only didn't engage, he profited. Made a deal with the rebel leader, bought and traded provisions. Not that Baer needed anything. Greed just got to him. Couldn't stand not making money. Fucker was always on the take." A tough guy like Jared didn't need soothing or sweet words. He probably didn't need anything. But she couldn't keep her anger from percolating as her appreciation for his need for revenge fully formed. "Profiteering asshole. Baer might as well have been a soldier of the devil. He started GSI with the goal of getting rich, and he's come a long way from ripping off African villages."

She turned to him as all the pieces fell into place. "The genocide was a pivotal reason for creating Titan?"

"*The* reason. I started Titan because I was the best. Could lead and recruit the best. Choose my assignments. Show up where I felt like it. Do what I thought needed doing."

The cold in the room was lifting. His personal confession warmed her heart. "You do a good job. No doubt, Titan's the best."

"A lot of jobs are gray. No clear right or wrong. But we have honor, and, for better or worse, we're the good guys."

"I never questioned that."

"And I will demolish GSI, taking down Baer. Hard. So you want the kid alive. I want Baer ruined, almost more than I want him dead. Though he's screwing with you, so I may re-evaluate that."

"You know, Jared." She dropped her shoulder against him. "At the risk of sounding like some fan-girl of yours, you have a good heart. It's hidden by that rusty exterior, but I like that about you. A lot."

He harrumphed.

Snuggling against him, she sighed. "Good thing you have a tough coating, because I'm a pain to put up with."

He hooked an arm over her shoulder. "You aren't so bad."

"I'm exhausted. Borderline delusional." He was so warm. His scent washed over her. "I... need your help."

"Fall asleep. I'm not going anywhere." His voice was low and coaxing.

She rested her chin on his shoulder. "Do you want to lie down?"

"I don't need to sleep. I need to watch over you. Nothing's getting by me. You might've forgotten there's a bounty on your head, but I haven't."

"Oh." So tired and so safe, she hadn't felt in danger before, but with Jared, she was sure no harm would come to her.

"As stubborn and pushy as you are, Sugar, as often as you ignore direct orders and common sense, we're partners. You and me, baby cakes. You need to sleep, and I don't." Eyes locked, they sat in silence. Jared pushed a non-existent strand of hair from her cheek, smoothing it behind her ear. "Sometimes, you have to rely on others."

She burrowed farther into the crook of his arm. "Partners works for me."

"Not much of a choice. I always get what I want." He leaned down and kissed the top of her head.

The kiss reminded her of one she surely imagined back in Afghanistan while curled into his body in a cave. She pulled back to study his face, searching to define how a brash man like him could dole out kisses as soft as that. "What do you want, Jared?"

"You." No pause. No moment. Only pure confidence.

Her stomach flipped, bursting into her throat. With a dry mouthed and a spinning head, she realized she needed him in ways that she couldn't grasp. She interlaced her fingers with his. "Come to bed with me. Awake, asleep. Next to me, in a chair. I don't care. Just be near me."

The whispered request against his ear earned a nod, and he tightened his hold on her. Forget the rest of the world, he was all she could handle. All she wanted.

His cell phone vibrated. Phone calls before the crack of dawn were never good.

"Go lie down. I'll find you in a minute." He squeezed her hand, then answered his phone as he stood and walked to a corner.

Moving wasn't on the agenda, not without him. Curiosity played a part, and she stayed put.

He turned back on his heels, clicking off the phone. "Did you hurt Kip Pearson?"

A cold knot immediately formed in her stomach. *Back to work.* His voice was all business, and his expression said he was taking charge. It shook her out of her lovey-dovey headspace.

"Nothing more than his pride."

"Well, the fucker's dead. Shackled and shot in his bed. No weapon to be found. I told you not to fuckin' kill him. Goddamn it, Sugar."

"I didn't! You don't believe me?" *Of course not. Why would he?* He trusted only Titan, not her, not even when he was feeling all hearts and flowers. Somewhere in the back of her mind, she could see her mother shaking a finger at her, chiding her because she should've known better.

"Damn it." Jared paced her living room, his boots leaving a path in the carpet. "I never should have left you alone."

"Partners?" She laughed because they were back to the beginning. "Believe what you want, asshole. I didn't kill him."

He glared. "Asshole? Really?"

Jared's phone rang again, and she was up the stairs before he had it against his ear. *Time to get the hell out of the house.*

CHAPTER SIXTEEN

Rubbing his temples, Jared continued to pace Sugar's living room. Kip was dead, Sugar was pissed, and he'd had about enough of all the random headaches tied to what should've been a tidy operation. His skin prickled. Sugar was being set up by someone close. There were too many coincidences, and too many sure things had fallen apart. Overly aware of the tingle racing the length of his spine, Jared tossed his phone from one hand to the other. His heart thumped in his ears. *Think, think, think.* The beats pushed his mind to position the puzzle pieces.

He didn't have many options to consider. Either GSI had eyes and ears on his team, or…

His heartbeat still spoke to him. *Think, think, think.* Its demand grew more impatient when he wouldn't admit the possibility staring him in the face. Someone within Titan had screwed him.

He dialed Parker. Gut feelings were worth investigating, even if it meant the worst-case scenario could exist. Jared checked his watch, oh dark thirty. He gave Parker an extra minute to answer the phone before irritation fueled their conversation.

"Boss Man, what can I do?" Parker's voice splintered with sleep-heavy dryness.

"Get to a computer, and light up everyone's phone signals." He cracked his knuckles, not believing he had to ask this. "Locate everyone on the team."

Jared heard a shuffling in the background, which he could only guess was Parker getting out of bed. "Give me two, and I'll hit you back."

"I'll wait."

A blasting noise screamed from the driveway. His breath caught in his lungs. Surprise, then concern jumped his blood pressure. *Car alarm? What the hell?* He put the phone on a side table.

"Sugar," he yelled up the stairs.

No answer.

He ran to the closest window, ducking for cover, and peeked out. *Va-voom, rumble, rumble, rumble.* The hood to his Expedition was up. Sugar's car floored into reverse, screeching out of the driveway as the lights flipped on.

"Sugar!" Jared ran up the stairs, then kicked open every door.

Each was empty. Instinct said he was alone, but his mind couldn't wrap around it. Jared scrambled down the stairs, swiping his cell phone, and then out the front door, keys in hand.

He barked at Parker, "Locate Sugar's phone."

"Okay."

How someone had slipped into her house and taken her was a question that should've made him question his chosen profession. If he couldn't pick up on an intruder who was an imminent threat to his woman, then he needed to pick up a new gig.

Still keeping Parker on the line, Jared walked outside, pocketed the phone, and withdrew his sidearm. His eyes scanned the perimeter, his senses honed for any danger. Nothing. All alone.

Why would Baer's team grab Sugar, knowing he was there? At the very least, someone had been there. They'd gone to the trouble of screwing with his truck. That didn't make sense. None of it did.

Gun in hand, Jared slammed down his hood and silenced the alarm. He opened the driver's door and slid in. His gut tightened. *Why'd I have to accuse her of—*

It took half a second before Sugar's brilliant plan slapped him across the face. His head dropped to the steering wheel, shaking slightly from side to side. He'd questioned her. Doubted her. She was gone, and there he was, analyzing his words.

"This woman will be the death of me."

Taking one long look at his car key, he popped open the hood again, instead of trying the ignition. He got out and checked the engine, knowing it would confirm his suspicion.

Missing spark plug. Well played, Sugar. Well played.

He paced in front of the Expedition and pulled out his phone. "What are you seeing?"

"Sugar's at home. Her phone's pinging at her address."

"I bet."

"Oh." Parker cleared his throat. "So... are... you."

Jared scrubbed his hand over his jaw. "So am I. Yup."

"And Brock."

The hairs on the back of his neck stood grenade-pin straight. "Brock?" *Brock was nearby? What the hell is happening?*

"Is everything okay?" Parker was typing in the background. "Brock's moving. Obviously, you know that. Everyone else seems to be where I'd expect them to be."

"Goddamn it." He slammed the hood closed. Of all the scenarios playing out in his brain, not one of them was good. "Get to Sugar's. Now."

Parker hesitated. "Okay."

"Tell no one where we are."

"Sure thing, Boss Man." Parker took a deep breath. "Honestly, whatever's going on, I'm more useful at Titan. Give me a few, and I'm there. I've got limited access to whatever we might need here at my home. And nothing that'd be much help on the road."

Jared got into his Expedition and tried the key in the ignition, knowing it would never turn over. Silence. No surprise there, given that his rig was missing a spark plug.

Parker was right. Jared needed him at Titan, using every resource they had. "Get to the office."

Without waiting for agreement, he hung up and dialed Rocco.

A sleep-thickened voice answered. Or maybe it was a hungover one. Jared didn't care. "Rocco, need you at Sugar's ASAP. Grab whatever gear you have. You need something, you call me. No one else. Radio silence."

Rocco cleared his throat. "Wake up, um… babe. Gotta go."

Christ. Jared didn't have time for one night-stand, next-morning conversations. "Rocco, are we clear?"

"Roger that. See you in twenty."

"And, Rocco? I'm trusting you. Until I don't. Then I kill."

Headlights flashed in Sugar's rearview mirror. *Damn it. What'd Jared do, travel with extra spark plugs?* She wouldn't put it past him, but it was a stretch. Tapping her fingers on the leather steering wheel, she became more furious over his murder accusation with each passing mile.

More headlights flashed. She glanced at the speedometer. She was going at least seventy in a forty-five, then slowed a little. "Just pass me. No one's coming." She waved to the mirror as if the driver behind could see her.

The horn honked, and she slowed down to the sixties, hoping the driver would pass her. She'd had enough of ego-centric pricks for the evening, and her mood was only worsening. It would be in this guy's best interest to go away.

Horn, again.

Sugar squinted and studied the rearview, then side mirrors. That was a truck, but not an Expedition. Strangers would've passed. Jared would've run her off the road. Her gut said call J-dawg, but her brain reminded her that she'd purposely left her cell phone by the back door.

Double whammy: Lights and honks.

She knew the two-lane highway better than most. No lights. No gas stations. Nothing that would say, "Hey, pull over here. It's safe."

Instead, she slammed the gas pedal to the floorboard. No point in having a baby like her '69 Mustang if she couldn't make the horses run. Power coursed through the muscle car and through her blood. The roar of the engine made her smile, even if her nerves would ask for a puke break.

The truck was losing steam. She rounded the serpentine turns with ease. A thrill of excitement made her tighten her hands on the wheel, flexing her fingers.

She took a breath as the lights flashed in her mirror again. The truck had caught up and was keeping pace.

Screw this.

Five hundred yards up, an empty commuter lot sat vacant. She floored it, pulled a hard left, and spun into the parking lot. Rocks flew. Tires smoked, and the burnt smell wafted into the car.

The truck was either going to pass her, or it wasn't. But she was prepared for the abrupt stop, and the other driver wasn't.

Hanging on through the g-force, she came to stop, facing oncoming lane—and the truck, which slammed on the brakes, screeching into the parking lot.

So that's how it's going to be. Fine with me, asshole.

She reached behind her and pulled out a loaded M2 tactical rifle. *Nothing like firepower when the going gets sketchy.* Throwing open the door, she positioned her body behind it, aiming the barrel over her side-view mirror.

The truck door opened.

"Go the fuck away, and you won't die tonight." Her finger caressed the trigger as she squinted for any recognition in the dark.

One boot, then the other landed in the gravel.

Bam! She fired a warning shot a few feet from the boots. "Get lost."

"Sugar."

The voice struck her as familiar, but she couldn't place it through her exhaustion and adrenaline. She pumped again, readying another round. "Go. Away."

"Damn it, Sugar. Just doing my job."

She couldn't see anything but a silhouette. "Kill your lights, or I'll shoot them out."

The man leaned over and turned out his headlights. "Take it easy, Sugar. It's just me." Brock walked around the corner of his door, his arms in the air. "Don't shoot. I'd never live it down."

Brock? He might be super important in the land of Titan, but the guy gave her the creeps. "What are you doing out here?"

He nudged his truck door shut like she didn't have an itchy trigger finger. So casual and carefree. "What do you think I'm doing out here?"

"Jared sent you?"

"Given whatever you did to his Expedition, seems plausible that I ended up on find-Sugar duty, doesn't it?"

Jared was going to tan her hide after she'd messed with his car. She didn't realize he could get someone lickety-split to track her down. *Only fuckin' Titan. What do they do, hang out together in pairs for moments like these?*

"Look, Brock." She tossed the gun into her car. Brock lowered his hands as he approached. The night had been such a headache, and she needed sleep. Or time alone with her thoughts. Something. "I need time by myself. Okay? Don't want to deal with your boss man. Don't want to deal with Kip Pearson. I just need some time to think. Okay?"

"We both know I can't do that." He shrugged.

"This again?" Mixing up with Titan was like hanging with a bunch of bullies. They threw their weight around to get what they wanted. "Tell Jared to screw off. I'm a grown damn woman. He can't keep sending you to find me and drag me home."

Brock stepped closer, and she shivered. A cold sweat broke out on her neck. Something was wrong. Brock's creep factor shot sky-high and kept going. Time for a new approach. "Fine. We'll drive back to my place. You can ride my tail the whole way to make sure I don't run off again."

"No can do, Sugar." Brock closed into her personal space. "One car."

Warning alarms screamed down her spine. "Back. The. Hell. Up."

His fist wrapped around her bicep, just as it had in Abu Dhabi. The bruise he'd left before flared under his grip. "Hard or easy way, Sugar. Your call."

A silver glint caught her eye. In his free hand, he held a syringe. Sugar stumbled back, then kicked for a groin shot. "No! No, no!"

Brock's hand tightened on her bicep, ripping her away as she tried to pull herself into her car. *Knife in my purse. Rifle on the seat.* She clawed and reached, letting him rip her arm out of its socket. Her heels kicked out, jabbing but losing footing. Just another couple of inches, and—

No! A sharp sting bit into her leg, followed by a slow burn. She stilled, looking down at the needle hanging from her thigh. Her head, suddenly so heavy, tilted. She couldn't keep her eyelids open.

"Gave you a choice." He released her bicep, and gravity dragged her to the blacktop.

The horizon became fuzzy. Her mouth filled with cotton. Her tongue was too thick, and her lips tingled. "Fuck... you."

CHAPTER SEVENTEEN

Brock's truck rumbled over the rocky back road that led to Buck Baer's mountain hideaway. His excitement surged, despite his deal with the devil. Soon, Brock would have his wife and children by his side, and they would walk out after handing over Sugar.

That part killed him, but sometimes, the end was worth the means. His family was worth everything.

He knew he would have to get them all out of the States because Jared would come looking for his blood. He wouldn't hurt Brock's wife or kids, but he saw no need for them to see his bloodshed.

Love and family were at the center of his world. They were why he existed. His gut churned, and he popped another handful of Tums into his mouth. He'd kept his family's existence a secret because of things exactly like his debacle with Baer. The life Brock chose kept them in constant danger. There would always be an enemy hell-bent on revenge or a rival willing to use his family for strategic gain. It was the same reason Winters had hidden Clara from the world before Mia came along.

He'd been scared of the possibilities, and the cloak of invisibility seemed the safest route. No one knew about them, and that was best.

"Damn it." He slapped the steering wheel as he maneuvered around a corner. He'd done everything right, and everything was still a mess.

He knew in his gut how dangerous falling for a woman and starting a family was. He hadn't been careful enough. Keeping his family life secret had never seemed self-centered, until the phone call from Buck Baer. Then it was clear—he was the most selfish prick to walk the planet.

Enough with the melodrama. He had a plan. Always a contingency. *Today's game day.* He had enough money in an offshore account to take Sarah and the kids someplace quiet, where Jared would never go. Far away from everything they knew...

Walking away from Titan would hurt almost as much as having his family taken. He'd been with Jared for years, since Boss Man had recruited him a decade ago, straight out of the military. He'd said he saw potential in Brock. At the time, that'd been funny because Brock had thought *he* was top dog. *Damn if Jared didn't show me how to excel.*

Brock glanced at Sugar slumped in her seat. "Jared'll know the score soon enough. Smart bastard."

It wouldn't take Jared long to piece together the night and to figure out that Sugar's escape hadn't ended well. *Why was she running anyway?* Brock hadn't expected many of the things he discovered when he'd arrived at her place. Jared's truck in the driveway. The lights on in her living room. Sugar sneaking out. Her jacking Boss Man's Expedition. Maybe fate was trying to help his family.

After an hour of driving on back roads into the mountains, Brock pulled up to a garage door, and it opened. He gave the truck a squeeze of gas, proceeding slowly into the darkness. The smooth asphalt driveway continued underneath Baer's compound, dropping him below the surface. The garage clamored shut, and not for the first time, Brock wished that one of the Titan guys was with him on this op.

Hell, it's not an op. It's a trade. A hostage negotiation. Why Baer needed it to go down like this, when Sugar was willing to walk straight into his lair, Brock didn't know. Didn't care. Just needed his family back.

At the bottom of the incline, a tall, broad man waited, his arms dangling by his side. He looked like a gym rat who was too old for his self-tanner that looked orange under the florescent lights.

Brock rolled his window down. "Baer."

"Where's Sugar?"

"Right there." He leaned back, gesturing to the woman leaned against the opposite door.

Baer took a step forward, his eyes searching over Brock's shoulder. "What's wrong with her?"

"She's knocked out. Made for an easier delivery."

A cruel, too-white smile flashed across Baer's face. "Impressive."

He looked around the parking area. "Where's my family?"

"Park your truck, grab Sugar, and we'll go check in on everybody."

Brock ignored the urge to kill Baer right there, in his parking lot. "Much rather drop my load and pick up what's mine."

"You're not calling the shots here. I'll tell you one more time, park and follow me. Sugar in tow."

"Goddamn it." Brock slipped into the nearest spot and slammed the gearshift into park.

Baer laughed and walked away, toward an elevator. Brock stuffed the keys into his back pocket and snagged the limp Sugar. This wasn't going according to his plan. Titan had never had hostage negotiations go like this, but that was okay. He would do what it took to save his family.

Still, this wasn't how he'd pictured the exchange taking place. None of the scenarios he'd imagined involved trapping his truck below ground and hoofing it with Sugar slung over his shoulder.

They reached the elevator, and Baer held it open. "She's a feisty one, isn't she?"

Feisty? Sugar was the living, breathing definition of the word. "You could have let her come in on her own. You sure as fuck didn't need to take my family. So let's cut the small talk."

"To have her come in on her own? What fun would that be?"

Brock shifted Sugar to a better position. Baer hit G2. They were on G1, and he wished they were headed above ground, not farther below.

"I assume you're armed in some capacity." Baer scrolled through his phone. "When we get to the holding area, you can disarm. One of my men will check."

"If it's all the same to you, I'd rather just head the hell home. I have no interest in games or gunplay. A fair trade, just like you requested. Then our business is done."

The doors opened to G2. The long hallway smelled like pancakes and bacon. Behind one of the closed doors, Brock heard his kids playing. His heart swelled. The urge to run toward the sound made his muscles twitch.

"Almost done. I have one more request of you, then we're done."

Almost done? Bullshit. Brock saw red. The lights, the hallway, everything was coated in blood-red fury. He launched toward Buck Baer, ready to kill him. Two men came from the shadows, pulling him back. He almost dropped Sugar.

Baer laughed. "Almost done. Don't worry, Brock. You have one more task to complete before they're all yours."

His teeth slammed together. Pressure building in his head threatened to explode. "I will kill you."

"Not before I kill them. So listen up. I'll ruin Titan Group. Think of it like a life goal. An item on my asshole bucket list. It's within reach. I can taste Jared's fall from *greatness*." Baer snorted. "Jared will lose his goddamn mind. His life's work and his girl? Not even that prick can handle that type of destruction."

Brock's chest ached for Jared and Sugar. "No one said anything about her being his girl. If that's what you're after, you're wrong."

Baer laughed. "That line of bullshit is too late. No reason lying. I already promised your family's safe return. Forget about what happens to your friend Sugar. It's a justifiable trade. Don't lose any sleep."

"She's nothing to him." *Shit, let him believe that.* Brock was turning her over to die. He knew that. But if she was to be a playtoy in this Baer-Jared game, there was no telling what she would go through before she hit lights-out for good. And God forbid his wife ever found out what he'd done to save their family. She wouldn't understand. She didn't know how much blood had coated his hands over the years, even if it had been for a greater good.

"No, I can tell these things. This one is special. And it'll be my pleasure to take that from him, too."

Brock shrugged, trying to seem indifferent. His heart sank, the guilt eating away his fortitude. "Believe what you want. Final job, what's it going to be?"

He produced a small envelope from his back pocket. "This is a USB drive. All you have to do is get to a computer terminal inside Titan's main building and plug it in."

Brock took the envelope and peeked inside. "What's it do?"

"Christ. Does it matter? Do your job. I'll know immediately if you have, and your family will be returned to you."

Brock's heart pounded. He couldn't believe he was betraying Jared this way, after everything that man had done for him and trusted him with. He pinched the bridge of his nose. Brock was helping ruin the man he most revered.

There was nothing that he wouldn't do for his woman and children. If that meant playing Buck Baer's game, than he would play.

CHAPTER EIGHTEEN

Jared cracked his knuckles while manning the range in Sugar's kitchen. He needed something to do with his hands since he didn't have enough intel to act on. If he couldn't kill, he would cook while scrutinizing every detail he had.

Brock's cell phone had suddenly turned off. No signal. No blips. Nothing. The hotel attack reeked of an informant after no listening devices had turned up. GSI had known where to hit and when. Brock had been outside Sugar's house for an unknown reason, and then he'd taken off after her. Parker had found her Mustang abandoned in a parking lot. Jared had nothing to go on.

After Rocco had arrived, Jared had laid out his suspicions. Neither had said a word since.

Waiting for intel normally wasn't a problem. Good intel meant a good operation and a high success rate. But this wasn't typical, and Jared was emotionally invested.

Flipping the bacon in a skillet, he ignored the kitchen clock that had ticked every minute, reminding him that he didn't have a plan. He flipped the bacon again and again. Trying to ignore the passing time wasn't working.

Sugar would be more pissed than scared. *Right*? She never saw the gravity of circumstances. Someone might want to kill her, but she would be more upset that they'd screwed her out of a good night's sleep. Chances were better that she had Brock by the balls, antagonizing him and making the situation worse—as long as she hadn't gotten herself killed. *Talk about a beauty with a dangerous attitude problem. Fuck, man, where's my intel?*

His foot tapped like automatic fire. He checked the clock again. And again, he scowled at it. Buck Baer could be a million places. Brock had a million ways to take her there. Jared's teeth ached; his clenched jaw was near a breaking point. He needed to move on this. Immediately.

The oven dinged, and he jerked it open, grabbing the baking sheet of biscuits and then pulled the bacon off the stove. The clatter on the counter did little to alleviate his rabid irritation at his lack of control.

"Bacon and biscuits." Jared shoved a plate at Rocco and pulled a stool up next to Rocco.

"She'll be fine." Rocco picked up the bacon and crunched. "Parker's working mach speed. Eat, dude. Do something other than fester."

"This isn't a normal gig. And she's not..." He grabbed a piece of bacon. It was organic and probably tasted awful. But it didn't. The irony wasn't lost. Lessons were everywhere. Organic bacon tasted fine, despite what he was prepared for. Labels and assumptions were worthless. Brock had served as Jared's loyal right-hand man, but Brock had the most important thing in Jared's life, making his second-in-command nothing more than a traitor.

Most important thing to me? Jared downed another strip of bacon. Other than Titan, Sugar held top billing. She made his gut feel something other than indigestion. She made his heart feel something, too.

Titan and Sugar. He tore apart a biscuit, then smeared organic butter on it. *Or was it Sugar,* then *Titan?* The question nearly knocked him off his barstool.

He wolfed down the biscuit and grabbed another. Why was he reprioritizing the basic tenets of his life? Sleep deprivation maybe? He hadn't slept much in the last week or so. But lack of sleep had never affected his judgment. He should've seen that Brock was a backstabber long before anything went down.

"You gonna kill him?" Rocco took a swig of water.

"If   he   hurts   Sugar.   No   question,   yes."

Rocco shook his head as he placed the water glass on the counter. "Somehow, I thought it'd be yes, *for betraying Titan*, no questions."

That's what he should've said. But it wasn't. "Don't be a dick."

"I'm not." Rocco downed a biscuit in a bite. "She's a good woman. A damn good fit for a jackass like you."

"Shut the—" Jared looked down at his ringing phone. *Parker*. He answered on the first ring. "What you got?"

"Brock's cell signal's back on. A mile or so south of Sugar's."

"Tell me where that fucker's been."

"Can't, Boss Man—wait, he's making a call."

Beep, beep. Jared took a breath and looked at his caller ID, then clicked over without saying goodbye to Parker.

His body scowled. Every muscle tensed, and his heart banged against his ribcage. If he could have reached through the phone and crushed Brock's windpipe with one finger at a time, the man would've been dead. Instead, Jared clenched his teeth together and waited for him to speak.

Brock cleared his throat. "I have to talk to you." His voice trembled.

Never had Jared heard Brock sound anything but confident. *I'd be scared, too, fucker. I'm coming after you.* "Where's Sugar?"

The groan into the phone pulled Jared's stomach into a spin. Rocco bounced his eyebrows, asking for a read on the conversation, for confirmation that Brock was playing them.

"Brock." His fingers flexed into the granite countertop. He wanted to break it off and throw it to alleviate his tension. "Where. Is. She?"

"You know, don't you?" The question was empty, void of emotion. More of an acknowledgement of impending death.

"I know enough. Tell me I'm wrong, or update your will."

A vehicle pulled into the driveway. Rocco jumped from the barstool, sidearm in hand. Jared grabbed his piece, and they headed toward the front door. Dipping his head out a window, Jared saw Brock's truck.

The rhythm of his blood throbbing in his ears was loud and irritating. Sweat tickled between his shoulder blades, despite the cool temperature in the foyer. He glanced at Rocco, who was pressed against the opposite wall, and nodded. Jared could taste the anticipation of Brock's arrival. Bitter and angry over the breach of his trust, Jared was enraged by the possibilities concerning Sugar.

He swallowed his emotions and ignored the dry crack in his throat. Never had he been *terrified*. But the seconds ticking by were like a hammer to his dome, and his heart squeezed with the unknown.

Phone still pressed to his ear, Jared couldn't wait to tangle. "Door's unlocked. Come on in." Clicking the phone off, he concentrated on the cool metal of the gun in his palm.

Outside, the roar of the engine silenced. The truck door opened and shut. Jared's pulse raced. His breath fought into his lungs, warring against the tank-sized weight pressing on his chest. With his eyes glued to the door handle, he needed it to jiggle, to turn slowly, and let the showdown begin with his most-trusted ally.

The handle twisted, and a boot toe nudged it open. Jared thought Brock would surely anticipate his move. They'd gone into battle together and forged side by side through the hell of missions gone wrong. They thought, they fought, and they reacted as though they had the same brain. Until they hadn't, and for that, Brock would pay.

A roar tore from his lungs. Jared rolled from his position, slamming the door open with his shoulder and wrapping an arm around Brock's neck.

Brock's arms were up. He had no weapon. Still, Jared locked hard and pulled Brock inside, smashing his weight against the man. Brock's head cracked against the wall, his mouth gaping at the lack of air flow.

Brock didn't flail or pull away. Jared knew enough about his training to know how long he could withstand the lack of oxygen. But he needed to know where Sugar was and why the hell Brock had taken her. As much as he wanted to pinch Brock out of existence, this wasn't the time. But soon.

Jared released the stranglehold, replacing the pressure on his throat with the barrel of his Glock. Pressing hard and deep into his trachea, Jared forced himself not to pull the trigger.

"Asshole." He was too emotional. His head wasn't in the game. "Roc, check him. Weapons. Listening devices. Anything."

Rocco did a thorough inspection, then gave a thumbs-up.

"Where is she?" Jared growled. Rage poured off him; his body vibrated. "Where the fuck is she?"

"I'm sorry."

Jamming the gun harder into Brock's neck, Jared fought to control the urge to destroy him. "*Where?*"

"With Baer."

His pulse pounded. Any shred of hope that he'd been wrong, that this was a massive misunderstanding, all blew up in his face. *Disloyal fuckin' bastard.* "Why?"

Brock's face was strained—his first reaction since he'd come through the door. "He has my wife and kids."

What? Jared's brain stuttered. Logic and control were quickly dissipating. "Excuse me?"

Rocco cursed in the background, reminding Jared that he would have a witness if he pulled the trigger on an unarmed man, no matter how disloyal the man was.

He shook his head, ignoring Brock's lie. *A wife and kids? No.* Brock was as single as they came. He wasn't a lady's man who trolled the bars for an easy lay post mission, but he wasn't *married with kids.* "Liar."

"He has my family. He has Asal. And I gave him Sugar."

Jared pulled his free hand back and landed a punch square on Brock's jaw. His head snapped to the side. Spittle and blood flew out, but he didn't react. No arms thrown up. No curse of pain. Only a straightforward gaze.

"You *gave* him my woman." His blood rushed, and he could barely hear his own words. "You took what was mine and put her in harm's way."

"I had no choice."

"There are always choices." He knocked Brock against the wall once more, tightening his fingers around the other man's throat. Tighter and tighter.

Jared's cheeks ached from the force of his sneer. Brock's eyelids fluttered. No oxygen. No tap out. Nothing. He would kill Brock and not have a thing to show for it. *God!* Taking a deep breath, Jared dropped his grip, then paced the hallway.

Sweat beaded on his brow and dampened his chest. *Make this a job. Do what it takes. Interrogate and move on.* He bounced a look to the men. Rocco stood ready, gun in hand and eyes trained on his *former* team leader. Brock didn't move. He waited for whatever came next, and whatever that was, Jared hadn't a clue.

He cracked his knuckles. "Why are you here?"

"Because I made the wrong choice."

Jared hurtled toward him, hissing through his clenched teeth. "You fuckin' think?"

Brock tilted his head a degree. A desperate, almost misty look formed in his eyes. "What wouldn't you do for the woman you love, Jared?"

"I don't—you come to me. You say this is what happened. This is my problem. You don't—enough of this."

Brock barely nodded. "Baer has it out for you. Wants to make it personal."

Jared's eyes narrowed, and he snarled. "Feeling's mutual."

"To get my family back, I handed over Sugar. But Baer screwed me, gave me a new... project. Go to Titan and plug a flash drive into a terminal computer. Baer's expecting it in less than an hour. If it doesn't happen, he'll kill my family. My head's been a mess. I wasn't thinking clearly before. I reacted. And now I'm trying to fix my fuckup."

"Not my problem."

"They're innocents. Do what you want with me. I made the wrong move. But you won't let them die without trying. You won't leave Sugar—"

"Of course I won't leave Sugar."

"Help them all. Kill me. I don't care."

Jared walked down the foyer and punched the wall, leaving a hole in the painted drywall. He flexed his knuckles. No broken bones. But the pain felt good, like a reprieve from the storm in his head. "Where's the drive?"

"Back pocket."

He scrubbed a hand over his face. *A stupid disk?* It didn't make sense. "What is it?"

"Don't know. But he said it would ruin Titan. That he intended to take the two things you hold dear. Titan and Sugar."

Sugar, then Titan. "Roc, grab the disk." Jared dialed Parker at the office.

"Yo, Boss Man."

"Parker, got a disk from Buck Baer. It was supposed to be patched into our system from inside HQ." Jared took a deep breath, thinking about Sugar, Asal, and Brock's out-of-nowhere family. "I've got some lives on the line. *Kids.* Baer needs to think it has happened. I need to know what it does."

Long seconds passed.

"Parker, damn it."

"Trying, Boss Man. Give me a second to think this out." Parker clacked computer keys in the background. "Maybe… it might…"

"Spit it out."

"I could build a dummy terminal. Given a time constraint, it'd be rough, but look like Titan's system. We could get a read on it. Baer'd get shit."

"How fast?"

"How long I got?"

They could get to Titan in thirty minutes, assuming they used a few highway shoulders and didn't hit less than seventy miles an hour. "We'll be there in twenty."

He clicked off the phone and stared at Brock. Disappointment threatened to throw Jared another headache. He gestured to Rocco. "Secure him and load up into your truck. Call in the team." *An order I used to give to Brock.* "I'll be out in a second."

Rocco nodded, and Brock complied, showing nothing on his face. *Good little prisoner.* Jared had taught him well. His eyes swept the foyer, and he walked into the living room, where he'd last seen Sugar. Heart in his throat, he vowed to bring her back, put her right back on that couch, and explain that he'd never meant to accuse her of killing Kip. He'd never meant to question her word.

With a deep breath and new resolve, Jared marched to Rocco's truck and jumped behind the wheel.

"Team's on their way in," Rocco said.

He nodded, noticing Brock was cuffed to the oh-shit bar in the backseat. A brief worry that Brock wasn't telling the whole truth struck him. *Why wouldn't Brock lie now? Why did I trust his whole wife-and-kids spiel? It could be a trap.*

He dialed Parker again and didn't wait for hello. "I need everything you can find on a family for Brock."

"What, like next of kin? Parents, sister, or something?"

"No. Wife and children."

"Wife and kids... okay."

He looked at Brock again. "But might as well dig up next of kin. Think there'll be a round of notifications coming soon."

CHAPTER NINETEEN

Grumbling voices echoed in the background, making Sugar's temples pulse. Her head was spinning, and her tongue was stuck to the roof of her mouth. The distinct feeling of rough carpet pressed against her cheek and forehead. As she swallowed a bout of nausea, everything came back with brilliant clarity. Kip's murder. Jared's distrust. Brock's attack.

The first one she didn't care about. She hadn't killed Kip, and he'd left her in Afghanistan to die. *So screw him.* She did wish she'd been able to exact a little retribution.

But the second one? Her lungs caught, aching. *Jared...* He made her head pound with an explosion of emotional shrapnel. Her heart felt the slice and dice of the pain, as well. But if he were just in the room... If she could just look into those dark eyes and crawl into his powerful hold... Everything would be better. It was more than her desperate hope the he would play the hero. She garnered comfort and the strength from his touch. The trust—

No. Not the trust. She swallowed a pathetic laugh. He questioned her words and her actions. That wasn't a trusting man. And she wasn't a trusting woman. She never had been, and Jared wouldn't change a life philosophy like that, no matter how she felt in his arms.

Her thigh throbbed where Brock had jabbed her with the needle. Its contents had burned like cold acid trailing into her leg for long seconds, then everything went bad-news black. *How long have I been out, and where is Brock?* She had several choice things to say to him.

Sugar listened without moving and tried to decipher the voices, not recognizing anyone. They echoed. One was dominant. The others only replied, never questioned. *Wait...* Maybe the dominant voice sounded familiar. She cracked a mascara-smeared eyelid to take in her surroundings.

Utilitarian room. Florescent lights. Two men in tactical uniforms. And Buck Baer—the voice she'd recognized. *Wait, what? Brock and Buck work together? In what world?*

Then again, Brock had hit her with the knockout juice. Brock and Buck. Why? She couldn't fit the pieces together, and her head was cloudy.

Minutes passed. The voices registered more clearly. Buck was irritated, and the two men with him were little more than armed sounding-boards. *Where are we?* They weren't at GSI's office. She'd been there before, selling wholesale deals on ammo. GSI's offices were obnoxious. Swank. Too much glitz and glitter. Nothing like Titan's fortress.

Sugar shifted her weight. Her arm tingled with pins and needles. Lying in an awkward crumple on the floor had stymied her blood flow. Slightly uncoordinated, she tried to move without attracting attention. Her cobwebbed mind cleared slightly, but she still had serious issues with her sleeping forearm.

"Ah, she wakes." The semi-familiar voice of Buck Baer sounded amused.

Great, no luck on avoiding his attention. She stilled like a statue, not daring a deep breath. Her pins-and-needle arm ached for her to shift positions again.

"No, don't bother pretending to sleep, Lilly."

Lilly. Her stomach turned. She hated that name, *except* when Jared used it. The jig was up. She pressed her chest off the ground, allowing the blood to rush into her arm. "Call me Sugar," she corrected him with a gutted whisper. Clearing her throat, she offered her name again and picked herself up to sit cross-legged.

Her head swam once she was vertical, but her eyes were nailed to Buck. His smirk and the way he held himself above her served only to stoke her irritation. Sugar swallowed until her throat worked like normal. With all the things she planned to say, with all the punches she didn't intend to pull, she needed a clear voice. Buck Baer would hear her out and answer her questions. If he'd thought she was a headache before, then she would convince him otherwise.

"So, Buck." She thanked God the sound of her words hadn't let her down. She sounded annoyed, confident, and ready to play his games. "What's with the big takedown when you already knew I was coming in to meet you? Thought you had me on your calendar already."

He laughed. His ruddy face was a little fuller than she remembered. "I was testing someone."

Testing someone? What am I? An item on a to-do list? "Brock?"

"Smart girl." Buck clapped slowly. "Very intuitive."

"He stabbed me with a needle, and I woke up here. Didn't take a lot of brains to figure that one out."

"You're a fun one. Not sure how I missed that when we met before." His eyes raked over her, and she wanted to punch him. "Yes, you're definitely good looking. And I like your attitude problem. No wonder Jared Westin has a thing for you."

Was he looking for confirmation? Had Brock told him? Or was Buck still extrapolating from the Abu Dhabi video chat when she'd barged in, wearing Jared's sweats? She refused to admit to anything. "You have the wrong idea about Jared. I'd have thought you had better intel."

Buck sneered at her without rebutting. *Maybe Brock did keep his mouth shut.* She held in the sad laugh. *What relationship? In bed a few times and a fun game of chase?* But when it came down to it, she'd walked away, and he didn't trust her. Jared was nowhere to be found. *He's probably still stewing over the spark plug.*

She laughed. Tough guy Jared was stranded at a chick's house because she'd disabled his Expedition. *Bet that defied his world of logic.* His spark plug was still in her purse, wherever that was.

"What's so funny?" Buck's shoes scuffed on the carpet when he walked.

How was he ever stealthy in the field with such obnoxious habits? Sugar couldn't imagine Buck and Jared on the same level. Buck was smarmy and obvious. Jared was competent and deadly. "Just thinking about how Jared's going to knock down GSI's front door and kick your ass." That was hardly what she was thinking. *But why fess up now?* "I imagine there'll be lots of damage. Your pristine carpets will get stained."

"Not that easy, sweet cheeks. You aren't in Kansas anymore."

So we're at Buck's mountain compound? Why hadn't that registered? Her brainwaves were still hazy from Brock's injection, but the pieces were coming together. *Where's Asal?* Sugar's heart beat faster. She needed intelligence to survive, and the more she needled Buck, the more he talked. "You'd be surprised what he's capable of."

Buck scoffed. "Well, let's find out. At any moment, I'll be able to tell you what the *great* Jared Westin is up to this morning."

Buck went to a metal table that held two computer monitors and other electronics. He stared at the black screens. GSI was attempting to hack into Titan? *Good luck.* Parker would recognize a problem faster than she could pull a trigger.

"Looking good there, Buck. I can totally tell why GSI has such a great reputation. Oh wait." She rolled her eyes and gave him an antagonistic laugh. "I'm not sure *that's* what I heard about your rep."

Buck whirled, his face a deeper shade of red. He was so easy to manipulate. *Almost too easy. Must be an insecurity thing.* Jared wouldn't get worked up over harmless pokes, even though her pokes were meant to cause harm.

"I'll have you know—" Behind Buck, the computer started to whir. The screen came to life, but it was too far away for Sugar to see the details. Turning his attention to the screens, he mumbled, "Never mind. You're nothing more than a pawn in this game."

He began banging away on his keyboard. Sugar felt his excitement build with every mouse click and key press. Even the two armed men looked on with interest.

"What are you doing over there?" Sugar pried, trying for a better look without getting caught. "You and Jared playing

Who Sank My Battleship? Or maybe it's a testy game of Go Fish?"

Buck smiled over his shoulder. "Hardly. This, *Sugar*, is Titan's mainframe. Their internal files. Access to every electronic document they have. Bank account information, contacts, and contract lists. This is *everything* that makes Titan."

A vulnerable Titan Group was inconceivable, and she hated that Jared's baby was under attack. Acid coated the back of her throat. A useless feeling haunted her. She could do nothing more than glean what she could from Buck and play the part of a semi-interested, mostly-inquisitive sarcastic woman. "So what? You can check their e-mails? Learn the latest Titan gossip? I'll save you the trouble. Jared has a dog that eats everything. Brock's apparently going to have to find a new job. Oh, and they'll soon be in the market for an upgraded computer-system firewall."

"You got the beauty and enough snark to drive a man insane, but you missed out on the brains? Tough break, Sugar."

Not really, since you keep explaining all of your plans. "So dumb it down for me, Buck. Explain how smart you are."

"Simple. While I'm in their system, I can drain their accounts, take their clients, and review their contracts. Think of the classified jobs they might have detailed. The covert projects that the trusting public wouldn't understand. Leak that, and Jared loses all of his clients who would rather remain anonymous. He goes to check his bank accounts and finds zip. Nothing. Nada. Titan-sized goose eggs."

Sugar stayed on her bottom, pressing her back into the wall. Was GSI talented enough to pull off that kind of cyber-attack? Were Titan's online defenses so poor that it could happen? "Nah, that'll never happen."

Buck gestured to the screens. "Easy. This has been like taking candy from a kid."

Easy? How could any fight with Titan be easy? "I'd say it'd be like trying to take it from a *killer*, not a kid, which is why it'll never happen."

"Killer?" Buck harrumphed. "More like Boy Scout."

Boy Scout? Now I've heard it all. If Jared was a Boy Scout, then she was a virginal gun protester.

Buck turned toward her. His body language looked confident, if not over-exaggerated. His hands on his hips, he shook his head knowingly. "Everything's downloading into our server. Very neat and orderly, almost one dimensional, just like Jared."

Do we even know the same man? Jared's twenty-second summary of Buck had been on point—greedy and oblivious to the big picture. Buck's memory of Jared had been whitewashed over the years, but Sugar did need to chime in on that point. "Great, Buck. Boys and their toys. Honestly, I don't care. Let's talk about Asal instead."

Buck rolled his eyes and paced. "Now *there's* a complication. Had I known how this would work out, I'd have made a different move with the kid."

His change in tone gave her chills. Sugar started to stand up, leaning her weight—

"No, stay seated."

On all fours, there was little to do but rock back onto her backside, which wasn't the most advantageous position.

Buck whined again about Asal. That was another difference between Buck and Jared. Jared knew each future move, no matter how far out an op was. He found all his info, then came up with contingency plans for his contingency plans. Except when it came to her. He'd never seen the stolen spark plug coming... or going.

Somehow, remembering that automotive part made her heart deflate. Why was she constantly screwing with him? *Oh yeah, because he chose not to trust me.*

Buck murmured to himself about Asal. "What to do. What to do. Both a headache and a complication."

Asal was the only thing that Sugar should concentrate on. Buck's face went ugly. Sugar's stomach soured as she watched him pace, his evil thinking cap in overdrive.

She didn't want to show how invested in Asal she was, so kneeing him in the junk was out. Instead, Sugar smirked, throwing her best sarcastic grin. "Fine, Asal's a *complication.* Tomato, to-mah-to."

He stopped pacing. "No lip, Sugar."

"She wouldn't have been such a headache if our plans had gone accordingly, if I'd shown up at the agreed-upon time. We could chat about Asal-the-*complication*, and you'd let me take the kid home. So here's my deal—"

He laughed. "Your deal? Priceless. Go on, Sugar. Tell me your *deal*."

Dick. "I forget about everything that happened in Afghanistan. I comp you a few major special orders from GUNS to show no hard feelings, and you let me walk out of here with Asal. Very clean."

"No can do, pretty girl."

"Why not?"

"I think you know why."

"I didn't kill Kip Pearson. I messed with him, but I left him alive."

Buck laughed and rubbed his forehead. "No, I know. Your restraint earns you a great deal of respect from me—the use of restraints in his bed, not necessarily your restraint in finishing him off. But as for Kip, the blame rests on my shoulders. Or rather"—he pointed to the armed men—"one of these two did the act, but I gave the order. You can't imagine the laughs we had when they explained how they found him."

Sugar bit her lip. *They'd laughed about killing their teammate?* Maybe they were more ruthless than she'd realized. "Entertainment wasn't my goal, but I'm *so* glad you're impressed. If not the Kip problem, what's the holdup with my offer? I rid you of the complications. You get a lucrative bonus from GUNS."

"The problem? Jared Westin, of course."

"Jared isn't *my* problem. He's a big boy. He can handle his glitches without my involvement. And, actually, I think he'd prefer it that way."

"Sugar, I think you're selling yourself short and lying to me in the process. There are two things important to Jared Westin. You and Titan."

The cold laugh fell from her lips before she could think better of it. "Correction, nothing would be ahead of Titan, and trust me, I'm not on the short list."

"We'll agree to disagree, though there's not much point."

"Why's that?"

"Because you and Titan are near to his heart. Dismantling, for lack of a better word, both will hurt him. And, well, between me and him, it's personal, so I want him to hurt. I'm just sick and tired of the goody-two-shoes act."

"Jared? A goody two-shoes? That's a riot." Sugar snorted and didn't touch the subject of her dismantling. She didn't need more details on that at the present. Maybe that was avoidance, but it might've been mental preservation.

"I've never been one to hide from the term "greedy." But I will enjoy poor Jared, penniless and heartbroken."

"Ah, heartbroken. That's me, right? I'm finding serious flaws in this plan, Buck. Sorry." Thinking better of her info-avoidance plan, Sugar did a complete mental turnabout. Knowledge was power. "Get to the point where you explain *dismantling* me. I find that far more interesting than your games with Titan."

"Your role is simple. He cares for you. You're his Achilles heel. Watching you suffer will almost kill the bastard. I want him to want death. To reach and beg for it. Anything to save you." Buck chuckled. "You're simply collateral damage."

Her nerves threatened to make her lose her trademark cool. Throwing snark back and forth was easy enough. But when the barbs came laced with deadly threats, explained with such business-like disinterest, it brought reality home. And fast. *Goddamn you, Jared, for not saving me already. Damn him. Damn the whole situation.*

"Sugar, nothing to say?"

"You're a sick fuck."

"Yes, I'm both greedy and sadistic. Comes with the job, I suppose."

She took a deep breath and tried to channel her inner Titan warrior. "I'm not big on threats, Buck. The whole make-me-suffer thing doesn't really have me quaking in my pants." It was a miracle she didn't scoff aloud, crying, "Bullshit" at her own lie.

"You have an attitude problem." He glanced at his computer screens, then back at her on the floor. "I bet he dreams of shoving a gag in your mouth."

"That'd be the day."

Buck crossed his arms. "It's almost a shame about the way this has to go down. You're growing on me."

She rolled her eyes because crying wasn't the right move. Buck liked her, in some screwed-up way. If she kept him talking, if she bought enough time, maybe Jared would realize Brock was a problem and that her plan had gone haywire. She wanted to believe that he would still want to go after Asal, even if he didn't come for her. Someone had to take care of Asal and get her out of the clutches of this jerk who'd called her a complication.

She swallowed against the lump in her throat and toyed with her hair. "Assuming you take down Titan, make me suffer, and Jared has some sort of nervous breakdown. What then?"

"I'll expand my team. Brock Gamble is already on board."

Brock was going to be dead as soon as Jared put a few pieces together. "*Already*? Like Team Titan is just going to join ranks with GSI?"

"A bunch of cold, heartless operatives? Why not? I offer competitive wages. They stay in the field. That type doesn't know any better. Just point them toward their next kill and pay them well."

"Interesting." Buck didn't bounce a look to her, apparently missing her sarcasm. Clearly, he had no idea about the people on Titan Group's payroll. *Heartless? Not a chance. Try loyal to a fault, with the exception of Brock.* They weren't mercenaries who were in it for the dough. They were good people who handled problems so people like Sugar could sleep safely at night. "And the kid?"

"Good question." He ran a hand over his chin. "How to clean up a complication?"

From the tone of his voice and the look in his eyes, Sugar already knew how Buck Baer would handle Asal. Her heart sank, and her eyes shut. *Screw the false bravado.* All she wanted to do was cry.

CHAPTER TWENTY

The Titan team circled the war room table and took their seats. Parker was present via the television screen so he didn't have to leave his post at Titan's electronic nerve center. Brock was noticeably absent, but none of the team had mentioned it yet.

Jared took his seat and chewed the inside of his mouth. His bulldog, Thelma, who'd been staying with Parker while Jared was out of the country, had plopped down on the toes of his boots, gnawing on a rawhide bone the size of a grenade launcher.

Brock's empty chair made his stomach roil. *Screw that traitorous son of a bitch.* When it was time, he would tear him to pieces.

"All right, let's get down to business." He cracked his neck, wanting to get this op into the done column soon as feasibly possible.

Roman knocked the empty chair next to him with an elbow. "We aren't waiting for Brock?"

"He's tied up at the moment." *Literally.*

Rocco failed to stifle a clucking cough, and Jared slammed him with a glare that the whole room took notice of. He would have to admit out loud that his team wasn't as loyal as he'd thought. It hurt. It physically made him ache. Loyalty was his credo, and Brock had screwed that up.

Insubordination was humiliating. His most-trusted man had hurt him in the worst way. Jared's pride had been drop-kicked to the dirt, and now he had to tell the team. As if knowing he was about to drop a bomb, Thelma nuzzled his leg to give him canine support. Jared reached down and rubbed her head with his fist. Now *she* was loyal. She hadn't betrayed him like Brock had. She wouldn't run off like Sugar had. All a man needed in life was his dog.

Between the Brock-Sugar double whammy, Jared was dealing with emotions that he'd never dealt with before. It was unpleasant.

"Forget about him." Shoving his shoulders back, he took a breath. Nothing showing. Nothing telling. Just a high-stakes mission to complete. Keeping his voice even, he told the team, "Brock's off the team. Gone."

Every eye went wide. The room was quiet, except for the rhythmic grinding from Thelma's teeth on her bone.

Ignoring the shock and awe, he looked at each member of his team, staring each in the eye. "Buck Baer has Sugar and Asal. He also has another woman and two more children in a mountain compound that we've tracked to outside Charlottesville." Jared lifted his chin to Rocco, who handed out a map of the area and an aerial view of the compound. "We've no idea what type of security or manpower we're dealing with. The area is rural, but we can't blow a hole in the side of the place without someone noticing. Our plan is to go in quiet. Extract our marks. Capture Buck if possible, but he's secondary."

Winters tapped his fingernails on the table, making a dull sound, and Roman leaned forward. Cash adjusted his cowboy hat, and Nicola looked from Rocco to Jared, then Parker.

She cleared her throat. "What aren't you telling us?"

On the screen, Parker shifted, and Rocco stared straight ahead. Jared dropped his head, hating to admit the betrayal. He looked at the empty seat, then met each of their eyes again, studying the team that he'd stake his life on. They deserved the truth. No matter what that said about him as leader.

"Brock kidnapped Sugar in exchange for his wife and children, who Baer had abducted. Baer, being the double-crossing asshole that he is, kept Brock's family. He'd been working with Baer during the Abu Dhabi mission. Each time we almost lost Sugar, you can thank Brock."

Another explosion of shock rolled through the room. Even Thelma stopped making her noises. Then the questions started: Brock was married? He had kids? How did he do that to Sugar?

"Not sure what more there is to say other than this: I walk into the field with you. I work side by side with you on every job. There is nothing I won't do to make sure my team makes it home. But to be betrayed like this, to have this level of deceit—it's far past unacceptable. I expect your loyalty, and you have mine in return. We walk a dark, jagged line of honor, but it *is* honorable. If that's not the case for any of you, walk out now."

No one moved.

"Good." Taking a deep breath, Jared weighed what'd been scratching at the back of his mind. "I didn't know he had a wife or kids, either. Can't understand what happened, but we're going to fix it." He slapped the table. "Let's bring them home."

Sugar walked down a hall, drawn by the sound of children and a television. *Other kids are here, just like Kip said.* Buck didn't seem like the type to have his own children. But even if he had them, he probably wouldn't mind a creepy windowless play area with armed men strolling about.

He'd given Sugar the freedom to walk around. He was no longer interested in conversing and was tinkering on his computer. Staring at the back of his head gave her no answers, so she hoofed it.

Utilitarian everything. Bland walls. Florescent lights. Locked doors. The more she explored, the more certain she became that she was in a bunker or insulated basement. The place was too large to be a home and too small to be… *What, a fortress?*

When she rounded a corner, the smell of pancakes wafted her way. *The sound of children and smell of pancakes? What the hell is this place?*

A uniformed man was resting on a barstool beside a slightly open door. She didn't know whether to look at him, ask directions, or—

"You looking for the food?" He looked her up and down. With his sidearm in easy reach, he seemed unconcerned that she was without a chaperone.

"Um, yeah. Sure."

He elbowed the door beside him, opening it a crack. The sound of children and cartoons spilled from the brightly lit room. Cautiously, Sugar peeked in. In the wide space, a television sat in the corner. Two girls about Asal's age, wearing brightly colored leggings and T-shirts, giggled in front of it.

She scanned the room to the far corner, where a woman sat on top of a folding table, pillows at her back against the wall and a few water bottles within arm's reach. She cradled a dark-haired child who was about the same size as the other two kids. Sugar instinctively knew who it was.

"Asal," she whispered, loud enough to get the attention of the woman and children.

They eyed her, but the woman went back to watching the child sleep soundly. Jealousy and anger rocketed through Sugar.

Three kids in an armored room—why were they there? What did GSI do with kids? Her heart banged. How soulless did a woman have to be to babysit kidnapped children?

Sugar's protective nature urged her to gather up all the children, hug them, and promise everything would be okay. But first, she had to scoop Asal into her arms. Somehow, someway, she would make the world okay for Asal.

There were no guards inside the room, only outside the door. The woman was quickly becoming her number-one enemy. Sugar marched forward, on a mission to extract what was hers. "Who are you?"

"Who are *you*?" The woman countered, barely lifting her gaze from the sleeping kiddo.

Sugar swore to God that she saw the woman's arms tighten around Asal. If children hadn't been present, there might've been bloodshed.

"Not playing a game where the kids are involved." Sugar stared at the woman. Fury approached a dangerous level, and she quickly tamped it down. "What kind of—" Pausing, she took in the items scattered around the woman. Water bottle. Ice pack. Thermometer. "What's going on here?"

"Back off, lady." The woman jutted her chin up, shifting Asal closer.

Sugar stared at Asal as she approached. Her dark curls were matted on her forehead. Her color had paled from what she remembered. Her lips were chapped. She didn't look right.

Taking her attitude down several notches, Sugar swallowed against the growing lump in her throat. "Something's wrong with her?"

"Get your pancakes and get out." She nodded toward a side table littered with McDonald's bags and fast-food breakfast items. "I don't care how tough and bossy you guys think you are. This is the one area that is ours. Now, take your nosiness and back off."

Say again? The woman's petite size didn't match the boldness of her order. The auburn hair and freckles screamed cute and sweet, despite the haggard lines and darkening circles under her eyes. Sugar tried to remember the last time someone had stood up to her and told her to back off. Never.

Sugar shifted in her high-heeled boots. "You think I'm one of them?"

"Yeah. No way you're a doctor or a nurse or a freakin' med student, so get your pancakes and go away."

"I'm not GSI. What's wrong with her?"

Nothing. Complete silence.

"Damn it." Sugar sucked down a breath, trying to keep her cool. Panic made her lungs tight. A thousand concerns rushed through her head. Rather than snatching Asal and running to nowhere, she swallowed a thick dose of snark and took another step forward. "I'm Sugar."

"Of course you are."

"I don't work with those guys. But I do have a vested interest in Asal. So, if you wouldn't mind telling me what the fuck is going on, I'll try to help." A staggered breath pursed through her lips. *So much for keeping my pissed-off on the down low.* "For all I know, you're some evil-hearted GSI babysitter, watching kidnapped kids for cold cash. Pardon me if I have a couple of questions about my girl."

"*Your* girl?"

"Tell me what's wrong with her."

The woman studied her. Sugar guessed her makeup had been smeared during her Brock debacle. Her hair was disheveled and tied into a makeshift bun. Nothing about her appearance was doing her any favors. Sugar tried again. "Please, let me know what's wrong."

The distressed pitch of her words floated into the air. Desperate and exhausted.

The woman hugged Asal tightly for a long second. "I don't know what's wrong with her. She needs a doctor. Has a fever. Went to sleep two days ago, and it's been impossible to keep her awake."

Tears stung in Sugar's eyes and behind her nose. "She's not from here. No vaccines. Never seen a real doctor."

"Oh."

Sugar nodded, didn't say anything, because her throat burned.

"How do you know that?"

"She's from Afghanistan. We... these men I work with occasionally, saved her. Only to lose her again."

"You do work for these men. Liar. Everyone here's a liar."

"Wrong." Sugar tried to watch Asal's breathing, which seemed slower than it should have been. "You're not babysitting kidnapped kids by choice?"

"No, I'm not." Her lips pressed into a tight line.

"You're their mom?"

"Yes." She nodded. "And I've never felt more useless."

Took the words right out of my mouth. "Same. Especially if Asal's sick."

The woman eyed Sugar. Hesitantly, she shook her head as if changing her mind. "I'm Sarah."

She looked like a housewife. Safe and unassuming. As much as Sugar wanted to hate her for holding Asal, she was thankful Asal had someone to comfort her. "Sorry about... my initial assumptions."

"I assumed that you were the female version of the men watching us." Sarah looked Sugar over. "Guess I didn't notice if you had a gun or not. They all do."

"And then some. The kids?"

Sarah laughed quietly. "My kids haven't *really* been scared, but I've told them they didn't need to be. That we were on vacation. A crappy one." A sad smile made an appearance, then drifted away. "They've been out of school. A new friend, TV, fast food for every meal, so they're buying it. But they're worried about her. Until Asal got sick, they were playing, teaching her English."

Sugar loved that Asal was with kids her age and that she was learning and thriving. It never occurred to her that the little girl would be susceptible to a whole new world of dangers once she was removed from her *husband* in Afghanistan.

"What've they given you to help? Medicine? Is a doc coming?"

Sarah shook her head. "First-aid kit had fever reducer, but it didn't work. The guy in charge called her a complication, and it scares me. I'm certain he hasn't called for a doctor."

Shit. Shit, shit, shit. Damn Buck Baer to hell.

"We need a damn superhero brigade," Sugar mumbled more to herself than to Sarah. *Damn, why hasn't Jared shown up yet?*

"Superhero brigade." Sarah muffled a quiet chuckle. "My husband does stuff like that. I think."

"Stuff like what?"

"I don't really know. Not supposed to anyway. I keep hoping that when he comes home, he'll know something's wrong and come find us. He's out of the country for work."

"Where'd he go? How long?" Sugar's fingertips tingled like she was on the verge of something important.

"I'm... not comfortable getting into it. We live quietly enough. Off the grid. All to protect our family. It didn't work, but when he comes home, he'll find us. He'll know how. Nothing can stop him." She smoothed the sweat-soaked hair at Asal's temple. "My superhero." Her whispered words sounded more like a prayer.

Chills ran down Sugar's spine. How many *superhero brigades* were there? She armed most of them, so she already knew the answer. Not many.

What was the likelihood that she was housed with the kidnapped family of an operative who wasn't related to Titan? It was a statistical improbability. "Sarah, what's your last name?"

"What's it matter? I could be a Rockefeller or a Kennedy, but it wouldn't get me out of this hellhole right now."

"What's your last name?" Sugar came back too quickly. She didn't mean to, but it happened. In the back of her mind, she knew what Sarah would say.

Sarah sighed, resigned. "Gamble."

"Fuck me." Sugar rubbed her temples. *This is bad.* "So Brock Gamble—"

"Is my husband!" Sarah's eyebrows arched in surprise, her mouth hanging open. "How do you know him?"

And it was suddenly clear. The Titan deceit. The needle in her thigh. Sugar was a payoff in exchange for his family. But Buck Baer was a piece of shit. He couldn't be trusted, and it seemed that Brock had done just that. Sugar shook her head, letting her chin fall into her palms.

Sarah's surprise wore away, and she urged Sugar, "You know my husband?"

A thousand things could've bubbled off her tongue, but instead she mumbled and nodded.

"Do you work with him? Maybe if Brock's company knows you're missing, they'll come and get you, finding us." Sarah's face brightened. Hope filled her eyes. Her head bobbed. "Yes. Brock might be out of town, but if they know you're gone, they'll rescue you!"

Sugar sucked on her bottom lip, thinking about what was happening in the outside world. Maybe Brock was still there. Maybe they could talk to him, explain how Asal was, and use his newfound allegiance to get her a doctor or something stronger than first-aid kit pills. Titan would still come for them, but at least Asal would be stronger.

"Sarah, Brock might… be here."

Her excitement washed away as quickly as it would have if Sugar had struck her. "He's been captured?"

She was treading a thin line, and she didn't want Sarah to hate her. She needed a partner in this situation, someone to bounce ideas off while they waited for Titan. "That's not exactly how I'd put it." Her needle-mark bruise throbbed as she remembered the struggle with Brock. "When were you taken?"

"About a week and a half ago."

"We were in Afghanistan. All of us. I was with Brock."

Sarah's bottom lip dropped, and her head tilted. "You were? Um, okay."

"He works for the Titan Group. They came to rescue me, but we also saved Asal." Sugar cleared her throat, not knowing how the next part would go. "I've known Brock for a while. I'm a gunsmith, and the guys make use of my range. Anyway, I'm getting off track."

Asal stirred in Sarah's lap, and she dabbed a wet washcloth on the girl's forehead.

"Can I sit with you guys?"

Sarah shrugged, and Sugar climbed onto the table and sat next to them.

"GSI, the men who have us captured, were after me. Titan Group saved me. Brock works for Titan." Sugar pivoted toward Sarah. "GSI and Titan have a longstanding feud, and Buck Baer, the man that owns GSI, wanted me. I think he may've had your family abducted in order to have Brock... *help* him."

"Help him?"

"Yes. You were bait. I was a job. He had to finish the job to get his life back."

Sarah's eyebrows furrowed. Her cheeks flamed an irritated red. "Excuse me?"

"Brock knocked me out and gave me to Buck." *There. I said it.* The fallout could go either way.

Sarah recoiled, sliding inches away from Sugar. "He hit you?"

"No, not really. He sedated me with an injection."

Sarah stared in silence, as if Sugar's words weren't jibing.

Why am I trying to explain? "Okay, different way to say this—I may've been a trade that didn't work out exactly as Brock had planned."

"I don't believe you," Sarah whispered. "He wouldn't have done that, and he couldn't be here and not"—her voice cracked—"come find me."

"Not sure it's like that." *And now why the hell am I reassuring Brock's wife? The fucker can rot in hell with Kip for all I care.*

Her temples pounded. That wasn't true. Brock and Kip were two different species. She'd known Brock, though she hadn't a clue he was married with kids. If his wife was in trouble, he would rain Titan's resources from the heavens to save her. He was that kind of man.

But if he couldn't use Titan? If he couldn't ask Jared? Nothing would stop him. He would sell his soul to Lucifer to save his family. Brock was that kind of man. That was the only way she could rationalize his betraying her.

"What's it like then, Sugar?" Sarah raised her voice in disbelief, then looked at Asal and breathed in deeply. Quieter, she said, "Why would my husband abandon me? He wouldn't. He loves us. We're his world."

"I think *that's* the reason. He can't leave here without you. He can't go back to Titan. Not with what he's done."

"And *what* has he done?" she hissed.

"I'm his boss's girl. More or less." Though after the spark plug incident, the chance of being Jared's girl was much, much less. "He took what Jared Westin has and brought it to his enemy. Brock can't go home. Can't go to Jared. He thought he was making the good move, saving his wife and all, but all he did was sign his death warrant. He can't leave here. He has to do whatever Buck asks of him, and when he gets the green light to leave, he'll swoop in, grab the family, and relocate to somewhere farther off the grid."

Sarah's eyes were round. "But..."

"That's if all works according to plan. Too bad nothing looks good for me and Asal. I'd kill for that kid." She sighed and reached out to touch her shoe. "To bring this convo full circle, Brock might be here. Asal needs a doctor. He might be able to reason with Buck and get her some medical treatment." She squeezed Asal's toe lightly and slid off the table. "Enough with chit-chat. I'm going to find someone—"

The door opened across the room. A large man in tactical pants with guns on his hips walked in. His jaw was set, and his eyes were cold. "Let's go, ladies. Grab the kids."

"We want to see Brock." Sugar put her hands on her hips.

"Let's go."

"Then I want to know when the doctor's coming."

"No idea. Not my problem. Move your asses."

Sarah's two girls had scampered to her side, and none of them moved.

Sugar walked toward him in full bitch mode. "Look, asshole. Take it down a notch. You're scaring the crap out of these kids."

"Yeah, and you're the picture of grade school fun. We're relocating. Grab what you need and move."

Doubtful hope jumped in her chest. "To the doctor's?"

"Sugar, I've been warned about you." The man stepped to the side, gesturing toward the door. "Shut up and do as you're told."

She marched to him and squared off. "Tone it down. Scare these kids again, and—"

The room went dark. The television died. Both the children cried out for their mom, and the armed man cursed. A surge of adrenaline ran through her. *Titan.*

"Damn it. Hold on." The man walked out.

In the darkness, Sugar turned toward Sarah. "They're here."

CHAPTER TWENTY-ONE

"This has been happening all week. We're in a shitty mountainside basement. Every so often, they use too much power, and the breakers flip." Sarah's voice bled through the dark room.

"No. Not this time. I know it in my gut." Sugar could feel his presence. The air tingled against skin. A raw and unfiltered aura blanketed her in Titan confidence. Jared was nearby, and her body knew it on a primal level.

A flashlight bobbled into the room, preceding the same armed man. His face didn't show, but the light moved in an imperative come-here motion. "Time to go. Move." His voice was clipped with unstated urgency.

Absolutely. Titan had arrived.

Before, their escort had acted impatient. This time, he was driven. The bunker's fuse box wasn't the problem. No, this electrical failure was tactical. Sugar shivered, amped up and excited for rescue. For the opportunity to get Asal to a doctor on the quick. For Jared.

The man approached her, bouncing the light in the space between her and Sarah. "I'll take the kid if you can't carry her."

"No. I've got her." She reached toward Sarah, who gently relinquished Asal, whose listless body felt hot, and her face was clammy against Sugar's bicep. Asal sleepily nuzzled into the repositioned hold, and despite the sick factor, holding her felt right. Whispered promises and prayers flitted silently from her lips as she pressed a kiss to Asal's temple.

The darkness was silent, except for the exasperated breaths from their captor. Sarah gathered her children in the dim light of the flashlight, taking each by a hand. The flickers of their faces in the flashlight bordered on terrified. *Poor kids.* Vacation's *over. Time to get them the hell out of captivity.*

"Follow my lead, Sarah," Sugar whispered. "And stick with me, no matter what."

The armed man turned on his boot, blowing in frustration. "What now?"

"Nothing. Sorry." Sugar needed a reason to slow their venue change. She bit her lip. "I forgot Asal's medicine."

"Hurry the hell up," he grunted.

Right. Hurrying at a turtle's pace, Sugar shuffled to the table. "Trying." She faked searching while still holding Asal close. "Sarah, I need help. Can't see anything."

The man beamed his flashlight on the table. Sarah joined her, catching Sugar's eye. A knowing look passed between the two women. Brock hadn't married someone stupid, thank God.

"Girls." Taking her time, Sarah looked each child in the eye. "Stay close while I help collect supplies."

"Come on, ladies. No time for this." He marched over, the flashlight scoring across the table. "Get what you need, or leave it. You've got three seconds."

Stakes raised, Sarah scrambled and grabbed a handful of cloths, a water bottle, and pill packets from the first-aid kit. "Got it."

"Good." He started toward the door again, swirling the light like a traffic cop. "Move your asses, ladies."

"Girls, hold hands," Sarah whispered and took the youngest's free hand.

They began their trek across the black room. Slow, heavy steps fell one after the other. Sugar held Asal against her chest and, without the constant beam of the light, let her eyes adjust to the room. Somewhat. It was still pitch black, but she could make out forms. Sarah both held Asal's supplies and guided her children.

Supply-holding arm in the air, Sarah tipped and leaned to an angle. She lost her balance, scattering supplies, and unsettling her   children.   "Ow!"

"Mom!"

"Mommy!"

Well, I'll be damned. Worst fake trip ever. Not only had Sarah received the let's-slow-our-departure message, but she was taking proactive measures. If the kids hadn't been worried that their mama had hit the ground under the irate gaze of a gun-toting jerk, Sugar would've had to contain an inner laugh. *But hell, job well done, Sarah.* Even if she couldn't have been a worse actor.

Sugar knelt next to Sarah, joining in on the theatrics. "You okay? That sounded awful."

"Ow. My ankle hurts."

Ow? Seriously, did she have to lob the *ow* twice? Sugar bit her lip, burying a grin in the dark and, instead, concentrating on Asal. How long would it take Titan to arrive? If they were *really* there... Of course they were.

Perfect timing for Titan to bust through the door.

Any minute.

That very second would be excellent.

But nope. No superhero brigade. Nothing.

"Get up." The man came back, his flashlight pinning Sarah to the ground. "Or I'll make you."

Sarah rubbed her ankle under the dim light. "I want to, obviously. No interest in sitting in the dark. Give me a minute, will ya?"

His aggravation was almost palpable. Tension vibrated in the room. But still no Titan. And the room was so quiet. Maybe it was all in her head. Maybe she'd given Sarah hope for no good reason.

Zap. Zap. A red dot flashed, and a shocked gurgle choked out of their captor. The flashlight hit the ground, rolling, rolling, rolling almost to Sugar. A shuffle of noise. Feet? Titan? The guard staggered, then crumpled to the floor.

Titan! Her ears were playing tricks on her. *Where are they?*

Clutching Asal tightly to her chest, Sugar reached for the flashlight. Contact. She grabbed it and spotlighted the shuffling noise—Titan in full tactical gear. *Thank God.*

Someone silently subdued their armed guard. She swung the light left. Someone else from Titan stood by the door, facing the hallway.

And a third person... She didn't need a flashlight to define the proximity of the third. She knew exactly where he stood, lording over her. She couldn't see his face. But his masked gaze burned through her clothes and set her blood on fire.

Jared.

Deciding between Baer and Sugar had been a no-brainer. Sugar was top priority, and Jared was certain she could lead him to the kid. All he wanted to do was to find Sugar. Fuck their mission. Screw GSI and Buck Baer. Having Sugar in his arms was all Jared could contemplate.

And then, there she was. Night vision aside, he would've known her in the dark, on the floor, with his eyes closed. Somehow, someway, he had a sixth sense for her. Each step he'd taken had held no logic. Instinct had marked his route. His head, even his heart, pulled him toward his girl.

But to see her cast in night vision, sprawled on the ground and clutching a child he knew she loved, was more than he'd expected. His throat went dry. An indescribable wave of relief coasted from his boots to the tips of his ears.

He took a deep breath. Sugar had Asal, and that shaved a solid ten minutes off their rescue mission. But a second glance screamed that something was wrong. The kid wasn't up and about. The two other kids had crawled on the ground to their mom, mewing in panic. Asal didn't. She didn't even stir. Curled into Sugar's arms, Asal was as still as a stone. Something was definitely wrong.

Sugar stayed on her haunches, her eyes reaching for him in the dark, but she stayed by Brock's wife. *Why?* The flashlight hung limp in her hand; she never bothered to shine it up. So he dropped to her level, grabbed it from her, and killed the light.

"Baby Cakes." His voice was barely audible, but she heard. She leaned a degree toward him, nodding, and his arms ached to gather both woman and child into an embrace. Nothing like he'd ever felt for a rescue victim before.

"I knew you'd come," Sugar whispered.

"Couldn't let you off the hook that easy." In the dark, on the job, he felt a smile tugging at his cheeks. "Mess with a man's truck, and he'll find you."

Nicola turned from the door, walking to the woman with the children. "Can you quiet your girls? It'll be okay."

Sarah nodded. "Girls." She looked at Sugar for confirmation in the dark, but she probably couldn't see much. "These are the good guys. It's okay," she told the girls.

Nicola reached for the woman's hand. "Can you stand up?"

"Yes. I'm fine." Sarah easily stood, gathering her kids to her sides.

"I'm Nicola." Her voice was one hundred percent trustworthy, and the anxiety drained out of Sarah's face. "The three of you stick with me."

Nicola nodded to him and staged her charges next to the exit. Jared looked at Roman, who stood in the corner. GSI's man was down and unarmed. Roman threw a thumbs-up and headed to the door to lead them out.

Sugar still crouched, clinging to Asal. Not good. He pulled off his mask. "What's wrong with her?"

"She's sick. Unconscious. Needs a doctor."

He didn't need night vision to tell him that tears brimmed in her eyes. Her voice nearly cracked. All the warm and feel-good thoughts vanished and were replaced by a vicious pounding in his chest. Buck Baer would pay. Whatever was wrong, whatever he'd done, the bastard deserved to be in Jared's grip that very second.

Lesson number one: do not mess with what was his.

Lesson number two: payback would be exponential.

Jared brushed his fingers over Sugar's cheek, and she sucked in the quietest of breaths. The softness of her skin penetrated the calloused tips of his fingers, calming his rage and focusing his mind. "We have to move. Is she stable?"

Sugar nodded. "Enough to roll out."

"Good. That's my girls."

One hand supporting her back, he helped Sugar stand.

A simple hand gesture got everyone ready to head for safety. Roman would go ahead, then meet up with Rocco. Nicola would take the lead, and he would follow at the rear.

In Jared's earpiece, Cash gave the all clear for their hallway exit plan. Nicola nodded to nobody and guided the group out the door. Slipping his night goggles back on, Jared watched the group move forward. As soon as he secured Sugar, Sarah, and kids into Titan's waiting vehicle, Cash and Nicola would haul ass for safety, leaving Jared to go Buck hunting.

Roman and Rocco were already scouting for him, but he wanted to be the one to pull Buck by his neck out of whatever rathole he'd stashed himself in.

Keeping pace with the group, Sugar glanced over her shoulder. No way could she see much in the dark. But he could see everything in goggled shades of green. Her expressive eyes went from unsure to settled, and with that, she surged on.

The hallway ended and dropped the group into an equally dark stairwell, which was safer than where they'd been, but not relief worthy. Nicola cracked two Day-Glo sticks and gave them to Brock's kids. They shuffled up the long flight of stairs and into a garage. As soon as the heavy door clicked shut behind Jared, a garage door began to rise and an engine turned over.

In the SUV, Cash flipped on the headlights. Pale light from the outdoors spilled in through the faraway garage door. He jumped out of the driver's side. Along with Nicola, they piled Sarah and her kids into the vehicle.

Sugar and Asal were the last ones to get in. Turning to him, her downcast eyes traveled from Asal back to him, and his heart clenched. *This was too easy. Almost textbook. It could've gone so many ways.* But he wasn't going down that road.

No one else in the world would believe it, but Sugar was vulnerable, sweet, and scared. He felt it all over. His heart lurched as he wished that he could've clicked his rifle and destroyed her problems before she'd gotten into this situation.

Jared took a step away from the stairwell door. It was against orders. *His* orders. But still, there he was. Not doing his damn job, not standing on post as he should've been. Needing to be closer, needing to say something, Jared closed the space between him and Sugar.

He should've been scanning the perimeter. He should've been watching for a thousand things that could go boom in the night. But his clouded mind chose that moment to remember how soft her skin had been on his fingertips and how much he would miss her. She'd absconded, leaving him madder than he'd ever been, for umpteen hours. Every lecture, each smart-ass thing he'd planned to say and school her on was forgotten.

"Thank you," she whispered.

Nicola stepped between them and eased Asal into the SUV. Ignoring the looks he was sure Nic and Cash were tossing him, Jared stole his body against hers. The tough-girl act was a front for everyone else. But Jared forgot them. It was just him and her. His mind churned with things to say. His heart had editorial comments. But his mouth stuttered for the words. "I'm…"

Sorry for the homicide accusations that I barked when we should've been partners.

Sorry that you were hurt.

Sorry that Asal's sick.

Sorry that I didn't make damn sure you knew how crazy I am about you.

The front doors shut, one after the other. Everyone had loaded up, and Cash was at the wheel. Nicola hung out the window, watching Jared's back because he wasn't watching anything but Sugar.

"Sugar, I—"

The muffled roar of an explosion echoed behind closed doors. *Fuck.*

He bumped Sugar into the vehicle, slamming the door behind her. "Go!" But the wheels were already spinning toward their exit.

Jared pivoted, running toward the blast. Smoke hit his face as he leapt down the stairs.

"Roman? Roc?" he called into his mic. "Come in. Status update. Now."

Nothing but dead silence.

CHAPTER TWENTY-TWO

The echo of the muffled explosion played on repeat in Sugar's head. Jared ran *toward* the sound. Toward his men. She knew what he did for a living and that he lived on the edge of danger, but to watch him run toward a big kaboom made her legs restless and her chest tight.

She needed a drink of water. The doors of the Explorer were closing in on her with each passing mile, and Cash was driving like he was under enemy fire. Sugar was convinced that the SUV was shrinking.

Couldn't someone call Jared to make sure everything was okay? Nicola might understand that request seeing as her brother was in there also, but Cash wouldn't. Plus, that was Jared at work. She couldn't freak out when he did his job. A mantra played in her mind. *Don't get hurt. Don't get hurt.* She was sure everyone could hear her silent plea for Jared.

She hoped that no one else would get hurt, but Jared was the only thing that really mattered. He'd run toward the explosion. *Son of a bitch.* She stifled an uneasy groan. The situation made her sick.

What was he thinking? That should be easy to guess. He would do whatever it took to bring his boys home, just like he'd brought her home. He was always saving the day, and she got it. Even when anxiety and apprehension trickled through her blood, she knew how loyal he was to Titan. It made her want to smile—and cry. She was all over the place, spouting emotions like a feelings fountain, one bad phone call away from a nervous breakdown.

Cash had the gas pedal pressed down, maybe as far as it would go. She couldn't see the speedometer, but if the passing cars were any indication, they were clocking some serious mph.

Cash adjusted his cowboy hat. He was brooding, blowing out deep breaths. Serious tension percolated in the SUV. Between the Titan team in danger and Brock's family sitting pretty in the Explorer, he looked like he might snap.

Nicola pulled out her earpiece out and shrugged out of her tactical vest. She disarmed, then turned toward the backseat. "Everyone, other than Asal, doing okay?"

Sarah's kids were in the third row of the SUV, silent and probably overwhelmed, just like their mother, who looked bad. Guilty. Dark circles. Red eyes. Brock's betrayal wasn't her fault, but she was ready for scapegoat duty. With pressure so thick that it was choking Sugar's air supply, she knew Sarah was feeling it, too.

"We're fine," Sarah whispered from next to Sugar, hardly moving to speak. Her cheeks were flushed, and she sucked in her chapped bottom lip. Tension still hung heavy as Sarah let out a slow breath. She didn't look Nicola in the eye, rather, stared at her shoulder. "You know Brock, too?" Sarah's voice broke, and she cleared it, then spoke louder. "You work with him?"

Sugar, still wondering about Jared, watched both women and Cash. Cash flexed his grip on the steering wheel, his knuckles straining a pinky-white color. He stared straight forward, clenching his jaw. Brock had betrayed the team, and Cash had lost a friend. The Titan boys were tight. And to have their team leader screw them like that? No wonder Cash looked like he'd sat on a pin-less grenade.

Couple that with having no news about Jared and the men they'd left behind, anger wasn't even the start of what was on Cash's face. More like explosive resentment and fury.

Nicola played it cool, being far less the hothead than her husband. Still pivoted toward the back seat, she flashed a weak smile. "We did work with him."

"*Did.*" Sarah nodded and interlaced her fingers, burying them in her lap. "Because he's..."

Dead is most likely the answer.

Cash slapped the steering wheel. "Because we trusted him, we worked with him, and he fucked us in the ass." He looked in the rearview mirror and growled through clamped teeth. "Sorry 'bout the language in front of your kids."

Sarah nodded. The AC blew on high, and Sugar could hardly swallow. She tried to breathe quietly, but her lungfuls sounded too loud in the screaming silence. She shifted Asal in her lap. Every move, every crinkle of fabric and shift in her seatbelt, wailed louder than the last.

Nicola glared at Cash, then turned back to Sarah. "We're all in shock right now. Nobody expected Brock to do anything other than follow the rules."

Sarah's lips pressed into a pale line as she re-knotted her fingers. "But still, you rescued us?"

"Well, yeah." Cash sounded like a teenager about to drop a *duh*. He probably rolled his eyes, too, but the backseat wasn't the best vantage point.

"Why?" Sarah asked.

Cash shrugged and changed lanes. "You shouldn't reap the consequences of his mistakes. Plus we were already going in for Asal anyway. Then the shit with Sugar went down." He scrunched his shoulders, blowing out another deep growl. "Fuckin' Brock."

Nicola glared at Cash again. "*Kids,*" she hissed under her breath. "Tone down the language." Looking back at them, she shook her head. "Sugar, what happened anyway? Jared was short on details."

That almost made Sugar laugh. *Short on the details? Bet he was.* "I ran off when he wasn't looking. He was being a dick. I was being... me."

"Hard to handle? Pain in the ass?" Cash volunteered over his shoulder, an impish grin hanging on his face. Nicola shoved him. They were a good couple, and Cash knew Sugar better than almost anyone did. Their history could've been awkward, but it never was, especially with Nicola.

"Forget him." Nicola nudged Cash again. "You ran off on Jared. Can only imagine that went over well."

"Never saw his reaction. I'd stolen a spark plug, so he couldn't chase after me."

Nicola snorted.

Cash swerved in shock, quickly righting the vehicle. "You did what?" All his tension disappeared when he threw his head back and roared with laughter.

"Look at the damn road, Cash." Nicola turned back to Sugar. "Are you serious?"

"Girl." Cash whistled. "Are you in some trouble. Holy hell."

Trouble, with all capitals and spelled out. That was so true. As soon as everyone was safe and sound and healthy, Jared would rip her to pieces or wring her neck. She saw it coming, and she could do nothing but wait. Her stomach churned at the thought, then sank. *God, let him be all right.*

"How'd Brock find you? Get you?" Nicola asked.

Sugar hadn't thought about it. Had he been watching and waiting? Mulling it over as she looked out the window, she shrugged. "No idea. He got me to pull over and stuck my leg with a needle. I was lights-out in seconds. Never saw it coming."

Just like that, the tension was back.

Sarah leaned toward Sugar. "I'm so sorry. So very sorry." Fresh tears welled in her eyes. "That's not the Brock I know. The man I love wouldn't... wouldn't do that."

Sugar loosened one hand from Asal and patted Sarah's knee. Not her typical MO, but the lady looked like she needed reassurance. "It's not your fault. He thought he was making the right play for you guys."

"Screw that, Sugar." Angry Cash was back. "He handed you over, knowing damn well what would happen. And who you belong to. *Screw that.*"

She snorted. "I don't *belong* to anyone, Cash."

He mumbled, Nicola rolled her eyes, and Sugar didn't know if that was meant for her or him.

"I want to pretend this never happened," Sarah whispered. "But I don't really know who my husband is."

"Sure you do." Sugar continued to pat her knee as though that would help. *When did I become so damn empathetic?*

"We sure as hell didn't know about you." Cash made a sharp change of lanes. "Or your kids."

Sugar looked over her shoulder. The two kids in the back were asleep, probably worn out from the overstimulation and grown-up bickering. How they could sleep was a mystery.

Sarah also glanced at her kids and went back to knitting her fingers. "I don't understand why he didn't turn to the people he trusted most."

"You and everyone else." Cash slammed on his horn, then hit an exit ramp going top speed.

"Chill, Cowboy. Geez." *Could Cash be more of a prick right now?*

His grip flexed on the steering wheel again. "Time to get Asal checked out and find out where the hell the guys are."

The explosion sounded in her head again. *Forget the drama. Forget the tension.* She had two objectives: find out what was wrong with Asal and grovel an apology to Jared once he was home safe. Both items on her to-do list made her want to retch.

CHAPTER TWENTY-THREE

Smoke billowed down the hallway, and even with night vision, Jared saw zip. No activity. No signs of life. Only static in his earpiece. His finely tuned skill of observation was turning up big, fat goose eggs.

"Roman. Rocco." He tried again, retracing their initial path through the corridors. The hallway ended, forcing him to go right or left. He stilled, listened, and watched. The smoke hung heavier on the right side. *Maybe? Fuck it, no sense in wasting time. Right it is.* He pounded down the hall, sweeping glances through any door he passed. Still nothing.

Another dead end. How was this possible? Tightness pooled in his chest, his eyes pinching behind his mask. Losing men wasn't on the agenda. That just wasn't going to happen. Not again. He couldn't handle it. Not after Brock had defected to the enemy.

Jared raged and roared, punching the wall with a gloved fist. Twice in one week, he'd punched a wall. The impact should've split his skin on impact. But instead the wall… echoed?

False wall. Has to be.

Jared kicked it. Hands out, he ran a pattern around the wall panel, knocking for the perimeter like he was checking for wall studs. Slow seconds ticked by. No telling if Roman and Rocco were in trouble.

Screw this. He didn't have time. Issuing two kicks as a warning just in case his boys had set up camp nearby, Jared placed a charge at the bottom of the hollow panel. If the hollow panel wasn't a door, then it was a way into a hidden passage.

He bumped his fists against the panel a few times, then hollered, "Move your asses if you hear me."

He bent, lit the fuse, and hustled back around the corner. Dropping to a knee and shielding his ears and face, he counted to three before it blew.

Bam!

It sounded just like the explosion he'd heard earlier. A flicker of hope passed. Maybe Roman and Rocco had done the same thing, and maybe they weren't victims of a GSI-made bomb.

Maglite in hand, he beamed through the smoke-filled, dusty passageway and stepped in. The floor sloped at a sharp angle. Spent shells littered the ground, and remnants of spent gunpowder floated, mingling with the particles from his C4 charge. The air tasted metallic, and his nostrils burned.

He looked both directions. Simple choice: up the slope or down. Buck Baer would want out. If Titan chased, he would run. *Up it is.*

The tunneled slope doglegged, and he rounded the sharp turn. A few hundred yards farther, it did the same thing. The path wove higher, so much that he was sure he would have to hit the surface soon unless somehow they were pushing farther into the side of the Blue Ridge Mountains.

But that wouldn't make sense. Baer would want to escape. He was a runner, a pansy. All talk and no back up. No way would Baer want a fair fight.

Pop, pop, pop.

Muffled, muted, and far away, was the unquestionable sound of a gun battle. He hauled ass toward the noise. Far ahead, a sliver of light crept into the impossible darkness. *Maybe a door, a hatch. Who knows?* As long as it was access to the ground game, he could make it work.

"You're mine, asshole." Jared tore through the remainder of the distance and stopped short of a door. Sunlight bled through a crack, and he nudged it open. As his eyes adjusted to daylight, the scene focused.

On a wide mountainside clearing, Baer had taken cover behind boulders and was throwing out shots like beads during Mardi Gras. They pinged everywhere. Ricocheted bullets and splintering rocks exploded around Roman and Rocco, and his boys had Baer pinned. He couldn't go anywhere, except down, and judging by the horizon, that looked like a hell of a fall. Buck Baer wasn't the kamikaze type.

But for all Baer's willy-nilly shooting, he was covered. Jared tried to mic Roman and Rocco again. "On your six."

Neither turned, but Rocco cursed in his ear. "About damn time."

"This asshole has an artillery stashed up here." Roman grunted. "And no clear shot."

Their pissed off voices made him smile. *Alive and angry, just the way I like my team on a mission.* The radios must've been down because of underground distance. He never should've doubted his team.

"We're waiting him out." Rocco's rifle banged out on full auto, slicing and dicing against Baer's boulder. "Mostly waiting him out. The fucker."

"Has to run out of bullets sometime." Roman picked up shooting where Rocco left off.

Baer sprayed rapid fire toward them, his aim off. He hadn't noticed Jared, but Baer wasn't known for his field acuity. His motives were always selfish, and if Buck Baer was burning through a couple of thousand dollars' worth of ammo in an hour, then something was—

Womp, womp, womp.

Bingo.

Baer had been waiting on his getaway vehicle. A helicopter roared nearby.

"Hold your fire. Don't shoot that bird." He could almost feel his men drop their jaws, but Jared didn't need a chopper smashing into the side of a mountain. He would have too much to explain and too many people to deal with. This engagement needed to be quiet, strictly Titan versus GSI.

Rocks and dirt flipped and fragmented as Baer continued to fire indiscriminately. He hadn't noticed that the scene had turned into the Buck-Baer-one-man gun show.

He was such a bad shot. The helicopter approached, dangling a ladder. Two men hung out the cabin door, ready to provide cover. Instead of an assault, Roman and Rocco crouched down, giving Baer's cover nothing to shoot at.

Baer scuttled over—no finesse or strategy to his awkward departure—and jumped onto the ladder. Watching his unsteady climb was almost worth the hell of the day. He'd obviously not been out of his cushy office in a while. *Too damn bad I didn't bring a video recorder. YouTube gold.*

The chopper hovered steadily as the pilot accounted for the novice on the swaying ladder. As the chopper pulled up in a slow climb, it was more than evident that *everyone* knew GSI's boss man was as uncoordinated as a new recruit.

Jared shook his head. This was his adversary? Titan wouldn't take down that pathetic mess with a shot to the back of the head. Too easy. Jared didn't even want Baer dead—not at that second, at least. Baer needed to suffer. He needed to know that his demise was solely at the hands of Jared Westin, not just the company he'd built.

As slowly as any retreat Jared had ever seen, the GSI helicopter finally left view. Roman and Rocco remained in place. He was betting they had a few choice words for him, but they were smart enough to keep their mouths shut.

"Take it easy, boys." Jared walked toward them while keeping an eye out for any leftover GSI headaches. "I want Baer myself. He'll deal with me, that pansy-assed motherfucker." After Baer had targeted Sugar, Jared wanted him to really *feel* his revenge.

Sugar and Asal were safe. That was all that mattered on this job. *What kind of son of a bitch uses a kid as leverage?* If Sugar hadn't been the reason for the compression in his chest, then Asal would've been. *Focus on the job well done.* Jared cracked his neck, took a deep breath, and wrangled his reactions. "Rocco, touch base with Cash. Tell him we're still kicking."

"What the hell?" Roman wiped sweat off his brow.

"Our goal was simple. Extract the innocents. They're out, so we're done." *If it were only that simple.*

He could picture Baer stumbling around the chopper cabin, asking for high-fives like he was the man. Jared wanted blood. He wanted to watch GSI crumble. But *he* wanted to be the ones, his men, who took out Baer. A boring gunfight wouldn't do justice to the ongoing feud with Baer. That required something bigger. Something in Baer's face. Something so extravagant that Buck Baer would be jealous he hadn't done it first. *God, I hate that fucker.*

Roman kicked at a pile of empty shells near his boots. "Dude deserves to—"

"I get that. More than you do. Shut your face and trust me. There's a bigger picture."

Rocco clicked off his cell phone. Bad news poured from his stance and downturned smile. "Cash took 'em to see Doc Tuska. Something was seriously wrong with the kid, and he had her transferred to a children's hospital. Kid went by ambulance. Cash and crew followed behind."

Jared ground his teeth and clenched his fists. He couldn't speak and didn't know what he would've said anyway. Of course Sugar would be upset, but his stomach turned. It was more than empathizing with Sugar. He didn't know when or how it'd happened, but Asal had become more than a job. It could've been all the courage she'd shown escaping Afghanistan. Some people are brought together by fate. Not interested in analyzing that sentiment, he turned and retraced his steps. The sooner he was behind the wheel of a vehicle, the sooner he could check on that kid.

CHAPTER TWENTY-FOUR

Speed-walking back from the ladies room was pointless. Asal would still be asleep in her hospital bed, right where Sugar had left her. But after a nurse sidetracked her into a pointlessly long discussion, she'd easily been gone for fifteen minutes. That killed her. If Asal so much as batted an eyelash, she wanted to be there just in case.

The hospital room door was open a crack, though she swore she'd shut it. *Damn doctors and nurses.* She was in a restricted hallway, but there was still noise. Sounds drifted from the nurse's station, and Asal needed to rest, not be bothered by—

The air in Sugar's lungs held in place, stuck in her throat and her chest. Her heart hammered like the beat of a drum as she faltered, clinging to the doorjamb. She didn't dare move forward or breathe. She could only watch.

Jared's hulking body was perched on the edge of a bedside chair in the dimly lit room. The expanse of his shoulders hung forward, and his chin dipped toward his clavicle. From the side, he looked rumpled, like he'd walked out of battle and into the hospital. *Probably because he did.*

Asal's limp fingers were clasped in his steepled hands, almost as though he held her hand in silent prayer. He was massive to her tiny. Powerful to her weak. His black tactical pants and shirt contrasted harshly against the white hospital linens. Jared was her guardian angel, her warrior, praying for the girl in his grip.

Sugar's heart stole away as she watched him move Asal's tiny knuckles to his chin and speak too softly for Sugar to hear.

His quiet words were lost in the sterile room, amid the beeping machines.

Jared turned his gaze from Asal to the door. Her little hand still encapsulated in his, he nodded hello, then gingerly tucked Asal's arm under the sheet. Smoothing a bump in the covers, he stood.

Never in Sugar's life had she seen a collision of opposites that looked so right together. The back of her throat burned, and she still couldn't swallow. The three of them, together, felt right inside her heart. A special part of destiny's plan had just revealed itself.

He met her at the doorway. Standing to his full height, Jared towered over her, and she wasn't short. He loomed larger than memory served and swallowed the space between them with his dark, brooding eyes and chiseled jaw. His shoulders could carry the weight of the world. She saw his Adam's apple bob as he swallowed, and her body craved his arms, just to be wrapped against him. Maybe there, she could let go of her concerns and exhaustion.

"Sugar." He grasped her elbow. "We need to talk."

His stern words bit like an ice bath. *Who am I kidding? Destiny and secret life plans? Anxiety-erasing hugs? Christ.* Maybe she did need to see a doctor. No telling what kind of aftereffects she'd suffered from Brock's sedative. Occasional lovely-dovey delusions were obviously a severe byproduct, and she needed to be hypervigilant to avoid falling into the land of make-believe happiness.

He led her away from the doorway, down the hallway, and her boots dragged. Heavy and lead-laden, they scuffed on the tile floor. Her muscles went on strike, refusing to help, and Jared half-dragged her to their destination.

Sugar didn't want to hear a lecture about the spark plug, and she didn't want to talk about GSI or Brock. All she wanted was her mini-fantasy, but the tick flexing in his jaw said that wasn't a possibility. It never would be, and she needed to pressure-wash the warm fuzzies from her memory.

With a deep breath in, she had her invisible armor up. She still owed him an apology for making Titan's job harder and for endangering her friends' lives. A big, fat "I'm sorry" was needed. But she appreciated that he'd made it back to her in one piece.

"You're safe," she whispered, thankful that her pleas for safety had worked.

"I am." His eyes narrowed, maybe trying to read her mind.

Good luck with that, buddy. It was all over the place. But right then, their safety was forefront. "The team is, too?"

He gave a curt nod. "They are."

"Did you get Buck?"

His face darkened and tension flexed through the chiseled planes of his cheeks. "Baer and I will handle our issues privately. The mission wasn't to kill him. It was to rescue you."

She'd never thought that angrily walking out of her house would have had such severe consequences. Guilt bubbled up more quickly than she could choke it down. "I'm sorry. I was wrong. I shouldn't have left."

Jared's jaw flexed again. His full lips were pressed into a tight line. Energy, anticipation, and tension swirled around them, and she struggled to find the right words. She stared at the ceiling, refusing to cry in front of him.

He wrapped his arms tightly around her, pulling her into his solid hold. "Damn, Sugar. I've wanted to hold you since the second I saw you." On the scale of one to ten—ten being completely caught off guard—she hovered around a fifteen and watched as he kept on going. "Don't know what goes on in that pretty head of yours, but, baby cakes…"

Every muscle shivered. She leaned into his embrace, shaking off the astonishment and basking in… him. He smelled of gunsmoke and hard work. Both were delicious and comforting. His solid body warmed her as she lost her mind while surrounded by his strength. Her legs melted, and she nuzzled her torso and head into his hug.

Jared squeezed her and threaded one hand into her hair, pulling it from its disheveled ponytail. His fingers combed, and her eyes closed. She could finally breathe.

"Sweet, sweet, Sugar." His lips buried behind her ear. "Don't do that to me again."

She nodded. "'Kay."

He pressed a gentle kiss into her hair. "You were wrong. *I was wrong.* But hell, never again. I can't handle that again."

He was wrong? There was something the great Jared Westin couldn't handle? She wanted to call BS. She wanted to push away and scoff. But nothing in her brain worked, except the head-nodding receptors that she rarely used.

"Promise me, Sugar."

She nodded again. "Promise. Okay."

He gave her one more squeeze, then held her in his outstretched arms. His intense gaze could've kindled fire, and it turned her insides to a hot, distracted mess.

His rough thumb caressed her cheek. She wanted to lean her cheek into his palm. If his hug could lighten her anxiety, then his kiss could ease life's burdens. She needed him for more than sating a sexual craving. His touch offered comfort and stability. His caress held the promise of so much more.

He cleared his throat. "I'm assuming you got the same spiel I did. We can't stay with her tonight."

Sugar sighed. "It's frustrating to have her again, then have to leave." She'd asked, but visiting hours were minimal and almost up. "I'm worried about her safety. Security."

"Trust me, that's covered. No one in this world will be under better eyes, with the exception of you with me."

"I've been alone for at least an hour."

"That's what you think. You needed some quiet time with your girl. No one would intrude on that."

"What?"

"I've got eyes most places. Even if it's not my hospital of choice, I'm still able to get the job done."

Cash and Nicola had dropped her at the hospital. She'd thought they'd left. But had they? And how long had Jared been there? And more importantly, he believed she was still a GSI target, and why wouldn't she be?

She shook her head. She wasn't the kind of chick who ran scared and hid. She would take the protection Jared offered for the time being, but her goal was to get her life back in order.

The image of him hovering over Asal flitted through her mind. That was the life she wanted—Jared, Asal, a cohesive little family. The realization hit her like a half-ton tank. *A family?* She'd never wanted something like that before. Family was a four-letter word. She had a sister, but they were more like friends than family. Mom and Dad were place-holding names for people who'd had the burden of raising her. That didn't constitute family.

"What's going through your mind, Baby Cakes?"

A whole bunch of craziness. Jared might have put up a good game when he'd chased her down, convincing her that two people who didn't *do* relationships could fudge their own version of it. But if she mentioned absurd thoughts like *family*, she bet she would see the back of his head as he ran down the hospital hall. "Nothing. Just worried about Asal. The usual." The *usual* lies. An omission was still a lie.

"If you say so." He shrugged, eyeing her suspiciously. "Why don't you say goodbye to our girl, and then let's go."

Our girl. Her heart fluttered. Jared tortured her even when he didn't know he was doing it. *But he said "our girl."* Sugar's mind went on a roll. *We could be the three amigos, the three musketeers, the three...* She couldn't go there, not just because she couldn't come up with a third. Jared had tossed out a simple comment, and she was circling them into one big, happy family.

He leaned forward and kissed her forehead as if the little gestures weren't already killing her. He had no idea, but with every word and every touch, Sugar was losing her mind and dreaming of the impossible. With a quick hug, he spun her toward the door and patted her bottom, scooting her off.

Jared watched as Sugar slipped into Asal's hospital room, and he let his weight fall back against the wall. His head dipped back too hard, but the knock did little to right his brain. His legs wanted to move beside Sugar's, to follow her closely and keep her within sight. That had nothing to do with any looming threats and everything to do with the woman and, if he admitted it, the kid inside that room.

Sugar reappeared, and his stomach tightened. Her soft smile nearly made him flatline as she whispered, "I'm ready. You?"

More than I've ever been. His hands caught hers, and like some love-struck puppy dog, he was pulling close to her and smiling. "Let's go."

"What about Asal?"

"Cash has got her."

"He's still here? I should've known." Sugar stopped in front of the elevators.

"No elevators today. Let's take the stairs. Just to be safe." Abu Dhabi was a mistake he should've seen coming, just like when Sugar walked out and into Brock's arms. He wasn't taking any more chances.

She studied him before they walked into the stairwell. "Guess it's my turn now. What are you thinking about? I can't read you."

"Sure you can."

She scoffed. "Yeah, just like I *really* knew someone was watching out for me and Asal in that hospital room."

They descended another flight of stairs, both their boots echoing. "What's on my mind?" He squeezed her hand. "I'm worried about Asal—"

"You're not a worrier. Doc said with special antibiotics, she'll be fine in a few days."

"I'm worried about you."

"I've got the best protection that's out there. You."

"Lot of good I've done you lately."

"Now you're talking crazy."

They reached the bottom of the stairs. She reached for the door, and he reached for her, knotting her arms around her and locking her into place, with her back against the wall. "You want crazy talk? You went missing, and I couldn't think straight. You're in front of me, and I still can't think straight. I want to touch you, kiss you. Tan your ass for being such a pain and love on you so you know how damn much I need you."

He tried for a breath, then noticed the rapid rise and fall of his chest and hers. His hands framed her cheeks, and the bluest eyes he'd ever seen went wild and wide. "Shit, Sugar. I want to be buried in you for all the wrong reasons. Nothing to do with relief or release, and everything to do with pulling you closer. So that's crazy talk, woman."

Her pink lips parted, probably out of shock. But he couldn't resist. Not giving her a chance to run, he closed the distance, whispering more tender-hearted words, which even he couldn't hear or understand against her pouted mouth. She was so soft and delicious that he had to groan. His eyelids drooped closed. His eyes might as well have rolled back into his head. Sugar opened her kiss to him, allowing him to savor it so deeply that he felt it roll from his tongue to his boots.

She pulled back. "Thank you."

Hell, what for? He'd just molested her in a hallway and dropped a bomb's worth of heavy-duty on a woman who didn't seem to believe in… love.

Blinking, she tilted her head. "You okay? Look like you've just seen a ghost."

More like the light. Tucking her under his arm, he opened the door to the parking garage. "Never better. Let's roll."

CHAPTER TWENTY-FIVE

Jared couldn't blame Sugar. She'd had a rough few days since they'd been home from overseas, and recovering from that trip would've taken anyone time. Maybe *rough* was downplaying it a little. Brutal. Exhausting. Harrowing. Those might be better descriptors.

During the hour-long drive to his place, he hadn't been the king of conversation starters. He was busy thinking about revelations and consequences. About Sugar. About the future.

Sugar snoozed, leaning up against the passenger door, and he let her sleep. But driving didn't keep him from stealing glances every half mile. It wasn't until they arrived at his home that he could ignore the road completely and just stare at her.

If he were honest, seeing what she thought of his place would stroke his ego. It wasn't fancy, but it was his. He had lots of land, no neighbors, and more space than he could ever use. But Titan Group raked in the moolah, so he had bought a place that worked with his persona and paid homage to the superb job he'd done building his black-ops empire.

He shifted the Expedition into park, and Sugar let out a tired sigh, but didn't wake. He rubbed her shoulder, admiring the view and savoring the smoothness of her skin more than actually trying to wake her. Her beauty was so much more than skin deep. Asleep, she looked sweet and vulnerable. She sighed again, and he was cemented to the seat. Minutes, maybe an hour ticked by, and still, they sat. Still, he watched her. No woman had ever made him think about consistency or the long haul. Never had he chased a woman as he did Sugar. Correction, never had he chased a woman. Period.

Sugar murmured in her sleep, and he would've killed to know what she'd said. In that moment, there was no question. He never wanted easy and simple again.

He finally had her at his home, and he wanted... *Hell, what do you want? Her to stay? Play house?* The answer was categorically complicated. But he knew he wanted more. The need to have her there was primitive. He wanted her to stay, and it was about more than screaming orgasms and a beautiful babe. She'd burrowed into his heart. And his life. He wanted her there because having her elsewhere was unnatural. He needed her for no other reason than because he loved her.

Ding, ding, ding. That was it. *Congratulations for figuring that one out.*

Until that point he hadn't defined love. He'd never had a reason, and it seemed all gushy Hallmark cards and candy-coated Valentine's Day. It was Cash and Nicola playing footsie under his war room table, not caring at the eye rolls, or Mia and Winters giggling over baby pictures.

That wasn't his scene. It never would be, and that wasn't Sugar's, either. A heart-covered greeting card would end up in her trash. But she would be crazy-girl happy over something like a special-order scope or an antique pistol.

Even Asal would fit with them. He had enough room for her to run around and enough money to make sure she had a good education and whatever else a third-world-meets-first-world kid might need. A good doctor. Nice clothes. Someone besides SpongeBob to teach her English. He cared about that kid in an entirely different way than he cared about Sugar, but it still felt damn near what he might call love.

Love had never seemed like a practical emotion, one that just happened without active, willing participants. But as sure as he was that she loved GUNS like he loved his bulldog, he knew he loved Sugar and Asal. They all were supposed to have found one another. That was worth a conversation.

Jared turned off the ignition and jumped out to open his front door. With her still sound asleep, Jared peeled open the passenger door so that Sugar didn't tumble out. The seatbelt held her in place, and when he unhooked it, she shifted into his arms.

He kicked the door shut behind them, but she didn't blink. She was out for the count, and it made him smile that she trusted him enough to fall into a deep slumber on his watch. He carried her toward his bedroom, enjoying the hell out of his realizations.

A loud snoring came from the master suite. Parker had dropped Thelma off earlier, and the bulldog lay sprawled across the king-sized bed. He whistled her down, but she stared, wrinkle-faced and wary of the woman in his arms.

"First time for everything, girl. Now get down." Bringing women to his home wasn't high on the to-do list, and none had ever been in his room. That was his space. His and Thelma's. Jared shook his head at his dog and realized that he needed to have serious conversations with two females, because Thelma wouldn't take Sugar lightly.

He whistled once more, and Thelma stood. Only then did he notice something that looked suspiciously like a destroyed beer koozie near her paws. He shooed her again, and Thelma grabbed the koozie and jumped off.

As carefully as he could, he laid Sugar in the center of the bed and wrapped part of the comforter over her legs. She sighed, rolled onto her side, nuzzling onto *his* side of the bed, and burrowed her head into *his* pillow. She could have it if she wanted it. He and Thelma would move to the other side.

Thelma plopped down by his boots, in a funk that she'd had to move her lazy butt. Jared scrubbed her head, scrunching her skin and wrinkles in his hands. "That's Sugar. Try making friends. It'll help when you have to learn to share the bed."

The pup groaned and rolled onto her back, and his gaze drifted back to Sugar. He had to get out of there. He felt creepy standing over her, watching like some kind of whack-job perv. But she was one of the more beautiful sights he'd ever seen. Her dark hair sprawled across the pillow, and her perfect lips let out sleepy breaths.

Thelma groaned again. He chuckled and took the destroyed koozie from her, thankful for the distraction. He and Sugar would have a conversation when she woke up. She stirred again, and her back arched, making her breasts press into her T-shirt. Perfect-sized mounds waited for him. Jared shut his eyes, thinking that his hunger for her covered so many levels. A conversation about their future would happen pronto. Or maybe that would be the second thing they handled once she woke up.

Warm light coaxed Sugar from her deep sleep. Not ready to wake, she turned away from the light and buried herself in the pillow. The scent from the linens acted like a shot of adrenaline. Her eyes flew open, and she lurched up, sweeping her gaze from one side of a masculine bedroom all the way to the other side of the huge bed she had been sleeping on. Curled on the pillow next to her was a dog that was snoring louder than a man could and was snuggled up with a rawhide bone the size of a Cadillac.

Where the hell am I? Jared's?

Her eyes peeled wider, if that was possible. The massive bedroom suite was decorated with dark wood furniture, but nothing personal, unless she counted the unused dog bed. There were no knickknacks or framed photos, but Jared wouldn't be all Martha Stewart about his home décor. His interest probably lay in functionality, which she could appreciate.

She studied the room. If this was Jared's bedroom, she could only imagine where he housed his weapons. Under the bed. In drawers. No doubt there was a safe somewhere, but he would want easy access. She rolled to the side and draped her arm over the edge, running her fingers along the underside of the mattress until she found—*gotcha*—a handgun holstered closer than his alarm clock.

She left it there, but that was her confirmation that she was in Jared's bed. She'd never slept in a man's bed before, nor had she ever allowed any guy to make use of hers. There she was, all alone except for a dog that had moved closer to her hip without so much as an off-beat snore. Then she laughed. Of course Jared would have a noisy, slobbery dog with a stealth mode.

A sudden memory of a sickly Asal lying in her arms wiped her from the moment. She needed to check on the girl. She noticed a note and a cell phone on the night stand. *Update from the hospital: Asal is doing well. Recovering quickly. Here's the phone number to call and check on her if I'm not there when you wake up. She's really a strong kid. -J*

After a call to the nurse's station had assured Sugar that Asal was healing, she relaxed against the pillows and stared at her furry bunkmate. The dog opened one eye, slowing the snore to a noisy breath.

"What's your name?" She rubbed the furry head, and the skin moved back and forth. "Must be a bulldog. Love your wrinkles."

"That's Thelma."

Sugar shot up and onto her knees, her adrenaline pounding. "Damn it, Jared." He propped an elbow overhead and leaned on the doorjamb. "You scared the crap out of me."

He laughed and smiled, and it made her tingly all over. A smile pulled at her lips as she sat back on her bottom. Thelma rolled onto her back, nosing Sugar's hand.

He was clean shaven and dressed in daydream-worthy jeans, a cotton shirt that may've been painted over his muscles, and no shoes. Cover model material.

"I think Thelma likes you. Wasn't sure in the beginning, but she's stood watch for a while now." His dog nosed her again. "Guess it's time for you to pay up. She likes petting, tug of war, and eating things she shouldn't."

That was right. Jared's dog had the stomach of steel. Her memory of passing conversations came back. "How long was I out?"

"About a day."

Like twenty-four hours? "Whoa."

He laughed again. "No kidding. Between you and Thelma snoring, I kicked it on the couch last night."

What? Her cheeks felt hot, and her jaw dropped open. "No way."

Shaking his head, he laughed *again.*

She didn't recall ever seeing him laugh so much. "You're a happy guy at home."

"Something like that." Looking too hot to touch, he approached the bed. With a flare in his eyes and a strut in his step, that man was on a mission.

"Hold up." She scooted back until the headboard stopped her. "I need a shower. And a toothbrush. Preferably some makeup, but that's a long shot at the Westin residence, I'd assume."

"You're gorgeous."

"You're crazy."

"Maybe I am." He leaned forward and put his hands on the bedspread. "Get lost, Thelma."

The pooch jumped up on little legs and soared off the bed.

"I will take the fastest shower of my life. But it's gotta happen. Trust me on this one." *Such a man.* He would be all hot and interested, until he felt up her legs and got a taste of her kiss. It made her want to puke. "Bathroom?" *Was he contemplating a rebuttal? How couldn't he be convinced?* Maybe she could show a little leg and scare him off. She wrinkled her nose. "Seriously. Trust me on this one, J-dawg."

"You win. It's that door." He pointed over his shoulder.

"Razor and a toothbrush?"

"It's all in there."

Okay. I can handle using his. That seemed natural, although maybe a little too close to home since she'd had thoughts about *family* back at the hospital. Playing house was fun, but if he'd known what was in her head, he wouldn't have made that offer.

Sugar swung her legs off the bed, then scurried for the shower. He would be waiting for her, and lust surged through her blood as she slammed a door between them. Lust and like. She really liked him. Even his dog. His bedroom. Probably his whole house. She liked his weapon choices and how he stashed them. She liked how he smiled and laughed when no one but her could see. More reasons to run. But she didn't want to. Not yet. Not when playing house felt so—

Sugar melted against the wall and stared at the shower.

Knock, knock.

She jumped away from the door, her hand automatically going for her concealed weapon, which wasn't there. *Old habits die hard.* "Yeah?"

"Everything okay? Need anything?"

She flushed the toilet. "Yeah, haven't been awake in a while. Had to pee." Much better to confess that instead of admitting her imagination had just walked that man down the aisle.

What? Wait. What? Her thoughts were moving from one major life moment to the next. Family. Marriage. That wasn't her. It sure wasn't him. She needed to get her head in gear, or all their great sex and all his babblings about how he'd caught her would turn into wilted memories.

She slapped the shower spigot to as hot as she could handle and slunk in, embarrassed that her mind had betrayed her.

CHAPTER TWENTY-SIX

Jared closed his front door and turned around to see Sugar standing in the hallway near the stairs, with nothing but a towel wrapped tightly around the swell of her breasts and barely covering her hips. *So damn beautiful.*

"Who was that?" She pushed strands of wet hair off her shoulder.

His eyes followed a trail down the slope of her neck. *Bet she tastes fresh and clean and smells like soap. My soap. In my towel, after showering in my home.* A possessive urge filled his lungs and made his fingertips tingle to touch her just-washed skin. He swallowed the urge to walk over and claim her in ways she couldn't imagine.

"One of the guys dropped off my Expedition *after* buying me a new spark plug."

"Oh." Her cheeks flushed, but she rebounded. "All you had to do was ask. I would've returned it to you. It's not like I threw it out the window. It's in my purse. In my car, and it would be great if we could go get it sometime today."

He had no intention of leaving the house, and she certainly wasn't going anywhere without him. "Maybe tomorrow."

"Why, J-dawg?" Her voice purred. "You got plans for us today?" She tilted her head to the side, raised one eyebrow, and then toyed with the top of her towel.

Scrubbed clean, she could still look so dirty. Far too much space separated them. He crossed the room and pinned her to the wall, making a wicked grin play on her pretty face. "Guess what I have planned."

"We could play a game." Her breath tickled his neck as her lips and tongue trailed to his collarbone. "Maybe Twister. That'd be fun."

She *did* smell like his soap—and his shampoo. He hadn't even known what his shampoo smelled like until he smelled it on her. "Twister, huh?" His fingers feathered down her arms, and her skin prickled under this touch. "How is it that you're always in a towel around me?"

"I'm strategic."

"You're something, all right."

Slipping her hands beneath the hem of his shirt, she rubbed his sides and massaged his lower back. Her touch melted across his skin, making him aware that he wore clothes and she was a cotton wrap away from naked.

As her kneading fingers drove into his muscles, sharp scratches of little fingernails made his teeth seal together. He held in a ragged breath, killing the urge to sink a bite into her shoulder.

"I want to play…" She layered kisses on his chest. The sear of her lips burned through his shirt. "A game."

Oh, the games I could play. "I don't like to lose."

"Neither do I."

"Just 'cause you're dream-come-true material, sexiest thing I've ever touched, tasted, I won't let you win."

Her fingers followed the back of his jeans to the front button, and bursts of sensations torpedoed across his skin. She rose on tiptoes and let her bottom lip drag across the base of his neck. "You promise?"

"Don't you want to know the game, Baby Cakes?"

Sugar pushed her hips forward, pressing against his swollen cock. All the blood in his body had gone there, throbbing and craving Sugar. He did his best not to drop his pants and yank that teasing towel.

It would be so easy to burrow deep inside her, to fuck until relief poured free. He needed it. *They* needed it, and the fire in her eyes said nothing about getting her warmed up. With every pouty sigh, every groan and moan, lick and kiss, she told him to   get   a   move   on.

"Long as those strong hands are playing with me, I don't care what our game is." She molded her soft torso against his. "Challenge me."

His mouth watered at how wet she had to be under that towel, and the irregular beat of his heart failed to normalize, knowing that soon enough, silken strokes of her tight pussy would coax him into oblivion. It'd been too long since he'd felt her come on his shaft and since he'd heard sweet cries fall from her tongue.

He tried for a deep breath, but she stole a kiss that sucked the air out of his soul. He was a goner. But she wanted a game, and a fun one percolated in the back of his mind—a challenge that would make her body *and mind* go into overdrive. It would make her vision blur with lust and maybe even prove that he respected her as much as he craved her. The perfect game for a firearm fanatic like Sugar.

On a deep exhale, he stepped back and smiled as she gawked at the canyon of space between them. "Go get dressed."

Reaching to him, she splayed her fingers across his stomach in a mixture of pushing him away and pulling him close. "Excuse me?"

"You wanted a game."

"I wanted sex, maybe with a little slap and tickle. Wasn't that clear?"

"Crystal. Move your sweet ass, Sugar."

Shocked, she stood there with her jaw gaping. It slapped shut, and her pink lips curled into a smirk. "No."

"I don't hear no very often." Stepping back into her space, he pressed his T-shirt to her towel until they couldn't back up any farther. The gentle thud of her shoulders flattening against the wall made her smile less of a snipe and more of a "Thank you, let's get back to the sex." He ducked his hand under the towel to caress her perfect behind. "Do you ever do what you're told?"

She shook her head.

Such a naughty girl. So much fun.

He parted the towel and slid his other hand down her warm stomach, letting his fingers graze the mound between her legs. "You wet for me, baby?"

"That'll all change if you make me find clothes."

The hell it would. Not once you know the terms of the game. He stroked her folds, and her sweet nectar coated his touch. She was turned on, and she would stay that way. Guaranteed. If only she would get dressed so he could strip her down. One last time, he smoothed his fingers over her sweetness, closing his eyes to savor her heat.

"Hell, Jared. You can't do that."

Teasing her was so much fun. Too much. Almost. He gave her just one more stroke before he sent her packing. "I do whatever I want."

"Me, too, buddy." She tried to jut her chin in a show of classic Sugar defiance.

But defiance wasn't in the cards. He would take care of that little stunt. When he brushed his thumb over her clit, she melted and burrowed against his chest, flexing her hips to grind for more contact.

"More of that," she whispered.

It was a seesaw of reaction. He teased. She cursed. She rocked in time, and he encouraged with more pressure. The insistent will of his fingers nudged her legs open. Sugar nodded and moaned her acceptance, and with a biting kiss, he speared into her wicked tightness. "There's always consequences, Baby Cakes."

"I run my mouth, you get me off." Her rapid breaths stuttered when he worked his fingers, curving fingertips along her canal. "I'm good with that."

When the blue of her eyes wasn't lost behind scrunched lids, they were filled with an intensity that stopped his heart, then reminded him that he had a challenge to dole out. He abandoned his sexual onslaught, dragging his hands over the towel, which felt like sandpaper compared to her smoothness.

Jared scooped her into his arms. Her barely covered backside tormented his forearm, making his hair prickle to attention, but he tamped the sensation down and moved down the hall. Her feet fluttered as she kicked, making the towel ride up under her ass. The woman was near wanton as her hands fisted into his shirt.

"What are you doing?" Exasperation colored her sultry voice.

Her clean scent of bodywash and shampoo swirled with her arousal. It proved more enticing than he knew possible. "What I promised."

Sugar bucked, begging for more. The tucked-in binding of her towel loosened with the increasing pitch of her fit, until it fell undone, pinned between her backside and his forearm. Whether it had been her plan or not, she was gloriously naked, flush, and taunting him to pleasure her.

"Forget it. I can't wait."

"Sugar," he growled in warning.

She arched in his arms, swollen breasts pressing high and long slender neck dropping back. Creamy skin covered flawlessly toned muscles. She froze as his gaze raked over her, lips to tits to hips, then back again.

He shook his head, accepting his new reality. The beauty in his arms was the only one he ever again wanted to possess. "Right here, right now isn't part of the game."

"Don't care."

His mouth found her puckered nipple, and he sucked the tip hard, razzing his teeth over it until she began to murmur nonsense. Strawberry-colored lips whispered his name again, then begged. Her need drove him to the edge of control, playing with his mind and screwing with his plans, and he loved every second.

At the base of the stairs, he put her down. Such a pretty picture, she was all his. No other man would see this again. He ran his hands from her bare shoulders to the swell of her hips, caressing the full mounds of her chest along the way.

Standing like a sensual statue, she was damn persuasive about changing his plans. Jared clucked. "You think you can do whatever you want, say whatever you want."

"Yes." Her eyes danced, and she owned the moment, standing on a stair, acting like it was a pedestal, and putting herself on display for his hunger. "That's me. You like it."

I love it. But that didn't matter, not once he had his mind set on a plan. "I told you to go get dressed." He spun her around to face the staircase and draped his eyes down the sleek contours of her back to the soft curves of her rear. "Go."

He stood close enough to feel the energy pouring off her. His fingers itched to palm her butt and squeeze. *Bet her hair would feel good wrapped around my fist.* Without warning, it slapped his chin when she snapped her head and glared over her shoulder. A sharp dare flashed in her eyes. "Finish the job you started, Jared."

"One last warning, Sugar baby." He positioned against her, using the added height of the stair to his advantage. Her ass fit against his erection and felt like heaven.

"You shouldn't send a woman away who's screaming to have sex with you."

"Then you should've trusted me." Unable to control the urge any longer, he took a step to the side and let his palm smack her ass. It wasn't a warm-up slap. Not hard. Just enough to cause her to pay attention. Just enough to satisfy his impulse, but in that regard, he'd failed. Huge failure. He wanted more.

"Fuck, yes," she whispered, surprised. She obviously hadn't expected it. The rigidity in her suddenly stiff muscles and the reflex of her luscious booty told him that and so much more. Sweet Sugar sucked in a greedy breath and arched her back, priming her ass for another swat.

He would have smiled if he hadn't been too busy trying not to salivate. His palm remained on her cheek, and the warmth of the spank heated his skin. He spread his fingers, circling and soothing the spot. "We've got a game I want to play. Get some clothes on."

"But—"

Smack.

There it was again. The same breathy moan. The same arched back. Her head rolled to the side. And again, he smoothed his rough hand over her delicate skin. With his other hand, Jared undid the button on his jeans. "You're ruining my plans."

"But *now* we're getting what we both want."

Nope. Not what he wanted. Well, he *did* want this…

Smack.

Her head lolled from side to side. Her shoulder blades poked up and down like she was a prize fighter readying for more. "Again, baby. Please."

Smack. His zipper came down along with his pants and boxers, and his cock was hard and hot in his hand. "You want it rough?"

She looked over her naked shoulder again and nodded. Her wild hair curled along her neck, down her back. Blue eyes sparkled bright, highlighting the pink flush across her porcelain skin. "From you I do."

His gaze fell to the red marks he'd left on the flawless curves of her backside. Perfect body. Perfect woman. He dropped down to kiss the irritated skin, then cupped her bottom softly, massaging her cheeks after he'd kissed each angry blotch.

Sugar whispered, and his hands found her hips. His teeth grazed over her skin, and he bit down until she groaned, harder until she asked for more.

"Like that?" Still stroking himself, he kissed where he'd bitten. Teased with his tongue. Scraped with his teeth. Her skin prickled up her back.

"Get me off, Jared. I need you, too." She dropped to the stairs on her knees and perched on her elbows. Her head rocked on a step as she dug her fingers into the carpet. "Please."

Smack. "You'll get off when I say."

"Goddamn, do that again."

So he did. And again. And a third time. His fingers drifted between her legs, and she wept for him. He'd never felt her so wet. One hand was entrenched in her sweet fire. The other wrapped his shaft, holding back his impending orgasm.

Enough.

Without additional prelude, he positioned his cock against her hottest spot and drove one thrust deep. *Sweet mercy.* His eyes closed, and Sugar called his name, loud and guttural. Her muscles swallowed him, squeezing and sending shockwaves of skin-on-skin shivers down his shaft. They ricocheted into every part of his body. He'd never felt such a sensation before, and it couldn't have been better with any other woman.

"Perfect," she breathed while the same word danced in his mind. What was better than perfect? *This.*

His cock took over while his mind went on sabbatical. In, out. Thrusting and driving. Working for every delicious cry. Owning every buck she gave back. He planted one hand on her hip and let the other slide into her hair. Its silk cut through the rough callouses on his hands, and she turned her head to watch him.

"Sexiest man. Ever. And all mine." She bit her lip, and velvet muscles went ripcord tight, holding him, releasing, and building again. Her eyes slammed shut, and her canal spasmed around his cock, clenching free a release that shook her whole body in his hold.

All mine. His balls tightened. His body readied to explode as she vibrated and pulsed, riding out her climax. *Use me, baby. I'm all yours.*

And did she use him. He loved it. Loved her. Needed this. Her twisting body came so hard that it hurt before the cataclysmic euphoria hit. That was what he wanted for her. That was what she deserved—better than her best ever.

"Good girl, baby."

His molars ached, and sweat covered the nape of his neck. No more holding back. He couldn't take another second without satisfaction. Jared pulled out, stroking the last seconds until he came on her back, spurting onto her immaculate skin. *Fuckin' perfect.*

Sugar went limp against the uneven surface of his stairs. He liked her sated and relaxed. Breathing like she'd run a marathon on his dick, she pressed her forehead to the carpet until she languidly repositioned to stare at the wall. A satisfied smile hung across her lips, and then her eyes drifted shut, like she wasn't sprawled, fucked within an inch of not breathing, on his stairs.

The hallway hummed around them. He pulled up his pants and grabbed the abandoned towel from the floor. Slow and methodically, he wiped off her back, then lay on the stairs next to her, reveling in their afterglow.

His forehead touched hers, and her eyes fluttered opened. *So damn blue. Deep like the ocean.* Like she could see into his soul, they sparkled, vivid and mesmerizing. He could stare all day.

"That was amazing." Her murmur was breathy. Dreamy. "You're amazing. More than that."

Right back at you. Maybe the time had come for their little talk. She curled into his arm, and together, they stared at the ceiling.

"You cold?" He rubbed her naked skin and tucked her under his arm.

"Kinda." She jumped up without warning. "But really, I'm rejuvenated. If I get dressed, do we still have *a game* to play?"

He had to laugh. *Naked Sugar. Bouncing up and down for more.* She was always a surprise. She pulled at his arms, ready for more rough and rowdy. He stood, wrapping his arms tightly around her. *This is love, or at least the best damn part of it.* He would never find a better woman out there, and their little talk could wait if she was raring for round two already.

"Course we do."

She squealed, already running up the stairs. He thought he saw a fist pump before she rounded the corner toward his bedroom. His heart swelled, and his dick jumped. That woman rocked his world.

CHAPTER TWENTY-SEVEN

Sugar's dirty clothes lay at her feet. She poked them with her bare toe, lamenting her lack of fashion options. Re-wearing without running them through the wash wasn't going to happen, and after a few nights at Buck Baer's basement bungalow, she never wanted to see that outfit again.

In one swift pinch-and-toss, she dumped them in the bathroom trashcan and walked into the bedroom. Her boots had been discarded in the corner, but if they were just playing a game, she didn't need to pull those babies back on.

Having failed with her search-and-seize mission for a robe, she opted for a fresh towel. She eyed his chest of drawers while Thelma watched from her perch in the middle of his bed. The dog looked uncomfortable as Sugar approached the dresser. She didn't growl, but she gave Sugar a look that said, "Back the hell off. This isn't your place."

"Come on, Thelma. Thought we were friends."

Thelma groaned and buried her wrinkled face under huge paws, as if she couldn't watch the trouble Sugar was about to stumble into. Was there some kind of rule about rifling through a man's clothes? Probably, but she wasn't much for protocol.

"I'm grabbing some of your clothes," she called out the door.

No response.

So... she was going to rummage through his drawers. Not a big deal, despite the strong opinion of her four-legged companion. The worst she would find was a stash of porn. Big deal. Running across a weapon or two was far more likely. As long as the damned bureau wasn't booby-trapped, she would be okay.

Her brows pulled down, and she tapped her index finger against her chin. *Would Jared set up his personal space to detonate?* A smile pulled at her lips. *Hell yeah, he totally would.* But he also would have given her a little notice if the room had a trip wire or two.

She looked at Thelma. "If this thing is going to blow, a heads-up would be nice."

One paw allowed an eye to peek at her. No more growls or groans, though.

"Last chance, girl. If I go, you go."

Thelma snorted, and Sugar was one hundred percent positive that the dog had laughed at her.

Fine. No trip wire. But just to be safe, she grabbed an envelope off the top of the dresser and slid it carefully along the crack between the drawers. Nothing caught. No explosions or ticking time bombs activated. She inspected the back panel and didn't see anything that would make the room go *kaboom.*

"Safe," she breathed out. Thelma snorted again and it made Sugar laugh. The whole last five minutes was a laugh. She'd taken the *exploding dresser* concern too seriously and that was ridiculous... *Right?* Her fingertips tingled with excitement. A wave of adrenaline pulsed through her veins as she opened the top drawer to find... socks and underwear.

She shook the craziness out of her mind. *Paranoia much?* What was wrong with her?

Not a thing was wrong, at least in the safe confines of Jared's mega-home. Outside his brick-and-mortar safety net, where Buck Baer had a hit team canvassing neighborhoods, that was another, very bad, story.

But here, when they were about to play some kind of game, she could relax, at least as much as possible with excitement pounding through her body. *That* wasn't just the thought of trip-wired drawers. *That* was knowing J-dawg was downstairs, plotting her next orgasms.

She opened a second drawer and found undershirts, then another drawer to find sweatpants. Sweats and a T-shirt would have to do. She could wash her bra and thong later. She doubted she would need layers of clothes for whatever game he had up his sleeve.

Sugar petted Thelma's head after she pulled on her makeshift outfit, rolling the waist and knotting the shirt at its hem so she didn't drown in cotton, and went to find Jared.

Like the king of his castle, he sat at his kitchen table and looked up, his eyes slowly drifting from her bare feet to her chest. The look smoldered, and her nipples let him know, tightening to the point of being painful. "That's what you're wearing?"

Heat crawled up her neck and into her cheeks, and arousal continued its rapid descent from her banging heart straight down between her legs. A sensual soreness reminded her that he'd just taken her on the stairs, but her body was crying out for more.

He looked starved for her. His eyes narrowed and jaw flexed. Waves of sex appeal stole her breath, so much that she could hardly think. She couldn't swallow away the need to pounce and crawl all over his hard body, then lick his neck, his chest, his... everything. He could make her hot and bothered in record time, at mach speed, but he didn't need to know that. She slapped her hands on her hips and emphasized her chest and the curves of her body—everything she knew he liked. His black eyes flared. *God, he's too much fun.* "You don't like, baby?"

"I like." His gaze laser-focused on her chest. "But I can see your nipples."

His scrutiny stroked her. The kitchen's atmosphere sparked with palpable intensity. They would never make it to the game he'd planned. *Too bad, curiosity's a bitch.* "You've seen my tits before. Don't distract me with your fuck-me gaze, or we won't make it to game time."

He chuckled. His kiss-swollen lips broke into a sinful smile, showing perfect teeth that had so recently bitten and grazed her sensitive skin. She knew that mouth felt better than heaven, and she caught herself licking her bottom lip.

"You sure that's what you want to wear, pretty girl?"

"We going somewhere?" She twisted the hem of her shirt in her fingertips. She tried to control her output of energy, but she failed, and he noticed.

"Nope. Not leaving home. You ready?"

She nodded. "What's the game?"

That sinful smile morphed into one that only the devil could've created. Too erotic. Too striking. And far too knowing. "Target practice with a twist, Baby Cakes. Strip shooting."

What? She took in his shirt, jeans, belt, and boots. She knew he was wearing boxers and socks, too. Then she looked at her two-piece ensemble. "Like strip poker?"

Her mind stumbled. She hated to lose—*hated* it. Statistically, she was fucked. Why hadn't she snagged a pair of his socks and put on her boots? *Damn, damn, damn.*

Losing to him might be all incredible orgasms and hot sex, but still, it wasn't her thing. Not if she could help it, and right then, she needed to find another layer or two.

She watched his Adam's apple bob as he tilted his head, and she knew he had thought about this from the moment she'd demanded a game. "Better than strip poker, Baby Cakes."

He stood from the table and, in one Titan-sized stride, crossed over to her to grab her hand. Wasn't the first time he'd pulled that move, but every time he did, it made her a little dizzy. Hardcore Jared was a hand holder who jumped toward her as if he couldn't touch her fast enough. Her heart swelled, and any sassy comebacks fizzled when his thumbs caressed her knuckles.

"Better than strip poker…" She mirrored his words, but in a love-struck whisper. Everything was better with Jared. Didn't he know that?

She bit her lips to keep from sharing anything and everything that would ruin the moment. She had only a finite amount of time before this fantasy life would pop like a bubble, and she wanted to float in the clouds with him for as long as possible.

Hands knitted together, they headed into his garage. It was everything she would've guessed. Expansive and expensive, it housed trucks and SUVs that somehow mimicked Jared.

Tough. Dark. Mysterious. Some of the vehicles were blacked out, from windows to headlights to car emblems. Some dared her to touch the gleaming chrome, while others were jacked ceiling high with lift kits and big tires that would make a country boy cream his pants. Collectively, all intimidated at a standstill, very much like their owner.

"Come on, Sugar. Nothing to see here."

His four-wheeled assembly certainly wasn't as modest as he was.

"Take me for a ride in one of these babies." She grabbed another glance over her shoulder as he tugged her along. His steering wheels were calling her name. Gas pedals were begging for a little floor action.

He chuckled but kept moving. "All in due time."

The fabric of her shirt swayed over her breasts. His handhold gripped tighter, and she dropped the garage distractions from her mind and concentrated on strip shooting—on winning.

You can do this. She could triumph, two articles of clothes and all. He might be an amazing shot in the field, but she lined up at a range to test weapons every single day. She could handle the boring conditions of a practice lot with precision *and* finesse.

Target.

Focus.

Bull's-eye.

With Titan Group, his only job requirement was to stay alive. He could make a kill shot when needed. But kill shots weren't tests of accuracy, just effective ways to survive.

He pulled her close before they walked through a closed door. "What are you smiling at? You're about to lose."

"I'm a damn good shot. You might lose *all* your clothes before I lose either piece of mine."

An eyebrow rose. "*Either?*"

"Nothing under these pants."

"Damn," he growled and opened the door. "Welcome to my little bit of relaxation."

"Holy shit, Jared." *Talk about a dream range.* His house was tactical, but this range was beyond impressive. Technically advanced, it had every gunslinger bell and whistle she could've come up with.

"What?"

Her eyes had gone wide, and she couldn't tamp down her admiration. "Nice digs. This place is... my wet dream."

He faked heart pains, clutching at his chest, crinkling his brow. "If that's the case, I have some work to do."

She shoved his shoulder. "You know what I mean. This is sweet. This whole place is... damn, just mind blowing."

He shrugged, playing down the humongous mansion, the elite-forces firing range, and the fancy-schmancy car garage he'd just strolled them through. Humble and Jared were two words never pinned together, but there they were. His eyes twinkled, and he squeezed her hand again.

"Glad you like it." He walked them toward a table and workbench. A cloth covered the display of weapons, but she could make out the shapes of various guns. "But don't forget why you're here."

"To whip your ass. Get you naked. Then take advantage of you."

"Fat chance." His coarse laugh coated her nerves in a way that made her pray to hear it again.

"Tell me the rules, and I'll show you how I'll win."

"Pick your weapons." Like a proud papa, he beamed, taking the cover off the table, and together, they stared at the beauties that'd been lying in wait. "We'll start easy and knock it back in twenty-five-yard increments. Every time you miss dead center, you lose your clothes. Looks like it'll be a quick game."

She rocked back on her bare heels and almost came when she studied the available guns. She knew two things well: sex and guns. She loved them both. Craved their feel. Their touch. And he stood there, offering her two things that she couldn't live without.

Only Jared would combine apocalyptic sex with weapons that could make collectors drool. Rare ones. Unknowns. Military grade, elite forces only. Every one of them was special. He'd pulled every one of them from his gun vault just for her to play with. It wasn't the sex and the guns she couldn't live without. It was the man.

"Go on, Sugar. Check them out."

God love him, because I sure as hell do.

"Good Lord..." Her fingers nearly vibrated with a need to slide over the cool metal and polished wood, to handle the specialty ammo, load up, and get ready for a hot range with him by her side.

"You like?" The deep timbre crashed over her in a sensual wave. It flooded her senses until all she could focus on was the firepower and the anticipation of violent explosions. "Sugar, baby?"

She nodded, her heart pounding to pull the triggers. "I like."

He stepped closer. A wall of warm muscle pressed against her back, and he wrapped his arms around her, to grab a Golden Desert Eagle in front of her. "Now this beauty." He took her hand in his and ran it down the barrel, smoothing her fingers against the polished gunmetal. "It packs a punch. Gotta hold it real tight. Because when it explodes..." He abandoned her fingers wrapped round the weapon to caress her wrist, crawling up her forearm.

Fireworks ignited as he trailed slowly. The hair on her arm stood, her skin prickled, and a swirling of need pooled between her legs. Jared moved to her shirt, his palm teasing her breast. "You feel the reverberations across your chest." He tweaked her nipple through the shirt. "All the way to here."

He dropped his hand and closed the minute distance between their bodies. His erection pressed against her backside, and he flexed his hips. Once. Twice. *Oh, hell...*

Her heart pounded. Jared's plan to win included a vicious lesson in the art of distraction. It *was* working, her concentration *was* slipping, and she tried to compartmentalize her arousal. "I know what it feels like to shoot a high-powered handgun."

"Do you now? How about this one?" He reached farther onto the display table, crushing against her. His breath tickled her ear, and, compartmentalization be damned, a full body shiver rocked from the nape of her neck to her toenails. His motives were clear. Caging her between his hard-on and a battery of firepower was a move only he knew would be so effective.

Her eyelids fluttered shut, and she absorbed the moment. His every muscle had muscles. He personified safety and security—an impenetrable force, designed to be solid and wide, ripped top to bottom. His sinewy strength was so evident that she didn't even need to look to see his sheer power. She could feel it all the way to her core.

His cock pressed through the rough fabric of his pants and the soft cotton of hers. His hips grazed her sore cheeks, sparking vivid memories of him slapping her until she came. The memory and friction made her moan, arching against his touch.

He bit her earlobe as he brought an assault rifle from the far edge of the table. "Feeling it now, aren't you, baby? You'll think of me every time you sit down, stand up. Every time you shimmy into those tight leather pants you wear. That soreness will burn, and you'll be wet for me."

She took a deep breath and locked her gaze to the rifle. "That's an M4 Carbine. Gas operated. Magazine fed. Selective fire."

He bit her lobe again, then trailed his lips down her neck. His tongue flicked out, and his teeth nibbled. "Smart girl. You're on to my game. I'll do whatever it takes to distract you."

"Whatever it takes?"

"No matter how good a shot you are, you can't hit bull's-eye creaming yourself, shaking for your next climax." He took her hands again, gliding them over the textured grip of the impressive rifle. "So much power. Almost too much kickback for a little girl like you to handle. But I bet you can tame this beast."

"Course I can." Her pulse pounded erratically. Her lungs burned as if he'd squeezed her breathless.

"Of course you can," he mimicked in a whisper that made her pussy shout for attention.

"I'm onto your distraction techniques, Jared."

He ignored her words, but not her body.

"You hold it here." His fingers lagged across her chest, massaging each perky mound. The sensation made her womb clench. Just as her ragged breaths sounded more like gasps, he moved on and arrived at the sweet spot where she would press the butt of a rifle.

"Now you're just trying to drive me crazy."

"With every little noise you try to hide from me, Sugar, I know it's working."

He lingered, teasing her control, then went lower, to the hem of the too-big shirt, and ducked under to press against her bare skin. Calloused hands roughly fanned over the width of her stomach, drawing circles around her belly button.

"Might be working," she whispered. "A little."

"A little, huh?" His hand slipped beneath the rolled waistband of her pants, and then he took his time, paying homage to the parts of her that begged for his devotion. "When you pull the trigger, I bet you'll feel it here, where you're already so sweet, so swollen, and so goddamn soaked."

"This isn't fair, Jared." Her betraying body abandoned her I'm-going-to-win attitude and rocked in motion with his hand, against the friction that she needed. If he would only give her just a little more. *A little more...*

His deep laugh rumbled against the top of her ear. "Didn't say anything about this game being fair, Baby Cakes."

Come on, Sugar. You can do this. She prayed her game face wasn't a joke and sucked in a pathetic breath, wriggling out of his hold. "Let's put lead downrange."

A suggestive smile tugged at his cheeks. "Love when you talk guns. It's almost as good as when you talk dirty."

She squeezed her legs together, but the pulsing need didn't disappear. "Prepare to lose, Jared."

"We'll see." He selected a custom .45 and walked to a waiting target. With a wink, he casually took a shot. It hit far off course. "Damn, whoops." He tore off his shirt with one hand and tossed it at her.

Ass... But what a chest. Broad and chiseled. Perfectly formed. Huge gun hanging in his hand and a cocky smile dangling off his face, he looked like an action hero.

"You're staring." He stretched, on purpose for sure.

She'd seen him without a shirt often enough that it shouldn't have affected her like that. Her eyes trailed from the fantastic planes of his shoulders and lingered over the smattering of dark, coarse hair that disappeared behind the fly of his pants.

"You missed that on purpose."

He tilted his head. "Looks like my strategy is working."

Following his gaze, she looked at her hands. They were practically trembling. *Can he see that? No way.* He was in her head, though, and his game *was* working. "Nah. No chance, Boss Man."

"Bullshit, pretty girl."

Throwing back her shoulders, holding her chin high, she smirked and took the gun from him. "I'll shoot whatever you shoot. And I'll hit better than you."

Oh, Sugar, tough talk when you're losing your mind. There was a serious chance that one wild kiss would make her fall apart in climax. She was too high-strung and too turned on.

He leaned back against a wall and watched. The scrutiny worked over her body, wrapping around her as though he was swaddling her in rough velvet. *Ignore him.*

She took aim at her target and ordered her breaths to regulate, but they ignored her. Instead, she zoned out and fought to find their irregular pattern. The concentration, the desire to win, burned almost as much as the need for his touch.

She shoved her earplugs in as Jared's mouth started moving. She knew he was talking, taunting. If she wanted, she could've heard him, but she decided to block him out. Her finger caressed the sleek trigger, and the surrounding world dissolved into a haze.

Sugar pictured the shot. She melded with the weapon. Dead center was hers for the taking.

Steady and... *fire.*

Center target, destroyed. A whoosh of breath flew from her lips, and her hands shook. "See, J-dawg? Easy."

He hit a button on the wall. The targets flew up, and he replaced them with fresh ones. With another punch of the button, they zoomed back, much farther than twenty-five yards. He snagged a Ruger P95 from the table. "You game?"

"Always." Her voice sounded a lot more sultry than she'd meant it to. *Good.*

He rolled his head, cracking his neck as he drew up to the line. His back was tan. Muscles cascaded down, creating a beautiful column of masculine splendor. She wanted to kiss him and walk her hands down his back to feel how—a brilliant thought worked into her hormone-overloaded brain. *She* should distract *him* this time.

She slinked behind him and looped her fingers into his belt loops. She still wanted to taste the salt of his skin and drink in his delicious scent, and she would, but her motives were more tactical than need-driven. But not by much.

Jared pulled an earplug out of one ear and turned to look over his shoulder. "You mind?"

"Just ignore me." Her tongue ran down the length of his shoulder blade. "Playing offense, if *you* don't mind."

She licked again and saw a chill prickle his skin. Her hand smoothed on his heated flesh. Her fingernails scratched his stomach, and she made a fist around the buckle of his belt.

"I can shoot like this. No problem." He didn't sound as confident as his words.

"So do it, tough guy."

She felt him ready for the shot, knew when he was about to pull the trigger. Three, two, one. He pulled the trigger as her hand dropped and cupped his length through his pants.

The shot hit off target, and that time, he *had* been trying. She giggled.

"Not fair, Baby Cakes."

"Oh, life's not fair." She undid the buckle of his pants and pulled. Every time the tail end of the belt skipped through a loop, it made a noise that echoed in the charged air between them. "I like strip shooting."

Their game went back and forth. He shot, dead center. She shot, dead center. A miss and a miss. Her shirt was gone. He'd kicked off both boots and socks when he'd missed outside the tiny center ring.

And they were tied. Her rolled sweatpants to his tented boxer shorts. As he readied to shoot, her mind raced. Arousal and adrenaline flooded her senses, scorching her body. She'd never been so turned on.

Shirtless and with his baggy pants hanging on her hipbones, she brushed behind him, purposely rubbing her bare breasts against his back.

"Tease," he said, sounding unaffected.

"Throw the game, Jared. Take the loss and then take me. I can't wait."

"Hush, pretty girl. Won't go down that easy."

"I'll go down that easy." She laughed, amused that the line had come to her. "Don't you want my mouth around you?"

His concentration could melt gunmetal. He wasn't listening or half-assing it. Her mind raced. Everything about them. About that moment. About how he'd put the game together just for her. She shook with a want for him that she couldn't control. Her fantasies about their future together had felt so right, but then he irritated the piss out of her, ignoring her half-naked body. *So he could what? Win?* Hell. That was exactly why.

No man in the world could compete with Jared. No man could compare, and she was done playing games.

With his finger pulling the trigger, she couldn't keep her mouth shut another thousandth of a second. "I love you."

The bullet pinged far, far off target, thudding downrange. She didn't even know where it had hit. He whirled around, jaw clenched. His eyes narrowed, *distracted.*

Mission accomplished. But she didn't give a fuck about winning anymore. She loved him, and the time had come to tell him. *To hell with the consequences. Fuck him if he walks away because he doesn't like to hear it.*

"Excuse me?"

She stood taller. "You heard me."

"You toss that bomb out to win a game?"

"Couldn't keep it in anymore. I'm done with this game. Question is, are you done with me?"

He narrowed his eyes and tilted his head just a degree. "Why the hell would I be done?"

"Don't hear you saying sweet nothings back, stud. I get it. But some things have to be said. So there you go."

"There you go?" The energy in the room electrified, with zips and zings rocketing around, but scarring and startling in their intensity.

"Fun game, though." Ready to get out before he got mad, she reached for her T-shirt. His hand caught her wrist. She looked at his knuckles, then his eyes, but she couldn't get a read on them.

"You should already know that I'd chase you to the end of the world. Don't run from me now."

He's going to spout that kind of shit? Either he loved her, or he didn't. If he did love her, he would've said it when the chance was there, but he'd let it pass. Despite knowing that she'd forced his hand, it hurt. Her eyes stung, but she refused to cry in front of him. "I gotta go—"

With her shirt clutched in her hand, Jared forced her knuckles toward his face. His full lips found her fist. Not taking his eyes off her, he laid the gentlest kisses she'd ever experienced across her clenched knuckles. "Don't run from me."

"I'm not." Her voice shook.

"You are. Have been from day one." He kissed her wrist, then her forearm, slowly reeling her closer to him. "I won't hurt you. I promised you that."

He'd said nothing about how he felt. Her stomach sank, and the mist threatening her eyes transformed into fat tears, which she refused to let fall. "I can't help who I love."

"Neither can I, Baby Cakes."

What? What does that mean? The bastard can't communicate worth a shit. His tongue was too busy swirling across her skin. He'd given up her wrist and jumped ship to her neck. His mouth worked a lot considering that he'd explained zip. "What are you talking about?"

"I've loved you since before I knew what it was to love a woman."

She shook her head. "You're in love with me?"

"You're surprised?"

Her mouth hung open. She was surprised. Relieved. Happy.

He lifted from her neck, placed both his hands on her shoulders, and held her outright. "Hell, had I known that you'd be stunned silent by a simple truth, I would've said it awhile back."

But what did that mean for their future? Maybe she needed to take it one monumental leap at a time. "Say it again."

A one-sided grin lit up his face. "Say what?"

She batted his chest. "Don't play with me, Jared Westin."

"Oh, Baby Cakes. I will play with you as much as I want." He smoothed his hands up and down her biceps, then pulled her in, wrapping his thick arms around her neck. She used them as a pillow, leaned back, and stared up, losing herself in the depths of his emotion. The cocky grin had been replaced by something deeper. "I love you, Sugar. You're mine. That's about as real and honest as it gets. Not sure that either of us had a choice. Life presents facts, and this is one. I was born to be with you. Hell, I only existed before I chased you down. Held you to me. Made you love me. And now I *live*."

CHAPTER TWENTY-EIGHT

Buck leaned back in his chair and pressed an ice pack to his forehead. His skin twitched under the cold burn. His adrenaline had long since drained away, leaving him feeling unsteady, unsure of his next move. Fieldwork wasn't his thing anymore, and giving commands had been much easier.

Find Sugar. Kill Jared.

But reality was, his GI Joe and Jane were probably together, plotting and planning, and as much as he wanted to downplay Titan Group as a threat, that wasn't smart. He was smart— smarter than smart. Some genius-level thoughts played out in his brain. That was how and why GSI had become so successful.

He had to think, even as his ears still rang and his muscles cried out for more Aspercreme after the scuffle yesterday. *Damn Jared and his team for blasting through my mountain compound.* Checking the small disk in his pocket, Buck smiled. At least he'd escaped with all of Titan's mainframe on disk. As soon as he had the energy, he would open up those files and begin Titan's corporate destruction, client by client. Golden boy Jared wouldn't know what had hit his sparkling reputation.

Jared. Titan. Jared. Titan. Buck was practically obsessed. He rolled forward in his chair and scrounged for headache medicine of any kind. An empty bottle of Tums didn't help. *Don't I pay people to keep this stuff stocked?*

His text-message alert shrieked in his ear. Finding three rogue Tylenol in his desk drawer, he swallowed them dry and grabbed the phone. *Found the kid. Children's hospital.*

Who the hell cares? He didn't. Not about the kid, or Brock's family, or even Sugar. She was a means to an end.

He wasn't concerned anymore that she could bring down his GSI empire. But Sugar had become so much more than an intelligence leak.

From Brock's snide remarks about the Jared-Sugar connection and her backhanded way of asking and answering questions about the GSI-Titan relationship, Buck could tell that Jared had done the unthinkable. He'd coupled up with the chick.

That made Sugar a powerful weapon. Destroying her meant destroying Jared. It was that simple.

Buck laughed, exacerbating the pounding in his temples. Jared was stupid enough to fall in love, showing his Achilles heel to the world. Buck hadn't seen that gem coming, but he couldn't have been more thrilled for the leverage.

His phone rang. The noise was so much louder than the text-message alert. His every muscle hurt, from his fingers to his trapezoids, as he reached for the thing, finally silencing the ringtone as he accepted the call. "What?"

His man gave him a rundown. The kid was sicker than they'd originally realized. *Big deal. Don't care.* Brock's family was with Titan. But he was betting that wouldn't last long, not since Buck coerced Brock into joining team GSI.

"Tell me something useful," he grumbled.

The man hesitated, like he had a sliver of doubt. "Sugar has a sister who's been running GUNS for the last few weeks."

"Round up your team. Get me eyes on the sister."

Jared's eyes were closed, and his body buzzed. Every part of him was alive. He was aware of every muscle every time the air shifted as Sugar breathed, sighed, or stirred. Every time his heart panged, it took him a while to figure out what the sensation was.

And his soul… hell, he could feel his soul, and not in a burn-in-hell kind of way. The feeling was more like everything in life had been just wasting time until he could get to this moment, with a sated Sugar wrapped around him in his bed, which   he   was   going   to   make   *their*   bed.

He combed his fingers through her soft, raven tangles of hair. Her wicked case of bedhead fell across her shoulders, tickling his bare chest.

He was in deep. And love wasn't so bad. He'd never been interested in a relationship before, but typical of his style, if he was going to do it, he was going to do it right.

"We should talk." He rolled onto his side and kept her pressed to his body. Cupping her chin, he forced her gaze to his.

Her pupils dilated. And a tight, little wrinkle above the bridge of her nose told him she was of the opinion that he should shut up. *No can do, sweetheart.*

"Nope. Not right now." A sassy little smile played on her swollen lips. Their rosier color turned him on all over again, and he could taste their sweetness.

He'd kissed the hell out of this woman, only stopping because they'd both been exhausted to the point of limp legs and arms, lungs that ached for a breath, and minds that needed to settle before another round of muscle-shaking, mind-bending climaxes.

She shook her head in an exhausted move that was barely discernible, and she languidly pressed a kiss to his shoulder. "Whatever you're going to say will ruin my moment. I'm basking, so keep it to yourself, J-dawg."

As he shifted in the sheets, the scratches on his back burned from where her fingernails had clawed. "I know I'm not Romeo and all, but I'm not going to ruin any damn moment."

"Romeo?" She scoffed, giggling. "Romeo died, stud. Not a good ending. All your I-love-ya stuff earlier was good enough for me. Leave it be."

He smoothed the pad of his thumb over her flushed cheek. Her eyelashes fluttered. That was the kind of reaction he wanted, so he did it again. "Sugar, you don't want more?"

The fluttering eyelashes slammed shut, then opened wide. Sugar blinked once, twice, and then avoided his face, bouncing her gaze from the ceiling to the headboard to the pillow behind his head.

"Sugar?" He knew what he wanted and believed to his very core that he knew what she wanted. But was she done running? With a sharp slice, her piercing eyes landed back on him. They were searching, trying to trust. He could feel her conjuring confidence in their relationship. A tingle ran from his scalp down his spine, radiating into every neuron, firing every synapse.

"Do you want more?" she whispered, and her uncharacteristic softness killed him, making his chin snap up and his chest thrust out.

Both were shocking reactions for a man who lived and died by his ability to control his body under any stress or circumstance. Determination flooded his senses. What had gone wrong before they'd met that would still cloud her judgment, after everything they'd shared and everything he'd said? Where had all the mistrust come from? She loved him, for God's sake.

Shaking her wouldn't do a bit of good. Convincing or conniving would be big failures, as well.

Instead, he closed the space between them, pulling her tighter, needing to feel the touch of her skin, needing... just needing her.

Do you want more? How could that still be a question? "Fuck yes, I do. I'm not gonna love someone, and—"

Ring. Ring. Ring.

Jared's eyes popped. The vein at his temple pulsed, and his fingers flexed against her, willing his phone to stop ringing. It didn't, and there was too much happening in their world to throw the thing out the window.

"This conversation isn't done." He leaned back, grabbed it off his nightstand, and checked the caller ID. *Nope, couldn't be ignored.* "Better be good, Rocco."

Rocco wouldn't have called unless it was important, not after Jared had put out the do-not-disturb command. He had told his team that unless life or limb was on the line, they needed to give him a day to recoup with Sugar.

Their conversation was brief. As he hung up the phone, Jared again gathered Sugar into his arms. He pressed the phone into her hand. "Jenny is fine, but give her a phone call."

Her mouth gaped, and she pressed her palm against his chest, her fingernails biting his flesh as she flexed her fingers. "My sister? What..." Tense and furious, she gathered the sheet around her breasts. "Why?"

Jared chose his words carefully. "She's fine. Tell her you're okay. We had to get her out of GUNS, and she wasn't—"

"What's going on?" Sugar spit her question, and he could almost see how hard it was for her to swallow the anxiety.

He dropped his voice an octave and willed her to listen. "She's fine, baby. Roman's taking her someplace safe."

Her fear disappeared from her face. "What *is* going on?"

"The guys saw something out of place, and Roc's checking it out."

"There's a Titan team at GUNS?" She pressed the phone to her ear.

He nodded. "Yes, I put a team on your sister."

"Phone's still ringing." She pinched her brow and moved restlessly under the covers.

He very much wanted to take away all of her problems. "Give her a second."

She grimaced, closing in on herself. "She's in danger because of me?"

"Baer's a vengeful ass. Not sure if he wants you more because you're mine or because of the threat you pose. We don't know how he'll find you. I've tried to cover a few bases, and I had figured your sister and GUNS were high priority."

"No answer. Voicemail." Sugar chewed her lip before leaving a message.

"Sugar—"

She struggled with the sheets. "Why wouldn't she answer her phone?"

"Sug—"

"She always answers that damn phone." Her fingers danced against the phone's SEND button, as though she were scared to redial.

Jared cupped her chin. Sugar was drowning in an internal battle. He knew her well enough to know both sides: wanting to be tough versus shying away from the gut-twisting, scared-shitless routine that came along with a loved one being in danger.

He should have known that routine well because he had just lived through it. "We got this, Sugar. No worries."

She threw the phone on the bed and glared at it. "Roman just forced my sister out of GUNS. She's probably scared to death and has no idea what's happening. Bring me to her."

"Can't right now. I have to go to GUNS."

Resolve painted her face. "So bring me there."

He didn't want to take Sugar into the action, but he couldn't lock her in a safe room, either. She wouldn't go willingly, and she wouldn't stay put. If he was planning to tie Sugar up, he wanted to stick around.

They slid out of bed, and for the first time in his life, he wished that life was normal. No saving the day. No concerns about death threats. No snipers or kill teams searching for Sugar. Just loving his woman, petting his dog, and manning his house. Simple.

Sugar walked toward his dresser, and he liked that she'd learned her way around. Her hair curled, ignoring her as she raked fingers through it. Her bottom was still pink from before. And when she looked at him, he wanted to beat his chest, stomp his feet, and holler to the world that she belonged to him.

"Thank God I keep spare clothes in my office. Got a comb in this place?"

He shook his head. If his hair got past a tight clip, he just buzzed it again. "Right, because we'll have time to work on your wardrobe."

"J-dawg dropping jokes. What comes next?" She opened his drawers and pulled out fresh clothes.

What comes next? First comes love, then comes marriage... Figure it out, woman.

Her makeshift outfit was too big and fit ridiculously. She rolled the waist of his sweatpants so they barely hung over her hipbones and then cuffed them at the ankles. Next she pulled on a white T-shirt. All he could focus on was her tits and the dark outlines of her nipples behind the cotton. "Nuh-uh. No white shirts for you. Find something else."

She checked the mirror and laughed. "Whoopsie."

"Whoopsie, my ass."

Somewhat satisfied that she could leave his house and not bare her goods to the world, he pulled on his tactical gear.

She watched as he strapped weapons into holsters, then double- and triple-checked his ammo supply. The process was nearly scientific. He could don enough gear to be a one-man unit in less than thirty seconds.

"This isn't a fluke, is it?" Concern etched her voice. "GSI is at GUNS, and there was a threat to my sister."

"Rocco is at GUNS, Jenny is fine, and I prepare for the worst case." He snagged a Beretta stashed behind his dresser. "Not sure where you're going to put this thing, but take it until we get there. Then arm yourself up. Deal?"

"I could—"

"Not playing, Sugar. It's your place. Your sister. I get that. But you have a history of running off and getting into trouble. Stay where I tell you. Agree now, or you stay home, tied to the bed, and that's a damn shame to walk out on."

Rolling her eyes, she waggled her head. "Agree. Agree. I'll behave."

They turned and walked toward the hall, and a spike of adrenaline shot through his system. Bringing Sugar into danger sucked on so many levels. Something could go wrong. She might do her own thing anyway. Maybe hell would turn arctic, and she would stay put, but things could still go wrong. A nasty headache cropped up. If he left her at home, he would be too far away if this was a set up.

Damn it. He slapped the wall as they rounded the corner for the stairs.

Her eyes peeled wide. "What's the matter?"

He kissed her. Hot and heady, his tongue moved over hers. She tasted so sweet; he might never be able to stop. But he made himself. *No time for this.* Breaking the kiss, she went slack in his arms, sighing as he pressed a kiss to her forehead, then her temple. He hugged her tightly.

"If something goes wrong," he whispered, shaking his head. "I can't live without you. Do you get that? I will do whatever it takes to end this with Baer. To protect you. Your sister. Your family. Whatever—"

"I don't have family. I have a sister."

"Okay. Not my point." He paused. "I need you to survive this hurdle because I want a future with you. I'm not a flowers-and-love-songs type guy, but I've got shit to say and no time to say it. So if you know anything else, know this. I love you. You're the reason for my beating heart, sweet Sugar. Once we kick Buck Baer's fuckin' ass, I promise you, I'll spell it out. Have it written in the sky or tattooed on my arm. Whatever it takes, you'll know it, believe it, breathe it, just like me. I love you."

"I *do* love you, Jared."

"I know you do. And now you know it's more than just a feeling. It's a way of life."

Their hands found each other, her Beretta clasped in one, and they moved toward the door. He was ready to end his blowout with Baer. By the day's end, Baer would know Jared's wrath firsthand.

CHAPTER TWENTY-NINE

Sugar watched Jared as he drove. He was so focused on his mission that she worried his jaw would shatter. Jared drove with one hand on the wheel, the other hand placed firmly on her knee as though he were holding her in place.

Her mind was already sprinting. Her legs felt the need to do a fifty-yard dash. Running was foremost on her mind. But she wasn't sure if Jared thought she would run from him or to GUNS.

She sure wasn't going to jump out of a speeding truck while it was barreling down the highway. But his grip above her knee never lessened, and it wasn't a sweet I-wanna-hold-you clutch. It was possessive, protective, and powerful. It strangled away her nerves and concern for Jenny, just as it had her worries for Asal.

When Jared was on duty, the logical response would be to relax and trust that everything would go according to his plan. But she couldn't. Her mouth tasted as though she'd sucked on the loose change in his console. Acrid and alkaline. Adrenaline coated the inside of her mouth, wrapped down her throat, and shredded her heart.

When Jared pulled into the parking lot at GUNS, Sugar's Mustang was sitting in its spot. Thanking Jared for retrieving it seemed so trivial. With a crunch of gravel, Jared slid his truck into a parking space. Another blacked-out vehicle was parked toward the end of the lot, and as Sugar narrowed her eyes to stare through its tinted windows, Rocco got out and advanced toward Jared's truck.

Both men had the faces of warriors. She'd known Roc for a while, but even in Afghanistan, she'd never seen him so ready to tangle with the devil. His eyes reached toward them like beams of dark fire. His jaw, very much like Jared's, looked chiseled out of granite.

Instinctively, Sugar clutched her rolling stomach. Her throat ached. More bad news was on its way, and that realization was strong enough to make her eyes burn with the need to cry.

She might not be Titan level—her undercover work with the ATF had been mostly intel and research—but she knew that crying wasn't going to make her mess go away. It wouldn't make Jenny answer her phone or ease the death grip on her insides.

Jared squeezed her leg, his thumb softening and smoothing back and forth. The motion was so simple and so needed. Without knowing it, he'd ordered her tears to stand down and made her mind focus.

"Sugar, whatever Rocco says, we'll handle."

"Sure," she lied.

Everything was going to be hunky-dory. Maybe if she said that aloud, she might believe it, too. Her leg began to bounce. Jared made a living off bad news, and she was unable to keep still. He would take whatever Rocco said, decide how to react, then execute a plan.

It was what he did. It was respectable. Commendable.

He did so to survive. But right then, she wished he would look at her and say, "Wake up, Sugar. You had a nightmare. Buck Baer never targeted your sister or GUNS." But no matter how hard she willed it, he didn't say anything. Instead, he clicked the window button.

As the tinted glass rolled down, soft twilight spilled into the truck cab. It did little to soften the hard edges on Jared's or Rocco's faces, and none of the tension was released with the infusion of fresh air.

Jared lifted his chin in greeting. "What do we know, Roc?"

"Roman took Jenny off-site. She's fine."

Jared looked at her. "See? Fine."

Yeah,   everything   is   just   fine.

Rocco continued, "GSI's on the perimeter. They had one man on the inside. Roman handled that headache on his way out. Parker picked up two heat signatures on the perimeter. GSI's good, but not undetectable. They're dropping transmission signals we've picked up. Bottom line, Buck Baer is nearby, but too chicken-shit to be onsite."

The faint taste of blood registered on her tongue, and the inside of her cheek was raw from gnawing her nerves silent. An exasperated tidal wave swept from her gut to her lips, and just like when she'd tried to smother her earlier declaration of love, she couldn't keep her trap shut. "If Jenny's safe, then go find Buck already. Finish this."

Jared shifted in his seat. "Sugar." His eyes bored into hers, cascading a wild ambush of goose bumps from her scalp to her hips. "Take out the emotion. Assess. React. That's our plan. Got it?"

"No, I don't." The hairs on her arms were at full attention. She was a bowl full of reaction and had no interest in assessing anything. *Go, go, go,* her panic chanted in her head. The sooner Titan wiped the floor with GSI, the sooner life would normalize. "I'm not a machine, Jared, and I'm running on adrenaline. I want this over with already."

"Love you, Baby Cakes. But calm it down and do as you're told." He turned his head to Rocco but kept his handhold on her.

Wide eyes. Raised brows. Hanging lips. Roc's priceless face had to be the results of hearing J-dawg choke out something like, "love you." But he pulled it together faster than Jared could tell him to stop the theatrics.

Jared scanned the mirrors. "Where's our team?"

"Cash has the perimeter." Rocco cleared his throat. "As does Brock. Nicola stayed with Asal."

The truck vibrated as Jared registered his words. "Back up and repeat." His words were intermixed with a growl. Sugar shivered at the overwhelming hostility in his voice. She wanted to slink back from the volcanic eruption readying to blow.

Rocco's lips formed a thick line. "I had to. Even with Winters covering the back entrance, we needed Brock. We needed manpower."

"He's a fuckin' traitor." Jared's fingers flexed into Sugar's leg.

"He's manpower, and he messed up. Deal with him later however you need to. We need his eyes and trigger finger right now."

Slapping the steering wheel with his freehand, Jared growled, "Goddamn it!"

"Delta Team's here, too."

"Fine." He gave a slight nod of approval. "I'll deal with Brock and your decisions later."

Rocco nodded and backtracked into GUNS.

Delta Team? What the hell is that? She wanted to hate Brock. She wanted Jared to destroy the bastard. But she'd known Brock for a while, and in a way, he was like Jared. Analytical. Emotionless. But she'd seen Jared lose his cool, spout romantic truths, and talk about the future. What if Brock was in the same situation? What if Brock couldn't see another way out and panic had driven him to a mistake?

Still, she could never forgive him for handing her to Buck Baer. But if Brock felt love the way Sugar felt love, then, in a backward, screwed-up way, she understood, because nothing in the world would keep her sane if she lost Jared. She shook her head, snapping back to reality when Jared's phone rang.

He snapped his fingers at Rocco, who spoke to a mic on his wrist. Rocco nodded back, and Jared accepted the call. "Baer, how am I not surprised a pussy like you would use women and children so often? Just when I thought you were the bottom of the shit-can, you take it down another notch." He shook his head. "Man up, dick. Show yourself, and let's do this."

He let go of Sugar's leg, and a wicked grin worked across his face. Jared was in the zone. This was his element, and he was good. Calm. Relaxed. Antagonizing. Exactly what he needed to be to provoke Buck Baer and let Titan, and whoever the hell Delta Team was, make life a-okay again.

He shook his head and gave a hand signal to Rocco, who powered into GUNS. "No go, Baer. But here's my counter—"

She could hear Buck yelling into the phone but couldn't make out the words. Jared reached over and squeezed her shoulder, mouthing, "It's okay." And she believed him. She felt it in her gut, which given the copper-penny taste she'd had in her mouth five minutes ago, was unexpected.

He laughed harshly. "Wrong again. Let me explain something to you. You might have used one of my men against me, but your trust was blind. That flash stick you gave Brock? You think you hacked Titan, but you didn't do anything but give me access to GSI."

There was a long pause interrupted by Buck's garbled barks.

Jared slowly shook his head. "My tech genius is better than GSI's. Here's how it's going to go. Show up in the next ten minutes. If you don't, every US Government-funded lie and cover-up will be e-mailed to Congress."

Buck started in again, and Sugar wished she could tell what he was saying.

Jared cut him off. "Better than that, it'll hit the inboxes of every reporter, from the *New York Times* to the *LA Times*. I know you, man. You love yourself too much. Your ego's too big to take this hit."

Jared paused, bounced eyebrows at Sugar, and cracked a knuckle against the steering wheel. He loved this back-and-forth routine. She couldn't wrap her head around it, but she understood him, so it all made sense—enough sense to give her a migraine, but sense, nonetheless. Sugar pinched her eyes shut. This relationship-connection mumbo jumbo was deeper than she'd realized.

He continued, "And if it could get any worse, Baer, then here it is. If you don't show up, I will personally make sure that every cartel king, every arms dealer, every fuckin' person you've ever made a buck off, knows who you are, where you live, and that you like eating cock for dinner. You've got eight minutes by my count. Show up, and may the best man win."

He hung up the phone and, with a cocky grin, threw it on the dash. "And that's how it's done."

"I don't know what to say." Never had her mind drawn a blank. This combination of tactical ability and psy-ops had stunned her speechless.

"Nothing to say. Let's go inside." He opened his door, then turned back and caught her wrist. She slid hard into an embrace of ripped muscles and weaponry. "There's nothing I wouldn't do for you. Trust me, and this will be over soon."

She nodded.

"You trust me?"

"Yeah."

"You love me?"

"I love you." Sugar sucked in a deep breath, not wanting to leave the confines of his truck tucked under his arm. "Damn it, Jared, you act like this isn't a big deal. You told me to stay alive, and you better do the same."

He pulled back and leveled her with confidence that made his eyes twinkle. "Piece of cake."

"I'm serious. You die, and I will never forgive you."

He nodded, amused. "Baer doesn't have a chance."

"Come home to me."

"Always." The amusement was replaced by a fierceness and a promise.

Always. That sounded good, because if he didn't, her sanity would shatter, never to be right again. "Promise me, Jared?"

His eyes intensified. An all-consuming force radiated from him. "You want a promise, Baby Cakes? How about this? Marry me. Crap timing, but there it is, Sugar. I'll come back to you. Always. Forever. But you gotta tell me that it's two ways."

What the... She couldn't comprehend the words he'd thrown down. They sounded familiar. They seemed logical, but as if she'd just looked at a simple word for too long, she was certain her understanding had to be wrong.

"Sugar?"

Dumbfounded, she shook her head. Jared had just proposed marriage while the countdown was on to kill Buck Baer. She didn't have time to think about her screwed-up parents, their cheating and lying, and how they had tarnished her views on the matrimonial institution. She had no time to ponder how her folks had driven her away with their gambling and lies. They defined her view of marriage. And she'd never taken the time to correct that idea.

But then, she'd known Winters and Cash. They were good men. They had married women they loved, and their lives were all smiles and sunshine. Sugar'd had those thoughts about Jared, as terrifying and impossible as they seemed. They were illogical, absolutely incomprehensible, because she had no idea why she would want to get married, especially when her parents' marriage had been so awful.

But now, marriage was offered up by an equal who respected her. He got her. He understood her mindset and liked her attitude.

She wasn't anything like her parents. She and Jared were a team. He loved her, and she loved him. They didn't fit into some Hallmark greeting card category, but they fit. Long term. Forever. Just like she wanted—

"Shouldn't take that long to answer me." He looked at his watch. "Like I said, I had a lot to talk to you about. This wasn't how I planned it. My proposing in a parking lot or you fumbling in shock."

"I'm not—"

Gunfire burst in the distance, and she jumped. Her gaze flew to his. His dark eyes narrowed, assessing. He readjusted his earpiece, and Sugar recapped what she knew. Rocco had just gone inside. Jenny was safe, but Winters was at the back of GUNS. Her throat went dry. Her breaths wouldn't come.

Jared had transformed to Titan commander without missing a second. "Winters. Roc. Come in, boys." With a quick flick of his wrist to check the time, he reached out again. "Who's got eyes on Winters or Roc?"

Someone answered. Not knowing killed her. Winters had a newborn. Rocco had... *Who the hell knows about any of these guys?* But Rocco's life was important, too.

"Good deal." Jared gave her a sharp nod and a thumbs-up. "Just keeping GSI on their toes. Let's go."

Jared was out of the truck and to her door before she could jump out. Snagging her hand, he pulled her toward the front door. They whipped inside, and he pounded them down the hall to her office. "Weapons and clothes?"

She placed her palm on the sensory reader of her gun safe, then pulled a change of clothes from her desk as Jared unloaded every gun and ammo box she had stored there. She would feel more in control the second she got out of his oversized clothes and into something that wouldn't trip her or fall off if she had to run.

Quickly ditching his sweatpants and shirt, she dressed in boots and a bra. Jared, still loading and laying out an artillery, stole a second to watch as she shimmied into her clothes.

He gave her a once-over, from her black baby-tee to her leather boots and the holsters strapped around her waist and to her thigh, then handed her a Glock. "Point the barrel at the door until I come back."

His thumb stroked her wrist as he placed the gun into her open palm. It was as much as she would get out of him right then. As quickly as they'd come in, he was out her office door, and she was alone. Raising the weapon in one hand, she used the other to switch on a television screen that showed the footage from each security camera stationed around GUNS.

CHAPTER THIRTY

Once Jared had stashed Sugar safely inside her office, he ducked down the hall to go back outside. Each security camera he passed pivoted, following his motions. Sugar had her eyes on him, and he wasn't sure if that was a good thing. She knew what Titan did. But she didn't need to see it. He would do whatever it took to eradicate anything dangerous to his world. And Sugar was his world. If that meant tearing apart Buck Baer, bare-knuckled and blood-flying, that's what he would do.

Occasional chatter crossed his earpiece—check-ins and status updates. Jared had plans for Buck Baer. Whatever Baer thought he was showing up for, they'd both agreed that this was their last stand. More formal than the usual Titan throw-downs, this one would be very different from the battles he waged against the usual sickos just to earn a paycheck. This would be nothing less than a duel.

He pictured Sugar's logo. Pink dueling pistols. *How appropriate.* A blacked-out Explorer pulled into GUNS as he pushed through the heavy front door and moved into position. Baer had made it with seconds to spare.

Parker's voice carried into his earpiece. "We have movement on GSI's perimeter positions."

"Shift. Stay on your targets," Rocco followed.

Confirmations came through. Brock's voice grated on Jared's nerves. As Delta Team checked in, Jared took a second to mentally commend Rocco for taking initiative. Delta Team was a good move. They were an arm of Titan that Jared let handle the grayer-meets-invisible ops. Titan had as many on-the-books assignments as they did off-the-books assignments. Delta Team had non-existent assignments. Titan versus GSI ranked as non-existent.

Under Jared's watchful eye, Baer's door cracked, and he emerged better suited for a business meeting than a field standoff. While bullets weren't flying and a chopper wasn't hovering, Jared could tell Baer had softened. The corrupt jerk might like a dirty fight, but he hadn't been the one pulling the trigger.

Jared's trigger finger was well practiced. His palm tingled as it hovered over his holster, ready to draw a weapon like a Wild West cowboy itching for a high-noon standoff.

A familiar feeling crawled down his back—an awareness that this showdown equated to more than finishing a job. Every job up to that point had helped or hindered someone else. His clients. Their victims. His marks. Their enemy.

This time, it was all about him.

He took a step forward, into the parking lot. Baer did the same. They didn't pass along pretend pleasantries.

No games. No small talk.

It was the end of their decades-long battle.

Both men locked eyes and readied to kill. Their dance continued, each sizing up prey to be slaughtered, taking slow steps forward. Each tactical-booted footfall crunched on tiny rocks. Jared's confidence made his lungs cool, refreshed. *Easy breezy breathing.* He readied his body and his mind as though he'd been preparing his whole life for—

Hell. A light-silver Volvo station wagon pulled into the parking lot and came to a stop in the middle of their standoff.

Remaining in place, Jared willed the car to pull out of the parking lot. It didn't, and his concern escalated when he glanced past the idling car toward his enemy. Baer was never interested in the well-being of the innocent. Women and children didn't garner any special treatment from GSI. Cases in point, Sugar, Asal, and Brock's family.

Adding as much menace and forewarning as he could manage in three words, Jared hollered as a woman stepped out, "GUNS   is   closed."

She kept her head down, unperturbed and not noticing Baer behind her. Then she leaned into her station wagon and... didn't get back in. Instead, she emerged with a purse the size of a Humvee and a hat pulled over her hair.

Is that...? Nah. She looked like Brock's wife, but that wouldn't make sense. Either way, she didn't look like the women who frequented GUNS. Those ladies defined "rowdy." One of *those* ladies would crack a beer bottle on a dude's head if he gave her the wrong pick-up line.

Volvo lady wasn't one of *those* ladies. She was in the wrong place and couldn't have picked a worse time. But damn if she didn't look like Sarah Gamble. *If only she would look up.*

Baer took another step forward, craning his neck to inspect the woman. *Fuck.* Buck Baer blowing away a random bystander wasn't in the game plan, and Jared wasn't in a position to handle a hostage.

"Closed?" Volvo lady asked, fiddling in her monster bag. Her voice shook, and Jared had a bad feeling. "I'm here to see Sugar."

"She's not here. Time to go." *Get your ass in the car and leave.*

One hand still lost in her purse and the other on her hip, she glanced up, her face unmistakable. *Sarah Gamble.*

"And why are you telling me and not Sugar?"

"I'm trying to save your life. Go home to Mayberry." Jared kept eyes on Baer in the periphery while he studied the back of Sarah's floppy hat. Baer wasn't stupid. If he hadn't figured out who she was, he might recognize Sarah's voice.

Rocco barked in Jared's ear. "Brock, hold your position."

"Sarah," Baer's slick voice slithered across Jared's skin.

Her head snapped to look over her shoulder. Her petite frame pivoted, partially obscured from Baer's line of sight by her station wagon.

Fuck.

"Goddamn it, Sugar's on the move," Rocco growled. "Winters, get in there and hold her ass down if you have to."

If she was watching the security feed, she had surely seen Sarah roll up. Only a titanium will kept Jared's head trained forward, to avoid alerting Baer before Sugar burst through the front door.

"Sarah." Jared took a step forward, his hand on his holstered Glock. "Get in your car and leave. Now's a bad time, sweetheart."

She looked from Jared to Buck, then back again. The woman had been abducted, her kids had been endangered, and only the Lord knew what she thought about Brock. She needed a Xanax far more than she needed to confront two men who were about to duel.

Jared pressed her. "Everything's all right. But you have to go."

She took off her sunglasses, squinting despite the dull early evening light. "You're going to kill Brock, my husband, if you haven't already."

"Where the fuck is Sugar?" Winters barked in his earpiece.

Damn it. I should've tied Sugar to the bed at home. He took a breath, controlled his heartbeat, and swallowed his emotion. "Wrong, Sarah. He's here. Alive. With me. Everything's all good, except you need to go."

Her purse slid down her shoulder and left her tiny hand exposed, wrapped around a .38 special. An instant tightness strangled his lungs. The only thing worse than a woman scorned was a woman hell-bent on revenge.

"I need to talk to Sugar. She's the only one I trust."

The wrought-iron security door at GUNS' front entrance slammed open. "Sarah, I'm here." Sugar sashayed into the parking lot as if the mess unfolding there was just two chicks chatting. "The boys have business, so you have to go. We'll catch up soon. Promise."

"Is Brock alive?"

"He would've been if you'd stayed with me." Baer cackled. "Now, Sugar, I've been looking for you, pretty lady."

Sarah spun toward Baer, the .38 held outstretched in an unsteady grip. "I hate you. You've ruined our lives."

Baer laughed again. Nothing good was unfolding. Sarah didn't need to be antagonized. She needed a swift kick toward calm-the-hell-down alley.

"Sugar, get inside. Sarah, get out of—"

Faster than Jared expected, Baer pulled his sidearm and trained it on Sugar. A half-ton tanker could've landed on Jared's chest, and it would've been lighter than the weight crushing him. On instinct, he had his Glock in hand. His heart thumped. His mouth went dry. A lifetime's worth of training and discipline skittered into the breeze as he watched a sadistic smile pull Baer's cheeks back and make his eyes shine.

Sarah was in Jared's kill-shot line of fire. This was all a game. Maybe Baer didn't have the balls to take out Sugar. Maybe he wanted Jared to suffer, to know that he could've saved his woman if he'd taken out Brock's wife.

A shot rang out. Sugar hit the ground as Jared dove toward her. Sarah screamed. Spinning. Falling. Someone cursed. Another shot fired in the background, and he crawled the remaining distance to cover Sugar's body. There was blood. Lots of it.

He ran his hands ran through her hair. Checked her face and her skull. Ran down her neck. *So much goddamn blood.*

Rocco's orders carried in his ear. Another scream followed another shot. Jared scooped Sugar against his chest. Her harsh voice didn't make sense as he hustled across the open space toward the front door of GUNS.

Out the corner of his eye, he saw Roman swoop in and head toward Sarah. None of that mattered. Jared had to secure Sugar. He wanted the kill shot on Baer, but more than that, he *needed* Sugar alive and in his arms. His head was spinning. There was just too much blood.

"Jared!" Sugar took a panicked breath. Her eyes reached past him. "Help me!"

Maybe the bullet hit her chest? Fuck, not good. Inside GUNS, he lifted her onto a table, searching with his eyes and fingers for the entry wound.

"Goddamn it, Jared," she screamed. "Listen to me!"

Her fists wrapped his collar. Sugar yanked him within inches of her eyes. All that blood on Sugar. It matted her dark hair to her cheeks and painted sickening streaks across her pale skin. He couldn't handle life without her. It made his body hurt. His mind ache. His world spin.

And then his world spun.

He and Sugar fell off the table, the weight of her body pulling him down into a pile of exhaustion. He paused, staring and studying the woman he would sacrifice his life for.

"I'm not shot." Again, she was in his face. "You were, goddamn it."

White-hot pain seared his neck. Realizing he'd been shot was less shocking than her being uninjured. The blood wasn't hers. She was okay. Everything was okay. Sugar wasn't shot. *Thank the fucking Lord.*

His terror dissipated, and his adrenaline drained away with it. Pain in his neck and numbness in his extremities hit him at the same time. Getting shot sucked. He'd done it more than he'd liked. But this time... this time... was different.

"I love you," he mumbled. His lips tingled. He tasted salt and metal. He smelled the blood. "Lilly Chase." Her name sounded too pretty to not say it.

"Stay with me, J-dawg." Sugar cupped his face. Her fingers were gentle and wet with his blood.

"Lilly... Chase." His words were slurred. *Such a pretty name.* He couldn't look away. Sugar'd been sexy. She'd been tough. But he never stopped and stared. Listened to her speak. Said her name. "I love you."

That was what he wanted to say, especially if they were his last words.

Tears ran down her face. Still she was so... pretty. That was the only word he could think of. He wasn't totally sure what she'd said, but if she kept talking just like that, he could close his eyes, and it would all be okay.

Jared listened, felt, and knew. He'd finally found life, but it was fading.

Sugar wrapped around him. He just knew it. He couldn't feel it... and he so badly wanted to feel her. A touch. Her warmth. But... nothing.

The voices of his team clamored in his earpiece, tickling his eardrum. Their words held no meaning. Somehow, his strength and coordination flickered back, but only long enough to pull the earbud out of his ear, and then his arm fell limp. He sucked a staggered breath, completely unable to help himself... or to take his eyes off Sugar.

Horrified, she screamed for help. For him. For...

CHAPTER THIRTY-ONE

All Sugar could do was cry. Her shoulders shook. Her eyes burned. She could barely hold them open because the scene was too horrific to commit to memory. But she couldn't close them, either. They were too raw, and shutting her eyes did nothing to erase the haunting blood and lifelessness on the ambulance gurney.

The sirens served only as screeching background music as the ambulance flew down the highway. The EMTs worked around Sugar while she clutched Jared's limp hand, kneading his lifeless fingers, and let tears fall down her face in stricken silence.

Bloody gauze and beeping machines kept the technicians busy, but nothing they did offered much hope. A medic in the front seat was on a radio, giving status updates to the emergency room and talking in codes Sugar didn't understand. But she knew each one transmitted was graver than the last.

It was in their tone. Their glances. The sympathetic looks sadly said they would be surprised if he pulled through.

Goddamn Jared. Damn him for loving her. Damn her for ever leaving his side, ever testing the boundaries of how far she could push him. Damn her screwed-up fears of love and relationships. If not for those mental hiccups, she would've had that much more time with him. She was prepared to barter with the devil for just long enough to nod yes to Jared's marriage proposal and declare that her love ran just as deeply and was just as strong as his.

She was a moron—a pathetic, scared moron.

Why had she stuttered? Why had she ever questioned... him? Them? Anything? She'd been cowardly and selfish. Self-preservation had been more important than the man who had stood before her, more than once, and told her how it would be. Him and her. Forever.

However long forever lasted. The slow beeps and the high-pitched alarms sounding around her announced that the grains of sand in the *forever* hourglass were settling at the bottom.

The sirens died. The vehicle came to a sudden halt, then the driver floored it in reverse. Before the driver had parked, the back doors flew open, and medical personnel rushed in.

A man crawled over Jared, unhooking wires and continuing to work on him while others unlatched the gurney and pulled it free. Sugar pulled her hand from Jared's, and a woman placed it across his chest without looking up.

Off he went, with his medical team working hard. No one had asked her to follow. Sugar watched his tethered body lie unresponsive, and she remained frozen in the back of the ambulance. She couldn't swallow the grenade-sized bulge in her throat. Tears came harder and faster, until she dropped to her knees amid discarded bandages and empty sterile package wrappers. Sugar held her shaking hands in front of herself. She squeezed her fingers together tightly and then turned over her dark-crimson-dyed palms. The vivid creases and lines in her skin were sketched by Jared's dried blood. She remembered years ago watching her mother study her palm.

A short love line and a long life line. That's exactly what you want. Long term-love isn't worth it, Lilly. It doesn't exist. That's the lesson I hope you take from me. Fall in love, and one day, you'll be me. Years drowning in a marriage, wishing to hell you hadn't done something so stupid. Men never stay true, and neither should you.

Sugar traced the lines on her palms, crying until her vision blurred and burned again. Her mother was wrong. Jared would've stayed by her side. And God help her, she never would have regretted a lifetime of moments with him.

Don't ever give your heart away.

"No," she moaned, because she already had given it away, and losing her heart to Jared was the best and worst decision of her life.

Hell, it wasn't a decision. And he wasn't dead... *yet.*

"Get it together, Sugar." She jumped to her feet and threw open the ambulance's cabinets and drawers. Tossing packages and wrappers around her, she searched and searched and searched. *Alcohol swabs.* She grabbed a handful and tore open the tiny packets. They were of little use, but she scrubbed clean her love line and her life line. The tiny squares dried quickly as they rouged, and she let them hit the floor, opening more packets, repeating the process of ridding her palms of the dark shading.

It wasn't working, and she didn't care if his blood coated her hands. Jared was alive. He would stay alive. Titan had access to the best doctors in the country, and Jared Westin, the master of the universe, wasn't going to die on an operation table.

Sugar spun to the ajar ambulance doors, then jumped out to the parking lot. The heels of her boots hit the ground, sending jolts of pain up her calves. For the first time in an hour, she felt something besides despair. Physical pain. And she would take that over the blanket of anguish.

No one else was around, and the ambulance entrance didn't offer much in the way of customer service options, just busy people who didn't notice her. She checked curtained rooms and looked down hallways, but didn't see Jared. A sign pointed her toward the emergency room lobby, and she pushed through doors until she found the triage desk. She marched to the front of the long line of waiting people.

"Jared Westin. Where is he?"

The nurses behind the desk dropped their jaws. She caught her reflection in the Plexiglas dividing wall. The dried blood covering her face was streaked with tears, and her hair was matted against her cheeks. She turned to see the people standing in line shuffle away.

"Ma'am," a young nurse stuttered. "Are you okay?"

Another nurse came from behind the desk. Maybe to check her injuries. Maybe to escape. Sugar looked ready to die or kill.

A wide-eyed baby-faced security officer approached her, his white-knuckled hand wrapped around a Taser gun. He mumbled into his walkie-talkie and held onto his Taser, unsure of her next move.

Like that Taser could stop me. "Where is Jared Westin?" She ignored him, placing both hands on the desk, and leaned into the nurse's space. "Find him for me."

"Step back from the nurse," Baby-face called to her. Sugar turned her head. He spread his legs shoulder-width apart and bent his knees in a classic shooting stance. Someone had taught him well. "Ma'am—"

"Oh, for fuck's sake." She reached over and tapped the nurse's computer screen. "Find Jared Westin. Tell me where he is."

Baby-face advanced. "Ma'am—"

A similarly uniformed grandpa-lookalike ran around the corner. "Wait! Wait. It's okay."

Baby-face kept his Taser trained on her and looked over, looked back, and over again. "Not sure about that."

Gramps rushed over and whispered to Baby-face. Slowly, the Taser dropped until it pointed to the tile floor. Everyone in the ER watched him. The janitor was holding his mop as though he had planned to fight like a ninja.

Then, turning a knowing glance to Sugar, Gramps cautiously approached her with his hands in the air. "Jared's in surgery. I'll take you to a private waiting room."

Other than the televisions hanging in the corners of the emergency room waiting area, the open space was silent.

"Okay." Sugar's tear-soaked voice cracked.

"Come on." The man dropped his hands and beckoned. "It's okay. You're with Titan. Come with me."

She nodded and followed. Her footfalls clacked with each step. Behind her, whispers and murmurs erupted. She didn't care. Jared was still *alive.*

The private waiting room was small and secluded. A few chairs faced a hanging television and a phone. The magazines fanned out on the table looked so foreign, so absurd. She couldn't contemplate how people could read or care about any issue outside the walls of the hospital when they sat on these couches.

She looked at the phone and wanted to call someone. Jenny. Titan. Maybe ask about Asal. But they would have questions for her, and she didn't know if she could string together a coherent sentence.

The door cracked, and Roman stuck his head in. "Sugar?"

She nodded, finding that she really couldn't string words together.

He pushed into the room, followed by Rocco. Both of them looked like hell. Worried eyes. Ruffled hair. They wore their tactical pants and black shirts. They carried their weapons, but Rocco wasn't armed with as many as he had been before. The battle was done. This was just their everyday weapons wear. Tactical chic.

Rocco nodded. Both men took a seat on the couches and stared at her. Her eyes darted between them, and the air felt heavy, trapped in her lungs. *Oh, no. Fuck, no. Please, God... no.* "If you have news to share, do it and be done with it."

If Jared's dead...

Her throat burned with pain. She needed to vomit. Bile coated the back of her tongue, and hot tears seared her eyes all over again. She couldn't find a breath. Her lungs stopped. Not one breath in or out, until she gasped, sputtering a cough. "Just tell me."

"We're sorry..." Roman shook his head.

"It shouldn't have happened like this." Rocco ran his palms over his knees, crossed his arms, and stared at the floor.

"No!"

There it was: the dreaded truth. Denying a fact did no good. Tears spilled onto her cheeks. Her body shook. Her blood-stained hands covered her mouth, her nose, and her eyes. She wanted to slip away and die, right along with Jared.

Strong arms wrapped around her, hoisting her back onto the seat. She hadn't realized she'd slid to the floor.

Rocco or Roman, one of them, hugged her tight. "It's okay. Everything will be okay."

Okay? In what universe? I don't need the bullshit life-will-go-on speech. She needed something to knock her out, to numb the pain, to erase the past, and rewrite the day. Anything. She needed anything but for someone to tell her things would be okay.

"Leave me alone." As hard and as fast as she could, she jabbed an elbow into her hugger's throat. "Go away."

Both men stilled. Neither said a word, which was good, because she didn't want to hear it.

Roman rubbed his throat. "Sugar—"

"Get out."

Rocco crouched in her line of sight. "Sug—"

"Get the fuck out!" she screamed, pushing past the men. She grabbed the magazines and threw them. "Go. Out. Now."

Collapsing to her knees, Sugar cradled herself. She craved the fetal position, needing to just curl up and drift away.

"Girl, when Jared wakes up, he's gonna—"

What? She looked up at the men. She mopped her face with the back of her hand and sat back on her heels. "What did you just say?"

Rocco's brow furrowed.

Roman nodded and whispered loud enough so she could hear, "Jared's gonna kick our asses if he ever hears we let you get this upset."

Sugar flew to her feet, swaying as the blood ran from her head. "Jared's... Jared's alive?"

Both men blinked.

"Well, yeah." Roman shrugged. "The bastard isn't going to die in surgery."

"But..." Her jaw fell, and they both stared at her. "You said, 'We're sorry.'"

They nodded. Roman mumbled, "We are."

"You said it shouldn't have happened like that." Sugar took a step toward them, and both men took a step closer to one another, unsure if she would attack. And she was about to. She closed the distance and struck Rocco in the chest. "You *said*— damn you, Roc. You don't walk into a waiting room and say bullshit like that unless someone's fucking dead."

They stood silently as seconds dragged by.

Finally, Rocco offered, "Today didn't go according to plan."

She crossed her arms. Indignant. Furious. Thrilled. "He's alive."

"Yes."

Relief was a cold splash of water, slapping her with emotion, and her legs gave out. A couch caught her. Tears welled all over again, and her lungs kick-started to a steady rhythm. "Jared's still alive?"

They nodded.

A nurse popped her head in. "Excuse me?" She laid eyes on the men, then Sugar. "Sorry to interrupt. I'll come back."

"No!" Sugar reached, needing outside assurance. "Please. Do you have an update?"

Giving them a nervous glance, the nurse stepped into the room and clicked shut the door. "Mr. Westin's surgery is going as expected. He'll be out in about an hour, and Dr. Tuska will give you an update then."

The men nodded. That was all they seemed to be doing.

The nurse shifted her weight and continued, apparently less concerned that their little group would kill her for delivering bad news. "As you know, Titan is a very welcome guest—"

"Guest?" Sugar looked at the nurse, then Roman and Rocco. "Very welcome guest?"

Rocco shrugged. "We do a lot of business with them. Titan has repeat-customer status or some shit."

The nurse smiled weakly. "We see them... often. Yes. Mr. Westin and Titan are very important to—"

"What have I gotten myself into?" Sugar almost needed to laugh. The absurdity of it all was far past comical. She'd fallen in love with a man who had a frequent-shopper card *at a hospital.* "Never mind. He's going to be okay. That's all that matters."

The nurse nodded again. "If you'd like, we can arrange for fresh clothes and a shower. That's if you like, Miss Chase—"

"Sugar."

The nurse tilted her head. "Come again?"

"It's my—never mind. A shower?"

Confusion stayed on the nurse's face. "And fresh clothes."

"Take the offer, Sugar." Roman laughed. "You look like hell. Boss Man will kick our asses regardless, but if you could look less like shit when he wakes up, we'd owe you."

A genuine happiness curved onto her cheeks. A few minutes before, she had known she would never smile again. Sugar looked at her palm, where the dried blood still dyed her life and love lines.

She was her own woman. No crinkled lines on her hands or motherly memories would dictate how she loved and lived. "Hell yes. I want a shower. But not before I call and check on Asal."

CHAPTER THIRTY-TWO

Jared took a deep breath. The smell of a hospital room hit him instantaneously, as did the feeling of dull pain and a foggy drug stupor. Trying to sit up made everything ache. His dry throat stifled a groan. He didn't know how long he'd been out or if Sugar was okay.

His fingers searched for the remote that would reposition his bed, and a warm hand with soft skin covered his. The touch startled him, forcing his eyes open.

Sugar. He didn't need to see her to know her, but she was the best thing to see.

"Hi ya, J-dawg," she whispered and interlocked his fingers with hers, giving him a squeeze.

She wore hospital scrubs, and her hair was no longer covered in blood. It hung loosely, framing her face. Her eyelids were red rimmed, and the tip of her nose was also red, but her smile was mega-watt, and again, *pretty* popped into his head. Pretty and perfect.

"Baby Cakes." His throat itched, and his mouth was dry, but she heard him. The mega-watt smile illuminated brighter than before, and he needed to hold her. "Come here."

No sooner had the words crossed his lips than Sugar gingerly crawled onto the bed and burrowed next to him. He threw his arm around her shoulder, and it hurt like hell, but he didn't care.

Sugar's hair fell across his bicep, and her cheek pressed against his hospital-gown covered chest. "I'm going to get into trouble for doing this."

He started to shake his head, but it ached, and he didn't want to make any sound that might drive her away. "They don't tell me no."

She laughed. "So I've learned."

He wanted to ask where she'd been while he was sleeping. He wanted to kiss her and…

He woke up again. Must've drifted off to sleep, but he'd had a good dream. He couldn't remember what it was, just that it'd been happy. Sugar was still nestled against him, and a blanket lay over them. Her breaths were soft, but she wasn't asleep. *How much time had passed?* Didn't matter as long as she never left his side again.

"Sugar…" He needed a sip of water. His throat was sore, his neck had a dull throb, and he wanted to tell her he loved her.

She didn't move. "You're awake?"

"Yeah."

"You hurting?"

"A little." Behind him, a machine beeped steadily.

Sugar rearranged the blanket. "Do you want some pain medicine?"

"No. But water would be—"

"Hold on a sec." She leaned to a side table, then offered him a giant plastic cup with a straw. "Here you go."

Gripping the cup's handle, his muscles weighed a million pounds. He was too tired and weak to grip it for long. "I hate being laid up like this."

"You lost a lot of blood. But the doc said you'll be running around in a couple days, although he's requested more than a couple months between gunshot wounds."

He chuckled and gave her back the water cup. "You met Doc Tuska, huh?"

Sugar snuggled against him again. "Whatever you pay him is not nearly enough."

A low rumble of a laugh escaped. The no-nonsense doctor handled all of Titan's medical problems without question. "He's worth his weight in gold-plated ammo. That's for damn sure."

"You want to talk to him?" She shifted. "I could go get him or the nurse or someone."

Soreness stopped him from shaking his head. "No, Sugar baby. I want to talk to you."

"Good, 'cause I want to talk to you, too. When you're ready." She pulled back and started to hurry her words. "I don't want to rush you. If you need to sleep or want medicine, that's fine."

She wasn't going anywhere. Not from this conversation. Not from his arms. His heart beat faster, his cheeks tingled, and warmth rushed through him. He'd had a lot to say for a while, and there was no better time. But what did she want to say? With Sugar, it could be anything.

"I'm ready now." He pulled her back into his hold, and she relaxed, drawing in a contented breath. "What's on your mind?"

"You," Sugar whispered and kissed his chest. "What do you want to talk to me about?"

Her lazy kiss melted through the cotton layer of his hospital gown. His chest felt tight, like it might explode from the emotional pressure building in his heart.

"You." Jared caressed her skin, smoothing the sleeve of her shirt and tangling with her hair. "I love you, baby. I shouldn't have dropped a bomb on you at GUNS before everything started, but I'm glad you knew where my head was before I ended up here."

Sugar's chin rested on his chest; her watery eyes looked up at him. The tips of her fingers stroked the stubble on his jaw. "I love you, too."

"I was never the kind of man who believed in the long haul. In settling down with one woman who I liked as much as I loved. Just thought it'd be me and Thelma." He brushed her hair with his fingertips.

A half-smile teased. "She's a good dog."

"She is. And she likes you. I think that makes me love you even more."

Sugar batted his chest. "Very funny."

"I know who I am. You do, too. We're one and the same. So to say I never thought fairytale bullshit and love was possible would be an understatement. But we belong together."

She nodded. "I know."

"And a family? Well, hell. It seemed like a concept for other people. Worked out well for Winters. One of these days, Nicola's going to show up, asking for maternity leave, and I'll be out my Bond girl for a while. Christ, Cash will be a pain in my ass come time for Princess to deliver. What I'm saying is, I thought family was nice for *them*. Not me. But I was wrong. Me. You. Asal. Maybe more. I don't know what we want, but that's family."

Tears streamed down her face. "I want that, too."

Damn. He hadn't meant to upset her, not after all she'd been through. "Now's not the time to cry." He wiped her cheeks, wanting her to smile and laugh, wanting her to feel the same detonation of love in her chest, burning to escape and explode, as he did. "What do you say, *Lilly*. You ready to stop running, give up the Chase, and become a Westin?"

A brilliant smile broke across her face, and her blue eyes beamed. If happiness and love had been tangible, it would've been Sugar, in his arms at that moment. "Join Team Westin? Hell yes, Jared. Hell. Yes."

"Good answer, Baby Cakes."

As he leaned down, his neck wound screamed, but he kissed Sugar. The top of her head. Her temple. Her cheek. It'd been one hell of a chase. He pulled her tight, vowing to never let go. He'd summited a hellacious battle between his head and heart and found victory with the secretly sweet Sugar, who was curled against him in his hospital bed.

EPILOGUE

"The happiest place on earth." Disney's tagline was no lie.

At first, Jared had raised an eyebrow to Sugar's suggestion, not only because the idea of bringing Titan to Disney World seemed more than a little absurd, but because, clad in leather pants, sexy heels, and polishing an automatic rifle, Sugar hadn't looked the Disney type.

But life had evolved. Winters and Mia had kids. *He* had a kid. Plus, as Jared found out, Disney wasn't just for the under-ten crowd. So it had been settled. Or rather, he'd agreed, which was an interesting part of marriage. With the backdrop of the Magic Kingdom, they were having a wedding reception and a belated Gotcha Day party.

Asal didn't know her birthday, so they celebrated the day they officially adopted Miss Asal Westin. Any girl of his deserved a big blowout for such a special occasion. Plus, Disney World gave Sugar an excuse to throw herself a wedding reception. Eloping in Vegas had been a ton of fun for them, but it hadn't given anyone else a chance to say congrats—or rib the hell out of them.

He couldn't blame them. If there were two people that looked less suited for marriage and a kid, it might've been Jared and Sugar. But looks were deceiving. And they could change. Case in point, he was holding a photograph of himself, with his arms around Asal and Sugar, while they rode *the teacups.* Giant, pastel *teacups* that spun, and sang, and made his girls smile.

But even better, he had identical pictures from the rest of his team and a few close friends who'd come along to help celebrate.

Roman had been chasing Nicola's best friend, Beth, who was doing an excellent job of ignoring him, although Sugar said Beth really wasn't. It wasn't his problem to figure out, but someone needed to put Roman out of his misery.

Rocco and Parker were on missions to meet-and-greet all the single women in the place, and neither was too concerned if they laid a good line on a married mom. They found far more interested ladies at the world of family and fun than Jared would've guessed.

The only one missing was Brock, and Jared still hadn't gotten over that wound. But he would forever owe the bastard for taking out Buck Baer when Jared didn't have a clean shot. The rumor mill churned out several stories about where Brock had headed off to, and the only thing Jared knew for certain was that his wife had taken his kids and left, saying something about being unsure that was the life she'd signed up for.

To each his own. He hadn't spoken to Sarah Gamble since, but Sugar had solid things to say about her. He only hoped that she found what made her and the kids happy and safe. He always wanted that for the direct or collateral victims whom he dealt with on jobs.

GSI shut down, and Titan absorbed all of their contracts. Jared had a lot of crap to sort through, but he'd been handed a few jobs that Delta Team could knock out immediately and let his home-based team take a breather. It was never a good idea to let those Delta boys sit around and stagnate. Without the structure of a mission, they went feral.

Jared placed the wallet-sized teacup photo next to the folded-up e-mail he still carried, that same one where Sugar said she wanted to kick him. He laughed because sometimes, she did.

Putting the wallet back in his pocket, he saw his wife and her sister, Jenny, walking arm-in-arm with Asal. The three of them were dragging a neon-pink stuffed animal that was as tall as Asal. Without a doubt, he knew that he would be carrying that damn thing within twenty minutes. But that was okay. He would do anything for his girls.

ABOUT THE AUTHOR

Cristin Harber is an award-winning author. She lives outside Washington, DC with her family and English Bulldog, and enjoys chatting with readers.

Facebook: https://www.facebook.com/cristinharberauthor
Twitter: https://twitter.com/CristinHarber
Website: http://cristinharber.com
Email: cristin@cristinharber.com
Newsletter: Stay in touch about all things Titan—releases, excerpts, and more—plus new series info. www.CristinHarber.com

For sexy, quick reads, check out two Titan novellas:
GAMBLED
CHASED

ACKNOWLEDGMENTS

Thank you to romance readers and for the support this series has received.

Stephanie Spangler Buswell, I learned a lot from you. Thank you for your guidance. Three cheers for Lynn McNamee and Red Adept.

Throwing CC stars on my critique partners. Jamie Salsbury, Victoria Van Tiem, Claudia Handel, Kaci Presnell, Racquel Reck, Amy Anhalt, and Sharon Cermak. I adore you.

And as always, huge love and thanks goes to my husband. XO.